"I—I . . . I THINK YOU HAVE DESIGNS UPON MY PERSON."

"Don't you know, Felicity, that turning into a prissy miss is the worst thing you could do?"

Logan eased nearer, one of his arms sliding around her back.

"There is nothing that a man finds more of a challenge than a woman who needs rumpling."

She swallowed, hoping to ease the dryness of her throat enough to speak. But it was a vain attempt, especially when he leaned toward her, his own lips parted, his hair, thick and wavy, falling around his face in such a way that she longed to push it back. To feel its weight. Its warmth.

"Shall I . . . rumple you, Miss Pedigrue?"

Books by Lisa Bingham

Silken Dreams
Eden Creek
Distant Thunder
The Bengal Rubies
Temptation's Kiss
Silken Promises
Sweet Dalliance
Sweet Defiance
Sweet Decadence
Wild Escapade

Published by POCKET BOOKS

LISA BINGHAM

WILD ESCAPADE

POCKET BOOKS

New York   London   Toronto   Sydney   Tokyo   Singapore

An *Original* Publication of POCKET BOOKS

POCKET BOOKS, a division of Simon & Schuster Inc.
1230 Avenue of the Americas, New York, NY 10020

ISBN: 0-671-52804-1

First Pocket Books printing October 1996

10 9 8 7 6 5 4 3 2 1

POCKET and colophon are registered trademarks of Simon & Schuster Inc.

Cover art by Matt Westrup

Printed in the U.S.A.

To my students,
who redefine
the meaning of
"adventure"
every
day

Prologue

"Tell me about my girls, Etienne."

Moments earlier, Louise Chevalier had burst into her dressing room amid a raucous round of backstage applause. Ignoring it all, she'd slammed the door in the stage manager's face, ignoring his grunt of pain. He would recover soon enough, she knew. Louise had taken twelve curtain calls after her performance as Mary Queen of Scots, so the theatrical production was an unqualified success.

"Well?" she demanded when Etienne did not respond. He should have known that she'd been watching for his arrival—or rather, that she'd been waiting for the news he brought her.

The heavy satin of her gown rustled as she moved to her dressing table. Tearing the elaborate headdress from her hair, she shook out the heavy tresses, ignoring the way Etienne's eyes flamed in response.

"How was the performance?"

She waved his question aside. "Don't tease me, *mon amour.*" She rushed to kiss him, having to stretch on tiptoes to meet his cheek. "You promised you would come here as soon as you'd finished, so I expect a report."

1

"Can't I kiss you properly first?"

"No." She dodged away from him, knowing that if he touched her more intimately, she would be lost. Especially now. Now that she was free.

Etienne dropped onto the swooning couch next to her changing screen. His pose was languid and blatantly sexual. Reaching toward the side table, he withdrew a cigar as well as a match from the box she kept for him there. A snail could have moved at a faster pace, Louise decided as he lit his ritual cheroot, then blew a stream of gray-white smoke toward the ceiling.

"They were there at the funeral," he finally admitted.

Louise greedily absorbed the words. "Then Alexander Pedigrue is dead. Really dead."

Etienne nodded, watching her carefully.

But Louise didn't satisfy his curiosity. Not by so much as a blink of her eye could she let Etienne know how deeply such information affected her. Not even Etienne, her friend, her admirer, could ever be allowed to know the extent of her hatred for her estranged husband.

"Yes, *ma petite*. He is dead."

"And the girls?" she asked eagerly. "They are pretty, vivacious young women, eh?"

He didn't immediately respond, and a coldness clutched her heart.

"They are . . . not so young anymore, Louise."

"But the youngest is but twenty. That cannot be considered so very old."

"In years perhaps. But I sense an experience on all of their countenances that belies their ages."

"They are married?" she asked hopefully. "They've given me grandchildren?"

"No."

Louise felt some of her excitement ebb.

2

"They have never married, Louise."

"None of them?"

"No. They were not allowed to marry."

It was then that she understood what Etienne was trying to say. "What did that bastard do to them?"

"Pedigrue was not kind, I'm afraid."

Louise sank onto the side of the couch, reaching for Etienne's hand, grinding the heavy wedding ring she wore into her skin.

She had been afraid that Alexander would take out his anger on the children. Louise had been only sixteen when she'd met Alexander Pedigrue. Her parents, performers in a traveling burlesque show, had been killed in a railway accident. Finding herself penniless and alone in the frontier town of Gerber, Illinois, she'd gone to a nearby church for solace and advice. There, she'd met Alexander.

He'd assumed that she was one of the young girls who lived in the parish and had come to the church for dancing lessons. The rapport between them had been instantaneous and the growth of their affections swift. When she'd dared to admit that she was an orphan, it had been Alexander who had insisted she marry him and follow him west where he planned to homestead. She'd agreed but only after vowing to herself that the past was over and that she should keep her unorthodox upbringing a secret. Alexander was so strict and didactic, he would never have approved.

She'd been happy in those early years. And if Alexander showed bursts of temper or occasionally hit her in rebuke, she'd thought that she deserved such treatment for not being all she should have been to him, for not feeling the same burning love her parents had felt for each other. Moreover, she'd lied about her past, and she knew that was something Alexander would never forgive. In some ways, she'd accepted his harshness as a twisted sort of penance.

3

Then, on a fateful fall day, Louise, her husband, and her three small daughters had been emerging from church when she'd been recognized. One of her father's old performing friends had been passing through town, and before Louise could stop him, he'd revealed her "shameful" secret to her husband.

Louise had felt sure that she would endure a beating that night. Instead, Alexander had been his usual self, even going so far as to laugh and tease and play with his daughters. By the next morning, she'd begun to believe she'd been mistaken about his attitudes toward the "ungodly" stage and the rampant sinners who performed. When Alexander had suggested she attend a quilting bee at the church the next day, she'd willingly complied.

Her eyes squeezed closed in remembered pain. She'd returned to an empty house and a scathing letter calling upon the hounds of hell to reclaim Louise's lying, unholy soul. He'd taken her babies away "for the sake of their own salvation" and had sworn she would never see them again.

"What has Alexander done to my girls?" Louise rasped, pushing away the aching memories.

Etienne offered her a Gaelic shrug. "He must have forced them to endure a horrible life. They could have been beautiful if there had been some shred of joy in their expressions."

"It could have been grief you saw in their faces. They must have loved him."

"No." His response was adamant. "No, there was no grief. No love. No regret. I sensed more . . . relief than anything else. I don't think they had a pleasant time of it with their papa."

He stroked Louise's wrist, her arm. "If you'd seen them as I did, you would understand what I'm attempting to explain. They stood huddled

4

around the grave like a trio of black-clad wrens. Their gowns"—he shuddered—"were absolutely wretched, worn, frayed. Their shoes were scuffed and reshod, their bonnets and gloves tattered as if they'd been supplied by a missionary barrel."

"But Alexander was quite wealthy."

"I was able to gather a morsel or two of gossip from the women around me. It seems that Alexander Pedigrue kept the girls locked in that moldering estate of his, forcing them to wait upon him hand and foot, promising them that only once they had proven their obedience to God and to their earthly patriarch would they be given any means of independence."

"Damn him."

"There's more, Louise. I managed to bribe one of Pedigrue's clerks into revealing a portion of the will. Alexander Pedigrue has decreed that his daughters are to receive nothing of their inheritance until they fulfill one last task on his behalf. From what I was able to uncover, the solicitor is unsure of the contents of Alexander's latest draft because the documents are sealed until tomorrow's reading. But in previous versions, Pedigrue stipulated that Felicity, the youngest child, is to serve in India for three years with the Heathen Aid Society. Patience is to remain the same amount of time as a resident companion at the Ingersol Women's Old Age Domicile. And Constance is to offer her talents as a seamstress and chaperone to the Whippleton Foundling Home. In addition, they are to have no outside contacts with anyone other than those with whom they work in these establishments."

Louise felt as if her long-lost husband had physically slapped her. *"Damn him."*

"If the three women succeed in their endeavors, they will be given five hundred dollars a year and partial ownership of his estates—provided they adhere to the rules of conduct he set forth during their childhood."

Louise's eyes closed as she fought the pain welling within her. "He means to enslave them from beyond the grave."

"I believe so."

Louise trembled with rage and helplessness. "We've got to help them, Etienne."

"How?"

"Who else knows the terms of the will?"

"I doubt anyone. As I said before, even the solicitor is unsure of all the details. No one will know the exact contents until the documents are read tomorrow morning."

"Good. Good!" Louise jumped to her feet, rushing to her dressing table and removing a small loaf-shaped trunk. Taking a key from the pocket sewn at the top of her corset, she released the latch and opened the lid. Inside was a pistol and a battered leather portfolio. "Help me, Etienne," she panted, lifting the scuffed case free. "Help me."

He rose from the couch. "What are you going to do?" he demanded, taking the portfolio and setting it on his lap.

But he knew. They both knew. Especially when she reached inside the container to remove a heavy old-fashioned signet ring. The same sort that had once been used for sealing letters.

"We're going to change that will somehow. Come hell or high water, Etienne, we're going to change that will and help my girls."

One

~

June 1859

The brigand stood in the fiery embers of a brilliant sunset, his huge shape girded in buckskin, the muscles of his arms bulging at the fabric like banded steel. He glared at her, the thrust of his audacious indigo gaze piercing the very bed curtains, tearing her equilibrium asunder.

"Madam," he murmured as he prowled forward with the grace of a panther stalking its next meal, "I have come for my prize."

Thump. Thump.

His boots echoed hollowly against the scarred parquet floor.

Thump. Thump.

The tone mimicked the increased pounding of her heart.

Lilybeth screamed and scooped the linens against her heaving bosom, shielding the sight of her lithesome body from his lustful gaze. But the display of modesty held no sway. He came closer, ever closer, until she felt honor bound to cry, "Stop! For I know you, sir! You are the fiend who murdered my father and destroyed our ancestral home!"

The ruffian laughed, "Ha, ha!" throwing his head

back and filling the room with his dank, fetid breath. "Yes, it was I," he proclaimed with great relish. "And now I will have what I truly came for. You, maiden. You!"

Lifting a knife from his belt, he held it high, creeping nearer, infinitely nearer. His eyes gleamed malevolently. His ominous spirit filled the room with its evil.

Lilybeth shuddered in distaste and dismay. If she did not stop him, he would take from her the one thing she must not give: her chastity. Her modesty. Her corporeal self.

Lunging from the bed, she whipped the saber from where she'd hidden it beneath the blankets. Sliding it free of the jeweled sheath, she held it high and . . .

"*Felicity!* How many times must we call you? You should be going."

Felicity Pedigrue started, glancing up from the novel in her lap. All too soon, the real world rushed into focus around her, bringing with it the blanketlike heat of the attic and the grim light that struggled to pierce through the single, small window.

"Going?" she whispered to herself, momentarily confused. She'd spent so much time here in this room, embroiled in her books and their make-believe worlds, that sometimes it was very difficult to reconcile what was real with what was not.

It was time to be going.

Her thoughts whirled, then took shape again in bits and pieces.

"Fe-li-city! Stop dithering and come downstairs at once."

Her sisters.

The train.

Miss Grimm.

It was time to leave home for the adventure of a lifetime.

"Coming!" Felicity shouted in response, jumping from the bare mattress flung over the narrow iron bedstead, one of the last pieces of furniture that hadn't been packed. "I'm coming, blast it all."

Hurriedly, she stuffed the dime novel she'd been reading into the battered leather satchel Constance had given her two Christmases ago. The book lay sandwiched on either side with the paper, pens, and writing supplies Patience had given her for her birthday only a month earlier.

She paused to touch the packet of notepads as if they were some secret talisman. One day, she would fill those pristine sheets with her own stunning epic—a novel of the highest caliber of entertainment. She wasn't sure when she would start such a project. It was too soon yet. Far too soon. She would have to live and suffer sufficiently to attain the clarity of thought and emotion demanded by such an art form. But one day, she would be an authoress. By hang, she would!

Gazing wildly around her, she tried to fathom whether she'd forgotten anything. But in the maze of trunks and crates and boxes, it was difficult to tell. Suffice it to say that she had done her level best to collect everything she possessed, stow it away, and label it for shipping or storage. It only remained to be seen if her belongings arrived at her final destination of Saint Joseph, Missouri, in any semblance of order.

"Felicity, hurry! You'll miss your train." This time it was Patience who called up the stairs. Patience, who was rarely patient and who was tested to the limit by Felicity's dallying.

Well, Felicity thought with a shrug, the delay couldn't be helped. She'd felt driven—no, *possessed*—to read the next chapter of *The Ruffian's Rampage*. Even the title caused her to shiver in delight. Felicity had all but decided that once she'd finished the tome, she would have to think of a suitable title for her own work. Something that would help her to plot her novel, an epic story of a woman tormented by the evils found in the world around her, a world that Felicity was finally going to join.

"Fe-li-ci-ty!"

"Tarnation. Hold on to your corset strings," Felicity whispered under her breath, grabbing her satchel and her bonnet. Racing out of the cramped, stuffy attic that had been her own private nest—and prison—for so long, she clattered down the narrow staircase and into the front parlor.

The disorder found there was no better than it had been upstairs. Each piece of furniture, each book, each sheet of music, had been carefully tucked into the sturdiest of containers, most of the items to be delivered to a rented warehouse for keeping and only the most necessary of personal items to be forwarded to the respective destinations of the Pedigrue sisters.

It astounded Felicity how quickly their lives had changed since their father's death. Felicity had once had a hand in helping to transcribe Papa's will, and she'd been so sure that she and her sisters would be shipped off to much more dire situations than a teaching post out west for Felicity, a stint as a chaperone to a young girl for Patience, and a cutting position with a New York costuming company for Constance. In fact, Felicity had been sure she'd heard the word *India* used in connection with her own name more than once.

But she wasn't about to quibble. Not when it meant she was going to travel by train and live in the Wicked West. The thought of such a delightful twist of events made her quiver in anticipation.

"Have you got everything?" Constance inquired,

her tone relaying that she doubted such an occur-
rence.

Felicity dropped her belongings on the bare floor
and planted her bonnet on her head, stabbing a hat
pin through the twist of braids at her nape as her two
older sisters fussed at a flounce here, a ruffle there.

"I've got everything I need. Stop that!" She batted
their hands away and tugged at the jacket of her
woolen traveling suit, then hopped up and down like a
jack rabbit as she'd been taught so the fullness of her
skirts settled properly over her new cane crinoline.

"You're far too flushed," Constance intoned dis-
mally. "Anyone who sees you will think you're ill."

"Nonsense." Felicity peeked in a mirror leaning
crazily against the wall. Her cheeks were a trifle pink,
her eyes bright, but no matter. It was the adventure
ahead that had caused the color, not her precipitous
dash down the steps. But she couldn't admit such a
thing to the other girls. Patience was already teary
eyed at the thought of the separation they must
endure for the next year, and Constance was still
disapproving of Felicity's plans to journey with only
one chaperone. One. And a stranger she'd found
through a personal ad to boot.

Knowing she must head off an emotional leave-
taking before it had a chance to develop, Felicity took
Patience's hands. But when she stared into her sister's
deep blue eyes, saw the artful sweep of auburn hair—
a color Felicity had always wanted more than her own
dark brown tresses—she couldn't help but offer a
gentle squeeze.

Maybe this day wouldn't be as easy, as exciting, as
invigorating, as she had supposed. What would she do
without Patience to confide in, without Constance to
annoy?

"I *will* miss you," she said, leaning close and kissing

Patience on the cheek. To her surprise, Felicity's throat tightened with a sense of nostalgia, fear, and regret, emotions she'd been so sure she wouldn't feel. Not with so many opportunities lying ahead of them all. Not when they would only be separated for a year. One single, brief year.

"You must write," Patience insisted as Felicity retreated. Her hands clung to Felicity's. "Every day."

"Every other, I think," Felicity said with a grin, hoping to banish the sting of tears lingering in her own eyes. She attempted to leave but had to tug her hands free from Patience's grip before her older sister would completely release her.

Constance, ever sober, ever ladylike, ever stalwart and reserved, broke down completely, enclosing Felicity in a fierce embrace that threatened to whip Felicity's skirts up to an indecent level.

"Make sure you eat properly. Lots of grains."

"Yes, ma'am."

"Get your rest—at least eight full hours."

"I will."

"And wear your woolens no matter the weather. A sudden storm could blow up, you know."

"Yes, ma'am." But even as she offered the meek answer, Felicity resisted the urge to roll her eyes. Constance was a proponent of wearing long woolen underwear no matter the heat. Felicity didn't tell her eldest sister that she'd already disobeyed her, that beneath Felicity's traveling costume, she was wearing a new pair of cotton pantalets—*pantalets*. Never in her life had she been allowed to own such a thing until now. Since her father wasn't here to dictate her wardrobe, she'd taken a portion of the money allowed her to prepare for her trip to augment her clothing. The crinoline made her feel free, and the pantalets were somehow wicked, decadent, as if she owned some sort of garment reserved for a man's use alone.

The precipitous ring of the front bell caused them all to start, sniff, and laugh halfheartedly at their own surprise.

"Miss Grimm is here," Felicity said needlessly, speaking of the tall, dour, scarecrow of a woman who would escort her west.

Suddenly, as much as she had wished this day to come, as much as she'd longed to escape, she wanted the minutes to stretch out and last forever. She needed one last hug from Patience, a pat on the back from Constance. She craved a chance for them to scold and tease and bully.

But there was no time for that. No time at all.

"My wardrobe trunks have been sent to the station?"

Patience nodded. "Early this morning."

"Good. Well . . ." Knowing there was no margin for delay, she gathered her carpetbag, a bandbox, and the portfolio with her latest supply of novels and writing equipment.

"Good-bye," she said.

Her sisters both embraced her.

"It's only a year," Constance murmured huskily.

"Twelve months to the day, we'll return here and spend weeks describing our exploits," Patience added.

Then they were moving forward, one to open the door, the other to gather a basket of food for the journey.

As soon as the morning sunlight spilled into the foyer and Miss Grimm's cadaverous frame cast a shadow across the hall, Felicity knew there was no going back. Not that she wanted to. Not really.

"Ready, miss?" Miss Grimm demanded shortly, obviously impatient to be on her way. "We must be off to the station."

Straightening her spine and filling her lungs with

the familiar scents of home, Felicity hurried outside, Miss Grimm trailing her like a piece of flotsam.

At the gate, she turned to wave, wishing that her sisters' arrangements had allowed them the opportunity to accompany her to the station.

But maybe it was better this way, she thought, seeing Patience and Constance in the early morning sunshine, the roses of the arbor framing their heads. Such a picture would linger much more clearly in her mind than the gloomy confines of the railway station.

"Good-bye," she called. Then Miss Grimm, toting the basket of goodies Patience had provided, took her arm and led her to the hired carriage.

"Come along, Miss Felicity," the older woman urged, and Felicity was glad that she'd chosen Miss Grimm as her companion. Her evident control of the situation was incredibly reassuring.

"We've got to hurry. We mustn't miss the train. It wouldn't do for us to be stranded here in Boston."

Felicity reluctantly complied. After all, there was no time for regrets.

Just dreams for the future.

Honey Valley, Missouri

Logan Campbell tugged on the rope attached to the train signal, watching as a small flag climbed to the top of the water tower. After securing the frayed strip of hemp in place, he guided his horse back to the shoulder of packed dirt that edged either side of the shimmering railway tracks. Idly, he thought that hundreds of travelers must have stopped to wait for hundreds of trains hundreds of times before him.

Lifting his hat from his head, he swiped at the sweat

that trickled from his hairline down over his fore-head.

Eleven-thirty and the day was already hot. Too damned hot. The sky hung azure white, shimmering with an oasislike haze that shouldn't have been apparent for weeks yet.

Logan had always hated the heat. It brought too many memories with it. Images of red-clay earth, the stink of ripened cotton, and the musky humidity of the swamps.

It had been ten years since he'd set foot on the Georgia plantation where he'd been born. A decade. So why, then, did the pictures of that place stay so fresh and pure on the fringes of his memory? He had only to close his eyes to see the big house as vividly as if it had been painted with barely set watercolors.

His fingers dug into the brim of his hat. *One, two, three . . .*

Automatically he began counting to twenty. Slowly. Methodically. Just as his mother had taught him. A mother who had sought to protect him from Isaac Campbell every day she drew breath. Janet Mac-Greagor had ignored the shame heaped upon her when the bachelor-master of the house had proclaimed to his friends that she was his mistress but had made it clear she would never be anything more. After all, for the first seven years of their relationship, she'd been an indentured house servant. To most people, she was nothing but a poor Scottish immigrant woman beneath his station. Even so, she'd ignored all custom and given her two sons their sire's family name, and for a time, Isaac had doted on his boys. So much so that she'd dared to hope he might name them his heirs.

But he hadn't. It had taken Janet until her sons were grown to realize that Isaac Campbell would never taint the legacy of his estate by willing it to anyone but a legitimate heir. So in the process of surviving the inevitable cruelties heaped upon them all, Janet had taught her sons to hold their heads high, to fall back on pride alone if no other emotion could save them.

He sighed, planting his hat back on his head. As far as Logan was concerned, she'd been the only woman to truly touch him deep inside, in his soul where it counted most. She'd taught him to love.

Then she'd taught him to hate. To hate injustice and cruelty and self-righteousness. He'd shed no tears when Isaac Campbell had died, nor would he. The only grief he'd ever shown had been when Janet MacGreagor had been shot while trying to help one of the plantation slaves escape.

Logan had blamed himself for not trying harder to convince her to leave that place. But time and again, she'd insisted she was too old to start a new life. She'd wanted to remain where she'd raised her family, where she shared all her close, intimate friendships.

She'd been gone now for nearly two years, but Logan hadn't forgotten her. Nor would he forget his promise to avenge her death.

Slipping his canteen from the pommel of his saddle, he removed the stopper and lifted it to his lips. Less than a mouthful remained, and swallowing it made him crave more. But there would be fresher supplies available as soon as he reached Saint Joseph—food, drink, and rest aplenty. He had only to make it that far. Just a few more hundred miles by rail.

The thought should have been reassuring, but oddly, it was not. Instead, he shifted in the saddle, touching the hilt of the knife strapped to his calf, sliding a hand over the butt of the rifle in the side scabbard.

He wasn't sure what unnerved him so much. Not the heat; he'd experienced worse. After his mother's death, he and his older brother, Everett, had decided that Janet's wishes would be fulfilled. They had not been present when she had tried to help a slave escape their father's plantation, but by damn, they would carry on where she'd left off.

It had been Everett who had first begun to work with the Underground Railroad—a mysterious network of abolitionists dedicated to helping slaves find their way to freedom. To this day, the entire system amazed Logan in how well it met its goals. For all intents and purposes, there was no organized leader, no board of directors, no written routes, no schedules, no list of contacts. Throughout the southern states, safe houses had been established one by one by abolitionist supporters who knew little more than the stop before their own and the one that came next.

Everett and Logan had started their own work in a similar manner. Buying a large house in Saint Joseph, they'd converted it into Mother LaRee's Boarding House—a bordello that with the help of two of the "girls" and a local doctor served as a successful safe house. But after nearly a year of such work, Logan had not been content with a passive role. It was then, with the help of his brother, that he became a "conductor," one of the few men and women that escorted slaves directly from their point of origin to Canada.

The work was far more dangerous when done in this manner, but because Logan could take as many as a dozen slaves at a time, the rewards were greater as well. Although Everett had been leery about taking such an active role in the cause, he'd eventually come to Logan's aid. Through his work as a sketch artist for the periodical *Western Travels,* Everett had been in a perfect position to organize the daring escapes. Because the magazine originated in Natchez, Mississippi, most of their "passengers" came from that state as well. But Logan had perfected five routes north, each with its own set of safe houses, railway lines, back roads, contacts, and hiding places should he need to elude the law or the bounty hunters that invariably tracked his groups.

There was no denying that Logan was good at what he did. He had yet to lose a slave to his pursuers, but he couldn't afford to drop his guard. Not even now, on a hot, dusty Missouri day. He could all but taste some nameless hint of danger crouched in the hot afternoon. Waiting. Always waiting. For Logan's first mistake. His first stray thought.

It didn't help to have Brant Rassmussen staring at him as if he'd never see him again, Logan thought wryly as he pulled his attention from the gleaming tracks to the matter at hand.

"It's spooky, isn't it?" his companion asked.

Logan's eyes narrowed, and he wondered how on earth Brant had been able to read his thoughts. At nineteen he was little more than a lad, but he has some very adult ideas. The boy continued.

"It's downright eerie the way that whippoorwill keeps saying, 'Lookie-loo, lookie-loo.'"

Frankly, Logan hadn't paid much attention to the faint sound of the bird, nor did he think the call sounded remotely like "lookie-loo." But Brant had always had a fertile imagination, and it had been working double time the past full week they'd been together.

In fact, if the truth were told, the kid's habits were beginning to wear on Logan's nerves. He didn't believe in the supernatural, wasn't even sure if he believed in any sort of God.

Not anymore.

No God could possibly condone what Logan had seen in the slave quarters of the South.

What he'd done to help bring about some sort of change in the South.

Reaching into his vest pocket, Logan withdrew a thin cigar and lit it, breathing deep of the smoke in an effort to calm himself. Only a few minutes more, a quarter hour at the most. In no time at all, the train would barrel down the track, see the signal, and stop. Then Logan could leave Brant here with the wagon and continue the rest of the way south alone.

Alone. Right now, he didn't think there was a sweeter word in all the English language.

Brant wriggled on the wagon seat. Lunging toward Logan, who had brought his mount close to the conveyance, Brant grabbed Logan's arm before the cigar could reach his mouth.

"Don't do it, Logan. Don't go back there," he said desperately. "Not so soon. Stay here with me 'n' Digger."

Logan stared at the boy hard, watching as bit by bit the ice of his demeanor conveyed itself to Rassmussen.

"Let go of me, Brant."

Rassmussen released his arm so abruptly it could have been a hot coal. Logan knew the boy had forgotten that Logan didn't like people to order him about or question his judgment.

"I only . . . Geez, Logan," he stammered. "I just wanted you to think twice about going back to Saint Joe so soon."

Logan didn't bother to give the boy's uneasiness a second thought. Rassmussen was an odd fellow, one of those fatalistic doomsayers who thought every run they made to Canada would be their last.

What Brant didn't know was that this was Logan's final trip to Saint Joseph. Then he would go back to Canada for good. After one more race for the border with a group of escaped slaves, one more flight for freedom. Then even Logan knew that to continue his activities would be foolhardy. The plantation-sponsored bounty hunters were suspicious of him. As it was, they would be on his trail much too closely for comfort.

Moreover, there was the added threat of the law— Saint Joseph's sheriff, Hap Grigsby, in particular. He and his henchman, Nathaniel Moon, were on the payrolls of at least two dozen southern businessmen and slave traders. They had a network of spies scouring the southern portion of the state that made even Logan's contacts in the Underground Railroad pale in comparison. Logan needed to lie low for at least a year, see to it that Mother LaRee's was used as nothing but a bordello. Then Logan could renew his efforts without the law growing any wiser to his activities.

The thought alone was enough to make Logan rub a knuckle at the spot high on his thigh where a Mississippi marshal had managed to wing him with a pistol ball. Logan hadn't been seen that night in Natchez. Not his face. But he also knew that it was only a matter of time before descriptions and alibis were pieced together enough to point the finger of blame his way.

Just one more run. One more promise to keep. Then he would be finished.

Grinding the barely smoked cigar against his belt buckle to extinguish it, Logan made sure the embers were out, then carefully replaced the cheroot in his pocket. Only then did he return his attention to Brant. "I'll meet you at the Wilmington crossroads outside of town two weeks from now, Brant."

He thought the kid would burst into tears at the suggestion. His cheeks grew red enough, the freckles beneath his carrot-red hair fading into muddy patches. Then all hint of color left his cheeks, and he became ashen.

"Geez, Logan. Do I have to be the one to go with

you? I thought I'd get out of this sorta business. I'm not like you. I don't have . . ."

When Logan met his stare, the boy's comment trailed into a wisely chosen silence. Even so, Logan didn't need him to finish the remark. *I don't have ice in my veins . . . I don't have balls of brass . . . I don't have the nerve of the devil . . .* He'd heard all the comparisons before. Heard them and disregarded them. What Logan did, the chances he took, didn't take courage. Just a whole lot of anger. At himself. At a father who had offered him an education but had never claimed him. At a world that continued to punish the weak.

"I'm counting on you, Brant. I need you and Digger to be at the crossroads with the wagons. On time. This will be our last run. I promise." Logan stared at him hard, and Brant finally relented, slouching in the wagon seat, resigned to the fact.

"Yes, sir," he mumbled with more humility than Logan had ever seen the kid extend to his mother or even his pastor. "I'll be waiting."

"Good boy." Logan knew that Brant had joined forces with the Underground Railroad thinking it would be a dashing and adventurous job. That notion had been drummed out of his head the first time a pack of hound dogs and bounty hunters had trailed him through Wilmington. The boy had since had more than one taste of real danger, and Logan supposed Brant had decided he'd had his fill.

A protracted silence settled over them like a woolen blanket. Long enough for the sweltering heat to sink into their bones and the cicadas to lull them into a false sense of peace.

Without warning, Brant slapped at the wagon box and said, "Logan? I've got to say it, damn it. I've got a bad feeling about this next trip."

Logan resisted the urge to sigh audibly. Brant was a

tenacious creature, he would give him that. Once he clamped onto an idea, there was no shaking him loose.

"Brant . . . ," he protested wearily. But Logan wasn't allowed to finish his thought.

"Look, why don't you cancel your plans and lie low for a while? I saw an owl fly 'cross the moon this morning—"

"Good hell almighty, Brant!" Logan snapped. His temper was already frayed, and he really wasn't in the mood to coddle the boy. He was tired, hot, and hungry. He wanted a bath, a bed, and a woman—not necessarily in that order—and he didn't care to hear about omens that had come to Brant in the form of owls or frogs or hair balls.

But Brant's stricken expression forced him to tamp down his impatience. "Brant, I swear," he said more calmly, "if I sense anything is wrong, anything at all, I'll send word to you to forget the whole trip. All right?"

Brant considered the offer with a good deal more caution than it deserved, but at long last, he agreed glumly. "Yes, sir. I won't let you down."

Again, Logan turned his eyes northeast, waiting for the train that would lead him south. One more trip. Just one more trip.

"'Course," Brant mumbled, partly to himself, partly to Logan, "the owl wasn't the worst of it. No, sir. There was that clump of grasshoppers resting in the middle of an open road . . ."

Logan took a deep breath, held it, and squinted more purposely down the tracks. Though he wasn't a religious man and hadn't prayed in years, he couldn't help thinking, *Dear Lord, send that train my way. Now. Before I lose all control and give Brant a sign of another kind to worry about.*

Two

Miss Grimm snored.

Felicity shifted on the hard train seat and bent her head as if she were reading the novel in her lap. Actually, she was peering through her lashes, hoping, praying, that no one else could hear Miss Grimm. Or if they could, they wouldn't think the two of them were together.

It was a faint wish. Miss Grimm's labored breathing could be heard with great ease over the pant of the locomotive, giving the impression that a grizzly bear had been imprisioned in this very car. Moreover, because there were very few passengers on the train as yet, it was also obvious that Miss Grimm was Felicity's companion.

Blast. How had a woman who had seemed so perfect in her advertisement have so many pitfalls in the flesh? Felicity glared at the elderly woman, but Miss Grimm remained oblivious, pale gray lashes splashed over sallow skin. She made a slight squeaking noise, a moan, then began to snore again, this time whistling through her teeth.

Hearing a snicker of amusement behind her, Felicity could have literally withered and died. She was finally about to indulge in the first taste of freedom she'd ever had, and she was shackled to the side of a prissy, scolding fussbudget who watched Felicity's every move with the intensity of a hawk and wouldn't let her so much as sneeze in public for fear it would ruin her reputation. Felicity had thanked heaven above when the old woman had finally fallen asleep.

Until she'd begun to snore.

Felicity smothered a groan. It was so disappointing. When the terms if her father's will had been disclosed, Felicity had immediately begun spinning pipe dreams of the adventure ahead. The tone of Miss Grimm's advertisement and the thrust of her answers during her interview had led Felicity to believe that she was a widow intent on seeing the world. Felicity had thought her sour attitude to be a result of nerves and had been so sure that once they became better acquainted Miss Grimm would blossom with spirit and laughter.

Instead, Felicity had unwittingly saddled herself with the closest thing to a female minister. A weary, fidgety spinster with the lungs of a dragon.

Shifting ever so slightly, Felicity tried to pull the edge of her skirt from beneath Miss Grimm's bony behind. It was a feat she'd been working on for the better part of an hour. She was sure the old woman had purposely planted herself on the folds so that Felicity would not be able to leave undetected. She must have known that Felicity wanted to stand, to stretch, to go out on the platform and feel the breeze whip through her hair.

Such a spontaneous display would have had Miss Grimm succumbing to a fit of apoplexy. The two of them had been together for only a few days and already Felicity was growing accustomed to the woman's patented response to whatever Felicity had wished to do: "It isn't done; it simply isn't done." A statement that was invariably followed by her lips pulling together like a drawstring bag.

Tarnation. How was Felicity supposed to do anything, *see* anything, if Miss Grimm wouldn't even let her stand up unescorted, for heaven's sake? She didn't seem to realize that Felicity had only one week to cater to her own whims. Then she would be taking her place as one of the literature teachers at Saint Joseph's Academy. From that moment on, even though she would be living in the heart of the American West, she would have to be the model citizen. Subdued, restrained.

Dull.

She tugged harder on her skirt, and at long last, it slid free. Felicity fought the urge to throw her hands into the air and shout "Hallelujah."

Easing sideways, inch by inch by inch, she finally managed to slide from the bench and stand. The sudden jarring of the train nearly sent her toppling into Miss Grimm's lap again, but she clutched at the worn upholstery until she regained her balance. Straightening, she smoothed her bodice with a glove-covered hand, and keeping her posture as stiff as possible, she made her way to the back of the car.

For the past hour, she'd been eyeing the barrel of water with its pewter spigot. She'd watched stray drops drip, drip, drip to the rough wooden boards beneath. The heat of the carriage and the prickliness of her gown had made the liquid that much more inviting, that much more luxurious. It didn't matter to her that Miss Grimm frowned upon the use of the public supply. She'd already heard the woman proclaim, "It isn't done; it simply isn't done" at least a dozen times. Such warnings held little sway now. Felicity wanted a drink. She would *have* a drink.

Her fingertips trailed over the backs of the seats as she walked, allowing her to keep her balance amid the shuddering of the train. But the farther she moved from her own place, the more the disturbances increased until, belatedly, she realized that they were slowing down.

The thought was enough to bring a wave of panic. This wasn't a scheduled stopping place, and so far, Miss Grimm had shown an amazing instinct for bristling like a porcupine at the first hint of trouble.

Blast and bother. If that woman found Felicity gone from her assigned place, she would never get her drink.

Felicity's pace quickened, and she grasped the metal dipper hooked over the rim of the barrel. The train began to shriek and hiss, grinding to a halt, and she prayed that she wouldn't be thrown to the ground with the precipitous stop. But soon, the jolting motions ceased, and the train panted and huffed as if the effort of drawing to a halt had been more than it could bear.

Knowing she had very little time, if any, Felicity twisted the spigot and filled the dipper to the rim. Only then did she dare to peer behind her.

To Felicity's ultimate relief, Miss Grimm remained asleep. Evidently, her dithering had exhausted her to the point of near unconsciousness.

Not about to trust her luck, Felicity took a hasty sip. The water was tepid at best but tasted good, so good, slipping down a throat caked with dust and soot and Miss Grimm's forced propriety. Manna from heaven could not have been sweeter.

Once her thirst had been momentarily quenched, Felicity bent at the waist to peer out the windows, hoping to see a reason for the delay. It had to be something exciting. Something wonderful.

But there was nothing there. Nothing but the steam that hissed through the windows the other passengers had left open to catch some air. Only Miss Grimm's panes and blinds had been left firmly closed—a weak attempt to prevent the ashes from the smokestack from settling on their clothing.

Something about the cessation of noise must have blasted its way through Miss Grimm's stupor because she shifted in her seat, and Felicity froze, sure she would receive a scolding.

The woman grunted. Wriggled. Huffed. Then she resumed her slumber.

For several seconds, Felicity stared, slack jawed, scarcely able to believe her good fortune. In a wink, she decided the time had come to test her freedom and see more of this fascinating world that had been whizzing by her window.

Filling the dipper once again; she tiptoed onto the rear platform of the train, catching the conspiratorial wink of the salesman slouched on the third to last seat. Offering him a weak smile that she wasn't sure she should have given at all, Felicity closed the door behind her.

Immediately, the tiny space was crowded with her skirts and petticoats and crinolines. But because no one appeared inclined to follow her, Felicity didn't let the fact worry her. Propping a hand against the iron railing, she gazed out at the rolling grazing land lining either side of the train.

How beautiful. How stark. How empty of the city bustle she was accustomed to viewing from her bedroom window.

This part of the country was inexplicably wonderful. Its vast array of flora and fauna intrigued her soul and calmed a clamoring corner she'd never known existed. It was as if there was something *right* about the place. Something . . . familiar.

Even as the thought appeared, she dismissed it.

She'd never been anywhere but Boston, so how could she possibly "remember" rolling prairies, sparkling streams?

And a house. She remembered a rough log house.

Shaking her head at such nonsense, Felicity decided she was experiencing some strange form of déjà vu.

Scanning the horizon again, she noted that the summer's heat had already begun to turn the grasses brown and there was a distinctly listless appearance to the trees in the distance, but she didn't care. It was so different from Boston. So different from anything she'd ever imagined. If she could manage to paint a picture with words, it could only add to her abilities as a writer, give her readers a greater depth of understanding. In fact, she would have to make a sketch or two . . . for . . .

Felicity grew still, the dipper suspended midway to her mouth as a figure materialized from the steam and soot and sunshine.

He was on horseback, coming from the front of the train at a speed that conveyed the fact that he knew he'd delayed them all, but he wasn't too concerned about it. He was dusty from the stained brim of his hat to the tips of his scuffed boots, but he moved with the assurance of a man who was accustomed to long hours spent in a saddle. His hips rocked with a familiar ease; his hands were loose on the reins but very much in control.

As he neared Felicity, he checked the pace of his animal, and Felicity gasped. He meant to stop. Here. Near her. Then she could have kicked herself for such an assumption, for such unmitigated conceit. Because this was the last passenger car in the train, he was not easing his gait on her behalf but obviously intended to load his mount in the boxcar behind her.

Her assumptions were confirmed when one of the elderly porters ran down the shoulder of the tracks and clambered up the outer ladder to open the heavy sliding door. Within seconds, a ramp appeared, and the stranger rode his horse inside, bending low and to the side of his saddle like an Indian to keep from knocking his head on the supporting beam.

Because she was momentarily unable to see him, Felicity took a sip of water, waiting, watching. Then she saw the stranger jump out again, his boots crunching on the gravel. Swinging his saddle over his shoulder, he said something to the porter, offered him a few coins, and made his way to Felicity.

Belatedly, she understood that the man meant to board. Right there. Right then. She took a step toward the door in order to clear the way, then stopped abruptly when there was a ripping sound from the direction of her hem.

Botheration. She was caught. One of the flounces of her petticoat had snagged on a loose nail.

There was no time to bend and extricate herself, no real space to move out of his way. But she also knew she couldn't very well tear her way free and chance leaving a scrap of her undergarments behind. Even *she* would be the first to admit such a thing "wasn't done." She couldn't allow any man to see so intimate a thing as a scrap of lace from her unmentionables. That rule applied even more so for *this* man. He was much too dusty and dirty and intense.

The stranger had come very close now, the musky scent of his saddle preceding him in a way that shocked her, his boots making small puffs in the dust. Then a hand sheathed in a stained leather glove grasped the railing, and he swung onto the first step.

Felicity was rooted to the spot, his nearness affecting her in a way no other person had ever done. She became unaccountably flustered and nervous. Not just because she had never been allowed such close proximity to someone of the opposite gender. No, there was much more to her consternation than that. This man caused a tight bud of emotion to form in her chest and aroused tingling sensations in her extremities that she didn't recognize or understand.

What should she do? What should she do?

At a loss, Felicity began tugging fruitlessly at her skirts. All to no avail. The stranger's eyes—brilliant indigo-blue eyes—were upon her. Hot and vibrant, their inspection was far more intimate than was proper as his gaze slipped from the tip of her modest bonnet, down her tightly corseted body, to her belled skirts and the peep of lace held by the board.

"You seem to be caught."

Even his voice was rich, flowing over her like a wave of rich chocolate.

Felicity opened her mouth but didn't respond. She couldn't. Not when she knew that an embarrassing squeak would emerge instead of a coherent word.

The man's lips curled in a crooked half smile. One that was more mocking than amused but had the ability to make her stomach do flip-flops all the same.

"Don't move, and I'll see if I can't get you loose."

She could only swallow against the tightness that continued to gather in her throat. An odd sort of scratchy self-consciousness that made any sort of a protest impossible.

To her horror, she saw him bend and watched the brim of his hat brush her skirts as his shoulder disappeared into the folds of her gown. Then those dusty, dirty gloves reached for the snippet of lace exposed to his view, and he carefully unhooked the ruffle from an exposed nail.

Felicity's face flamed, the scorching heat settling into her cheeks as he took the time to smooth the flounce into place and adjust the lowest rung of her crinoline. Although the gesture was entirely innocent, even helpful, she couldn't escape the fact that he was touching her undergarments. Worse yet, the crinoline provided no buffer between her body and his fingers. The heat of him seeped beneath her skirts, warming her skin.

Felicity's lashes flickered closed. Constance had been right. Felicity should have worn wool. If she had obeyed her eldest sister, she might not notice how his shoulder pressed into her thigh. Or how one knuckle grazed her ankle in a way that was quite unnecessary. Quite brazen. Quite shocking. Quite deliberate.

At long last, he stood, climbing up another step and crowding her unmercifully with his maleness. "That should do it."

A part of her heard the locomotive chug and hiss. They were about to leave. It didn't matter to anyone else that she and this man continued to cling to the platform. She hadn't even noticed that the elderly porter had returned to his place, merely another sign of her scattered wits.

The stranger was watching her closely, so closely that a tingling began at the base of her spine and radiated up and out.

Dear heaven above, she shouldn't be here. She shouldn't be staring so boldly at a total stranger, but she couldn't help it. The harsh set of his features and the golden-brown hair that hung to his shoulders held her transfixed. Like a fly in a spider's lair, she couldn't ignore the fact that she was unwillingly drawn to his narrowed eyes and haughty posture. She was attracted to him even as she was repelled. He fairly reeked of danger. Of a velvet-encased cruelty. A grim acceptance. He was like nothing, like no one, she'd ever met before.

When she would have escaped through the door, he caught her elbow quickly, easily. She sucked in a breath at the contact. She could feel each of his fingers through the layers of clothing that separated them.

"Is that all the thanks I get?"

His cockiness should have offended her. If he'd said such a thing to Patience or Constance—or even Miss Grimm—she knew that they would have had a crushing reply.

But Felicity had nothing to say. Nothing but "Thank you."

The words were so soft, so meek, so breathy, she could have kicked herself.

Again, he offered her that mocking half smile.

"So you *do* talk."

Felicity felt the heat crawling up her neck and into her cheeks. She must sound like an idiot schoolgirl.

But that didn't mean she was completely without pride. Her chin tipped ever so slightly. "Of course I talk."

The retort lost some of its indignation when the hiss of steam increased and the wheels of the train ground against the track in an effort to pull the heavy conveyance.

Through it all, Felicity didn't move. The searing tide of her blush made its way even farther, and try as she might, she couldn't do a thing to stop it. She could only stand there like a fool and gape at him.

He was beautiful. Absolutely beautiful.

Hard.

Lean.

Implacable.

Earthy.

Nerve-rattling.

The train shuddered into motion, and Felicity gasped when she lost her footing, pitching forward. But the stranger was there to stop her from going too far, his arms snapping around her waist, his back bracing against the rough wooden wall of the passenger car.

The action caused her own hands to fly out in self-defense, and the half-filled dipper of water knocked against the stranger's sleeve. Embarrassed, she unwittingly braced her free hand against his chest. A firm, masculine chest.

"Pardon me," she mumbled, mortified when one of her fingers strayed inside the shirt he'd left unbuttoned far lower than was customary in Boston. She encountered flesh. Tensile, summer-moist flesh and downy-soft hair that made themselves felt through the thin net of her gloves.

Felicity thought the man would rail at her for her inadvertent familiarity. But rather than being peeved, he stared even harder, his gaze adopting a decidedly wicked gleam.

Extricating herself from the possibility of an even more mortifying situation, Felicity sprang back. Grappling with the stubborn doorknob, she hurried into the railway car.

Once there, she stood uncertainly, trembling, wondering what she should do next. How was a woman supposed to act after encountering such a man? Especially when she could feel the impression of his body against her skin?

Shaking herself of such nonsense, Felicity tried to summon the stern control she'd seen her sisters use often enough. Rehooking the dipper to the barrel, she returned to her seat next to the sleeping Miss Grimm. But she had barely smoothed her skirts when she noted that the stranger had followed her. He hadn't even waited a discreet interval of time on the platform in order to avoid talk.

His boot heels thumped on the rough wooden floor and he dropped his saddle on an empty bench. With a glance in her direction, he reclaimed the dipper for himself. Filling it, he held it aloft in silent tribute. One that she prayed no one else saw. Then he drank greedily, the muscles of his throat moving fluidly, dribbles of moisture escaping down his chin into the stubble of a beard that darkened his chin.

Through it all, Felicity could only stare, stunned by the shuddering reaction that coursed throughout her body.

His lips were covering the spot where hers had been minutes earlier.

The exact spot.

After filling the metal scoop again, the stranger returned to the outer platform. Even as she damned herself for her curiosity, Felicity leaned sideways in order to see past the shape of the traveling salesman.

To her utter astonishment, the stranger removed his hat and vest, tossing them onto his seat inside. With his shirt unbuttoned to a point below midchest, he upended the dipper over his head, allowing the water to rush down his body. For several minutes, he stood with his chin tipped back, his feet braced apart, allowing the gusts of air to cool the moisture streaming down his face.

A grunt at her side brought Felicity's attention rudely aside.

Miss Grimm had awakened. Her mouth hung agape and her narrow bosom heaved in acute distress at discovering that such a man had boarded the train and now stood on the rear platform making a spectacle of himself.

"Indecent. Completely and utterly indecent," she snapped, already reaching for her handkerchief to fan some air in her direction.

When the man happened to glance Miss Grimm's way and tip his head in acknowledgment, the elderly woman's bony fingers clamped around Felicity's, causing her to jump. "Come along, Miss Pedigrue. We will sit facing the opposite direction."

The stranger raked his fingers through his wet hair, an action that caused Elmira Grimm to make a strangled mew of disgust. "Move, please. This instant. You shouldn't have to witness such carnalities."

Carnalities? Felicity wondered as she was forced to stand and exchange her seat for the one where their basket and satchel had been positioned. But as she moved, she couldn't prevent herself from taking one last peek at the stranger. An action that only increased her agitation.

The man continued to stare at her. He'd grown quite serious, quite sober, as if a goose had walked across his grave. Then, just when her interest was piqued again, her pity, her unconscious empathy, he had the nerve, the unmitigated gall, to smile.

And wink.

Three

～

The woman in the passenger car blushed.

If the reaction hadn't been something he'd been expecting, Logan might have chuckled. But after watching the tide of color rise and ebb in her cheeks time and time again, Logan had winked at her on purpose, hoping to see the spots of pink appear. It had been ages, perhaps even his whole life, since a woman had reacted so sweetly, so honestly, to any overtures made by him. Even the way she sat quickly in her seat, her back turned resolutely in his direction, her dainty hands rearranging her skirts with more fussiness than necessary, pleased him to no end.

Of course, her companion was not nearly so delightful to study. The older woman glared, her arms folding beneath her flat bosom, her gray eyes staring him down.

But Logan was not dissuaded. Not at all. He'd spent eight weeks on horseback eluding the law and a bevy of bounty hunters while he'd taken six slaves north to Canada. He'd slept in the dirt, lived in the saddle, and fed upon fear and tension. At this moment, that slip of a girl was the most inviting thing he'd seen in weeks.

Girl? The word caught in his consciousness and stuck there. No, she wasn't a girl. Not at all. Her molasses-colored hair and eyes might offer her a certain fragility, even a naïveté, but there was a strength and maturity to her form that bespoke a full-grown woman.

So why was she accompanied by such a protective old crone?

Logan swept back a lock of wet hair. He was puzzled by the contradiction of roles he saw before him. He'd been around the elderly lady's kind enough to know that they were paid companions, generally employed to follow young, impressionable charges as they traipsed from pillar to post. Their sort did not accompany women who were of an age to be married and have families of their own.

Unless, by some chance, the brown-haired creature was unmarried.

No. She wasn't the type to sit on the shelf long. Not with that face, that form. That delightful blush.

Returning to his seat, Logan settled sideways on the worn bench and propped his back against the wall. The ache of his shoulders and the throb of his knees conveyed to him eloquently enough that it was time he rested and readied himself for what awaited him at the journey's end. There was no time for intriguing bouts of "what if."

Especially not for a man like him. One who'd spent too much time in the company of the world's rougher characters. A man with no honorable background or breeding to speak of—a definite disadvantage with women who were taught to behave so properly.

Pulling his hat low over his eyes, he extended his legs into the aisle in an effort to ease his cramped muscles. But even though the weariness tugged at his brain, he couldn't bring himself to sleep. Not yet.

Instead, he peered beneath the brim, telling himself that it couldn't hurt to look. Just look.

For some time, he watched the young woman's back, noted the way her head bent over her book, allowing him a glimpse of the damp curls at her nape. The sway of the train caused her body to move from side to side ever so slightly, and he couldn't help wondering what her hair would look like unbound and free.

Pity he wouldn't have time to indulge in flirtation. It had been so long since he'd been with someone like that, so long since he'd smelled that clean, floral scent proper females carried with them wherever they went. He would like to hear her voice again, perhaps even touch her skin. Once.

But even if he had the time, such things could never be. He was the antithesis of everything a true lady desired in an acquaintance, and he could tell by studying her that this girl had been raised to adhere to a gentlewoman's high standards. He was surprised that she hadn't called out for help at the boldness he'd displayed on the platform. He'd been quite sure that his knuckles had grazed the cotton of the hose at her ankles, yet she hadn't said a word. Not a word.

Yes, it was a shame he didn't have more time. If he did, he might consider . . .

"Don't do it. Don't even think about it. That's not the kind of a woman you want to dally with."

When the familiar voice slid out of the hot air around him, Logan felt a shimmer of alarm. Peering around the brim of his hat, he met his older brother's gaze, then took in the conductor's uniform Everett wore over his lanky frame and the sheaf of tickets stuffed in his pocket.

What the hell was *he* doing here?

But the question wasn't voiced aloud. Not even as Logan's heart began to pound in his chest. Something was wrong, seriously wrong, if Everett had made a special trip to intercept him on the train south.

"Leave her alone, Logan." Everett gestured imperceptibly to the girl in black.

"Why?" Logan asked so softly that no one could have heard the response over the rumble of the train.

Beneath his visored cap, Everett Campbell frowned. "Later," he said, conveying that now was not the time to talk openly. Then, for the benefit of anyone who might be listening, he said more forcefully, "Ticket, please."

Logan dug into the pocket of his vest, withdrawing a twenty-dollar gold piece. "Take it out of that."

While Everett scribbled a receipt, he glanced at Logan and inquired carefully, "Everything go according to plan on your way to Canada?"

Logan's imperceptible nod was his only answer.

"You're sure?"

Again, a frisson of alarm slithered up Logan's spine. Brant's dire predictions of trouble rose to the fore of his memory, but he tamped them down. "Yes, why?"

Everett ignored him, asking, "How many did you get out of the country?"

"Six."

Six slaves. Six slaves who had managed to escape from a plantation in Natchez and had needed a guide to take them north to Canada. Logan had made a dozen such trips already that year—without having ever been caught. Just one more trip, he reminded himself for the hundredth time. Then he would retire, find some land and a new life. A purpose. Something beyond rebelling against his father's heritage and the man's views on slavery, he supposed.

"I think you should let someone else take this next batch, Logan," Everett said, handing him his ticket and a handful of change.

Logan took the coins, then slumped even deeper in

his seat, pulling his hat over his eyes. "Have you been talking to Brant?"

"No. Why?"

"Nothing," Logan mumbled, not in the mood to explain. "If you can't tell me what's got your knickers in a knot, then at least tell me why should I let someone else take the run I've been planning for the better part of a year."

"Where are you headed?"

"I've got a special family in mind."

"Who, Logan? Who is so all-fired important that you can't wait a month or two until interest in your activities dies down?"

Logan gauged his brother's reaction, knowing Everett wouldn't like what he was about to hear. "I've got a pair of slaves in mind . . . Ezekial's children."

Ezekial was the slave their mother had helped to escape. An act that had cost Janet MacGreagor her life.

The stub of a pencil Everett had been using clattered to the floor, and he swore as he scooped it up. When he straightened, there was no disguising the glare he sent Logan's way.

"Damn it, Logan—"

"I'm taking them north. I promised."

Everett swept a quick gaze over the occupants of the passenger car. His lips thinned, but he didn't express his obvious anger. Instead, he whispered, "Meet me on the siding next stop, Logan. We've run into trouble. Big trouble." Then he made his way down the aisle again, heading toward the front of the train.

With each step he took, Logan was left with the distinctly unpleasant idea that maybe, just maybe, he should have paid more attention to Brant Rassmussen's omens of doom. Because he didn't have a good feeling about any of this.

* * *

Blackness had descended by the time the train paused in its journey for fuel and water. Logan was one of the last passengers to alight—he and the pretty woman with her chaperone. The old hen had been clucking on and on with the girl about the evils of public waiting rooms and the inadvisability of eating restaurant food.

It amused him to think that there were people in the world who cared about such things. Appearances and propriety. Logan had abandoned such things years ago—the willingness to please, the craving for approval. He could thank Isaac Campbell for teaching him that such emotions were altogether useless. It wasn't the glossy finish of a person that mattered, it was the substance to be found underneath.

After casting little more than a glance in the female's direction, Logan walked quickly in the direction of the caboose. For part of the way, he was accompanied by a fading monologue on virtue that the girl's chaperone had continued to recite.

". . . lady must see to it that she is a vision of poise no matter what indignities she is forced to endure . . . primitive country . . . far from . . . decency . . ."

A lesson on indignities.

Did that mean the girl had confessed to meeting him on the platform?

He shook his head. No. If that were the case, he was sure that he would have received far more from the woman's chaperone than a warning glare.

Forcing his mind onto his own reason for prowling the rail yard so late at night, Logan passed the warm lamplight shining from the last car and continued on, making his way deeper into the tangle of tracks located beyond the station.

Here the evening gloom was deeper, quieter. The sound of his footsteps made an odd sort of intrusion, reminding him that he'd spent too much time skulking through the shadows of late.

Walking slowly, cautiously, he made his way farther and farther into the stillness until he reached the northwest spur where the empty boxcars were kept. Only then did he stop. Leaning a shoulder against the rotting wood of a flatbed carrier, Logan lit a cheroot and waited, knowing that in a matter of moments the glowing ember would be seen and the signal given.

Just as he'd supposed, barely a minute passed before he heard the rustle of cloth and Everett appeared. So tall, so stiff, so full of rules and procedure.

Not for the first time, Logan wondered why he couldn't be more like his brother, more convinced that there were people who could be honest and noble and self-sacrificing. Why did Logan always look at the blackness instead of the good?

Knowing that Everett would have wound himself up and was ready to deliver some sort of self-righteous scolding, Logan was the first to speak. "So what's the problem, Everett?" He gestured to the man's clothes. "Why are you here, all dressed up in that ridiculous monkey suit?"

The attempt at humor fell flat.

Everett scowled and snatched the cheroot from Logan, his own fingers shaking. Taking a deep drag, he peered into the blackness as if he were convinced some unseen foe might fire on them in a matter of seconds.

"Damn it all to hell, Logan!" he finally hissed. "What happened in Natchez?"

Logan resisted the urge to rub his aching thigh, to feel the wound that he had incurred during his last run through Mississippi. The bullet hole was nearly healed but remained angry, red, and sore.

"What do you mean?" he asked with apparent casualness.

"I mean you were *seen* taking those slaves!"

Logan shook his head to deny such an idea, but his pulse grew sluggish and each nerve in his body stood on end. "Impossible."

Everett took another deep drag of the cheroot. "Impossible, hell," he mocked, stabbing Logan in the chest with his finger. "One of my contacts in Mississippi had to put a stop to a circular being passed around—a circular with your description."

"My description could pass for a hundred men. How do you know it was me?"

Everett clamped the cigar between his teeth and reached into his pocket, withdrawing a piece of crumpled paper. "Because the circular was originally supposed to have this sketch attached to it, that's why."

Logan took the sheet, holding it up to the light. The artist had not been particularly gifted in his rendering, but the similarities between the man who had been drawn and his own face were too close for comfort.

"Who saw me?"

"Some woman. She said you were with her in Natchez that night, that you bought her a drink."

Logan shook his head. He would never be so careless as to expose himself socially in the same community where he'd gone to help those slaves who wished to "relocate."

"It's a lie. I didn't have a drink with anyone, let alone a woman."

"Well, that doesn't really matter, does it?" Everett snapped. *"Someone* has seen you. Your picture was almost sent all over the country. If it hadn't been brought to one of the print shops owned by a fellow abolitionist, your face would have been staring back at you from every fencepost north *and* south of the Mason–Dixon line. Luckily, the printer—Raddison is his name—altered your picture to look like something out of a bad dream. Now, all the wanted posters that have been circulated have enough inaccurate information to keep the bounty hunters away from you for a while."

Logan folded the paper in half once, twice, then tucked it deep in the pocket of his vest.

"Thank Raddison for me, will you?"

Everett stared at him in amazement, clasping the cheroot and throwing it to the ground in frustration. "Is that the only thing you can say?"

Logan grew icy. "What more do you want me to do, Everett?"

"I want you to get off that train and get back on the first one going north. I want you in Canada by the end of the week. I'll have Doc Wanger close down Mother LaRee's and both of us will take a nice, long vacation."

"What good will that do?"

"What good? What good?" Everett sputtered in disbelief. "Haven't you been listening? Someone has *seen* you. Even with the bad posters, it's only a matter of time before the bounty hunters realize Logan Campbell is the man responsible for moving forty-two slaves to Canada. They won't take kindly to your activities and neither will the plantation owners who employed them to find their property. Then to top it all off, there's Grigsby. Because you operate out of Saint Joseph, one of these days he's bound to figure out you aren't some saddle bum who makes frequent stops at Mother LaRee's. You know the slave holders would offer him a handsome reward for your capture—whether or not he apprehends you inside his own jurisdiction. He'd be happy to follow you all the way to Canada if he had to."

"Then I suppose I'll have to hurry and finish my business down south."

Everett's mouth dropped, but no sound came out.

He swept the peaked conductor's hat from his head and threw it into the dirt in frustration. "Let someone else do it!"

"No. I promised Ezekial—"

"Promised? Promised! What about your own *life*, damn you?"

Logan refused to respond. One more run. One more escape. Then he would retire from this business. Retire at the age of twenty-six.

"Did you send the telegraph to Doc Wanger?"

Everett huffed in indignation, then finally threw up his hands in defeat. "Yes. I let him know that the last group you escorted arrived safely in Canada."

"Then our mutual business for tonight is finished, Everett."

The moment the words were free, Logan knew he'd said the wrong thing. He'd diverted Everett from the problem at hand and unconsciously reminded him of his role as an older sibling.

Everett glared at his younger brother in a way that Logan had grown used to seeing. It was that you're-a-stubborn-fool-who's-going-to-get-yourself-killed gaze. Logan didn't really give a damn.

"I never should have let you take on this kind of work."

Logan shrugged. "Why not? You've been just as involved with these escapes as I have, and you've never complained about the job."

"I'm a messenger, no more. The law can't shoot me for that, but the plantation owners you tangle with would be more than happy to string you up."

Logan didn't bother to reply.

"At least call on someone to help you."

"Who? You know as well as I do that most of our contacts operate safe houses and nothing more."

"What about that fellow in Midville? Barker? Or the one in Greensboro? Wallace?"

Logan sighed and gazed regretfully at the crushed cheroot on the ground. Everett had never approved of his smoking, even though Everett had been the one to introduce Logan to the habit and continued to indulge in the activity himself.

Reaching into his pocket, Logan withdrew another thin cigar. His last one. The same cheroot he'd smoked while waiting for the train and listening to Rassmussen's tales of woe. "From what I hear, Barker's laid up with that broken leg and Wallace barely escaped the bounty hunters last week. He's got to spend time with the folks at home to convince anyone watching him that he's as sweet smelling as a rose."

"Don't you think you should do the same?"

Logan shrugged. He was a wanderer, he'd always been a wanderer. At sixteen, he'd left home to join the army. By that time, his mother had finished the terms of her indenture, and he'd begged her to join him. She'd refused, and five years out west had cured Logan of the sport of killing. Especially when he'd returned to discover all the ways Isaac Campbell had tried to humiliate his mother. How he'd grown cruel and cold and mean.

"No one expects me to stay anywhere."

It was true, and they both knew it.

"Let me do my job, Everett. Let me get Ezekial's boys out. Then I promise I'm through. I've got everything planned. Doc Wanger will give me some sleeping powder so that I can hide the kids in a steamer trunk. I'll load them on the train at Atlanta, make a straight run from Atlanta to Saint Joseph. Once the boys are rested, I'll move north on horseback to Wilmington where Brant and Digger will meet me with the wagons."

"Wagons? What in hell for?"

But Everett knew. There was a safe house there run

by a Quaker family. The Rosses. If any other slaves had managed to find their way that far north, Logan would retrieve them as well, hide them in the false bottoms of the special wagons he'd had built, and take them north.

Everett snatched the cheroot Logan had just lit out of his hands and put it to his own lips, inhaling deeply of the fragrant smoke. Logan frowned. Surely, Everett didn't mean to take this cigar from him too?

For several minutes, Everett studied Logan intently, but Logan didn't fear his brother's reaction. Everett had never been able to deny him anything. No one had. And it wasn't conceit talking. Logan knew far too much about people—when to coax and when to prod. His mother had once said he could lead the devil himself into redemption if he ever had a mind to do so.

"Go ahead and make your way to Saint Joe," Everett conceded at last. "Just be on your guard." He poked Logan in the chest a second time. "Especially with the women. Remember, it's was a woman who gave the authorities the sketch in Mississippi."

Even though Everett hadn't said anything truly worthy of arousing his unease, Logan felt the hair on his neck rising, the muscles of his gut tightening.

A woman had seen him?

It was impossible. No one had seen him in Mississippi, least of all some unknown female.

Then how had the sketch come about?

Logan roused from his thoughts in time to see Everett throw the second cheroot to the ground and mash it beneath his heel. "Go off to Saint Joseph and take up your position at Mother LaRee's. But I'll go on to Georgia. *I'll* get Ezekial's boys off Father's plantation and bring them to you there."

"Ev—"

"No, damn it! *I'll* do it! I want you to continue on to

47

Saint Joe and wait at the boarding house, you hear me? Otherwise I'll turn you in myself."

Logan almost believed the threat. Almost.

But he also knew this was a matter of pride with Everett. For too long, Logan had been the man behind the actual escapes while Everett had been the organizer. Instinctively, he sensed that Everett needed this. To prove to himself as well as to Logan that he could be an effective guide and not just a messenger.

Nodding, Logan tucked the tip of his thumb in his vest pocket. "I'll give you ten days."

"Fine."

"Ten days, Everett."

"Fine! I'll have them to you in less than that. Then you hightail it for safety, understood?"

Logan nodded, surprised at the way his brother's sudden initiative made him feel . . . well, proud. Everett had never been so determined before. So full of piss and vinegar.

"Be careful, Everett." This time it was his turn to express his concern. "The minute those boys are reported missing, we'll be top on the authorities' lists of suspects. Our mother died helping Ezekial. We've got a grudge to settle in that respect, and the whole state knows it. Isaac's heir will be the first man to point a finger our way."

The statement was enough to bring a picture of Isaac Campbell rushing into Logan's head. His father had been a proud, stubborn man who had brought himself from the slums of Scotland to the height of the southern "aristocracy," and after his death, the nephew he'd chosen as his heir was no different. Judd Campbell, the existing master of the Campbell estate, would not take kindly to Isaac's bastard stealing a pair of slaves from his plantation.

"Ten days, Everett," Logan said again, not entirely

comfortable with the larger role his brother wished to adopt. "If you aren't back by then, I'll—"

The crunch of gravel caused them both to stiffen. With a jerk of his head, Logan signaled for his brother to leave. After watching him fade into the darkness, he waited, barely breathing, his fingers closing around the bowie knife strapped to his calf.

Again there was the rasp of leather on stone, so stealthy, so secretive, the hairs at the back of his neck stood on end.

Pressing his back against the boxcar, Logan crept toward the sound. Whoever had been listening would never live to regret the fact.

Four

~

Felicity tiptoed forward, sure that she'd seen the
stranger heading in this direction.

From the moment she'd escaped Miss Grimm while
the woman searched the station for something appropriate for them to drink, she'd had only one goal in
mind. To see the man up close again. Once. Just once.
She didn't have to talk to him—indeed, she wouldn't
really want to. But since encountering him on the
platform, she'd been flooded with ideas and scenes for
her books. He was the sort of ruffian she was interested in writing about. She was sure that he was a
gunfighter or something equally horrible. If she could
just get close enough to see if such men actually
carved notches on their belts.

From somewhere up ahead, she heard a low murmur of voices. Rather than dissuading her from
approaching, the sound brought her closer. Who
could he possibly be talking to? Out here. In the dark.

But then the furtive conversation stopped and an
eerie silence settled around her. Belatedly, she realized she'd blundered into some dark portion of the
rail yard, too far from the station to be heard if she
should call for help.

She stopped, touching the side of a crate marked Farm Equipment. With each tension-fraught second, she knew she'd made a mistake. She'd surrendered to her impulses and allowed them to outweigh common sense.

She should go back. It had been the height of stupidity to come out this way. If Constance or Patience ever discovered that she'd left her chaperone and put herself in danger, they would chain her to their sides for the rest of their lives. Then she would never have a chance at adventure.

Nervously biting her lip, she turned toward the station. A figure spun out of the darkness, and she screamed as she saw the glint of a knife.

Before she knew what had occurred, the man's arms were around her and his palm had covered her mouth. Again, she screamed, but the sound was muffled and all but useless. Wriggling, she used what weapons she possessed, biting and kicking while she reached for her bonnet and the hat pin securing it. Her fingers closed around the sturdy brass ball just as a harsh whisper erupted next to her ear.

"Stop it!"

Her struggles immediately stopped. She knew that voice. That deep, melodic voice.

The strength fled from Felicity's limbs, and she gripped the arm around her chest as much to keep her balance as to allow her room to breathe.

"That's better," the man verbally congratulated her when she grew docile. His head had bent low, his breath skipping across her cheek. "You won't scream?"

She shook her head from side to side.

Bit by bit, he released her mouth, but the arm around her torso didn't budge. The knife hovered within inches of her neck, and she stared at it wide-eyed, realizing how close she'd come to feeling the blade prick her skin.

"Damn it, woman. What are you doing out here?" the stranger growled.

Her mouth opened, then closed again. How could she possibly respond to that? She couldn't tell him she'd been following him. She couldn't tell him she'd wanted to check his gun belt for notches. Her eyes squeezed closed, and a self-deprecating wave of shame swept over her. She'd been so stupid. So blasted stupid.

"Well?" His demand was accompanied by the tightening of his arm, bringing her so intimately near to his body that she could feel the brass buttons of his vest digging into her shoulder blades.

"I, uh . . ." She licked her lips, opening her lashes again and searching the indigo shadows for something—*anything*—that could give her a reason for being on a deserted portion of track.

"I felt sick," she finally said, knowing he wouldn't believe her, knowing she should have thought more carefully before responding.

"Sick?" His tone fairly rang with disbelief.

"Yes. The, uh . . . train . . . all that swaying and stopping and starting . . . riding backward."

Babbling. She was positively babbling.

Even so, something of her explanation must have rung true—either that or the trembling of her body convinced him—because the man relaxed ever so slightly.

He bent close, so close that his hair brushed the tiny sliver of bare skin exposed at her nape.

"Why did you come out here?"

"Air."

"Air?"

"Yes, I w-was feeling a trifle faint."

Not as much as she was feeling now, however. Her knees trembled horribly, and the effect had nothing to do with her acting.

"You could have gone in the waiting room."

"The . . . which?"

"The waiting room in the station."

"Yes." Again, she searched frantically for a logical line of reasoning. "But there was so much smoke."

"Smoke? In the ladies' waiting room?"

Darn. She hadn't known the facility was reserved for her own gender.

"Yes, it, uh . . . wafted in from the rooms beyond."

"I see."

It was clear he didn't believe her.

"I was also afraid I would . . . embarrass myself."

"How?"

"By . . . relieving my stomach of its contents."

That was enough to cause the man to let her go so quickly, she nearly fell to her knees. Judging by the expression he wore as he gave her a wide berth, he'd been afraid she might be tempted to do such a thing over his sleeve.

Felicity had to school her features quite carefully to keep from grinning in delight. To think that such a large man, such a handsome man, could be intimidated by the frailties of a woman.

"How are you feeling now?"

Frazzled. Enervated. Deliciously warm. The thoughts raced through her head, but she couldn't utter them aloud. Not even to herself.

Unfortunately, her hesitance in replying must have convinced the man that she felt woozy. Before she knew what he meant to do, he slid his hands beneath her arms and lifted her onto a flatbed car, then pulled her head resolutely toward her lap.

She could have died, just died, as her hoops

bounced up, thus exposing her pantalets while her face was pushed into the folds of her skirts. She'd only had the crinoline for a short time and hadn't quite learned what to expect from it. She was beginning to believe she should have invested in one of the newer, collapsible, watch-spring varieties.

But when she scrambled to put her skirts back into position, he held her where she was, instructing, "Breathe."

"I *am* breathing," she huffed indignantly, although the stays of her corset were pressing unmercifully into her ribs. If he didn't let her up soon—*now*—she *would* faint.

To her infinite relief, he let her go, and she sat straight, righting her bonnet and taking quick gasps of air.

"Better?"

She glared at the man. "Not really."

"Pity."

Felicity frowned at his terse replies. "Do you usually treat a woman in so cavalierly a fashion?"

"I was trying to help."

She glared at him, doubting such a statement. But then, she couldn't blame the man too much. Not when it was her own fault that she was in this predicament. She was the one who'd startled him to the extent that he'd felt it necessary to draw a knife.

"Could you put that thing away?" she asked, waggling a finger in the direction of the blade.

He wasn't inclined to obey but relented at last and slid it into the scabbard strapped to his leg. Amazing. She'd never seen a weapon kept in such a surprising place. She would have to remember that detail for later.

"Tell me, miss," he said softly, distracting Felicity from her examination. "Where are you from?"

She was studying the strong, muscular calves,

equally well formed thighs, narrow hips, whipcord stomach, then up, up, up to a strong jaw and firm lips.

"Boston." The word was a mere puff of sound.

"Oh." He said it in such a way that it was clear he did not approve of the place.

She frowned. "What's wrong with Boston?"

"Not a thing."

A tense silence stretched between them, becoming so electric, so disturbing, that Felicity felt the overwhelming need to fill it with some sort of talk.

"My name is Felicity Pedigrue," she said, extending her hand for him to shake.

He didn't move.

She kept her hand out for some time before withdrawing it again. Needing something to do, she smoothed her skirts to keep her hoop in place.

"Will you lift me down, please?"

"No."

She shifted uncomfortably, wishing she weren't so high off the ground that she didn't dare jump herself.

"You're playing a dangerous game, Felicity."

It should not have been so shocking to her system to have him call her that, but it was. Other than her father, she didn't think any male had ever addressed her by her first name.

"I'm not sure what you mean, Mister. . . ."

He did not respond to her prompting. Instead, he moved closer than was necessary, his body crowding against her skirts, his arms bracketing her legs and effectively pinning her in place.

"I'm not one of those Bostonian gentleman," he began.

She blinked at his strange statement. "Beg pardon?"

"You must be used to the type. Men who are taught from infancy the proper words to use, all the pleases and thank-yous and such. The kind who wear expensive suits and shiny shoes and wouldn't sit astride a horse for fear of creasing their pants."

But she wasn't used to those types at all. Oh, she could see them in her mind's eye—just as she'd once watched them traversing the streets of Boston from her bedroom window. But other than her tutors and her father's business associates, she'd been strictly forbidden to have contact with anyone of the opposite persuasion. Time and time again, her father had insisted that such wanton company could only hasten her doom.

But then again, she thought as she tried in vain to put some distance between herself and the stranger, maybe her father had been right. Maybe he'd been aware that people like this man existed. Maybe he'd known how easily she would be tempted to succumb.

To succumb to what?

Her gaze sought to explore his in the darkness, but the moon was shrouded in clouds and offered no help. Nor did the lights from the station reach this far. She could only trust her senses, senses that informed her that the man was much too near, much too large, much too overwhelming.

"What's the matter, Felicity?"

His voice was like a feather stroke against her skin.

"Have you suddenly realized your precarious position? That you are alone in a place you shouldn't be with a man you shouldn't acknowledge?"

He edged closer, flattening her hoop and flounces against her as if they were no real barrier at all, as indeed, she supposed, they were not.

"You won't harm me." But the statement she'd meant to emerge with utmost certainty emerged as more of a question.

"Won't I? How do you know?"

"B-because . . ." A real reason eluded her. How could she explain to this stranger that she believed what she'd said, that on some elemental level she trusted him as she had never trusted anyone before?

"You should fear me."

"No."

"You should run screaming into the night."

"No."

"I can only hurt you."

"Perhaps. But I don't think you would."

His hand shot out with the swiftness of a snake and he cupped her cheek, forcing her to look at him.

She was startled by the fierceness she found in his expression, the anger, the rebellion, the bitterness. Even so, she didn't cringe. Her response was foolhardy at best, she was sure, but there was something in his manner, a hidden part of his soul she saw gleaming in his eyes, that warned her not to retreat.

Several long, agonizing minutes passed, his stare growing so hard and flinty she felt a trembling deep inside her. Then he released her just as abruptly as he'd grabbed her. Turning, he took three steps before whirling to face her.

He opened his mouth as if to utter some sort of scathing comment, paused, lifted a finger, and pointed at the air in front of him. Again, he appeared ready to speak, then reconsidered and dropped his arm.

"Damn it," he muttered to himself. Then he was striding back in her direction. His hands slid around her waist, and he was lifting her, holding her high, before allowing her body to slide down his as he lowered her to the ground.

"I hope this isn't your usual method of dealing with strangers, Miss Pedigrue."

"No." The reply was barely audible.

"Good."

To her infinite amazement, his head began to bend.

"I mean to kiss you, Felicity Pedigrue."

She could only shiver in response—the reaction one part anticipation and another part dread. Staring up at him, at the tense set of his jaw, the crease of his brow, she knew that she would never be the same again, could never be the same again.

His lips touched hers so softly, gently, that she could have wept that such a hard man, one so rough and tumble and infinitely dangerous, had somehow known what she needed. A slow start. Time to absorb it all.

His arms slid around her body, pulling her tightly to his frame—dear sweet heaven above, how tightly. Her palms rested high on his chest, on the same spot where she'd braced herself once before to catch her balance. Yet, this time, it was he who helped to keep her upright when the quivering of her knees threatened to undo her.

She'd never been kissed before. Such a fact was obvious to him, she was sure. But he didn't chide or tease. Instead, he deepened the intimate caress bit by bit, teaching her how to respond and return the warmth of desire he'd stoked deep in her own heart.

Just when she feared she would not be able to breathe—or, worse yet, would surrender her very soul to this man—he withdrew. She damned the fact that the darkness hid his precise expression. She wanted to know what he was thinking, if his body thrummed with the same pleasure as hers.

But he gave her no clue. Setting her firmly on her own two feet, he gently disengaged himself. Without another word, he turned and began to leave.

Stunned, it took several seconds for Felicity to realize he didn't mean to speak, not even to say good-bye.

"Wait!"

He paused but did not face her.

"What's your name?"

When he didn't immediately speak, she feared he would leave her then without telling her the one thing she wanted most to hear. Then, melting quietly out of the darkness, she heard his reply.

"Logan Campbell, ma'am. At your service."

Logan didn't return to the train. Not right away. Instead, he waited in the black shadows next to the boxcar that contained his horse.

He watched as Felicity hurried back to the station. He smiled when she caught her reflection in the glass and hastened to repair her disheveled hair and the definite list to her bonnet. He thought he even heard her companion begin a sermon on responsibility as soon as she entered the waiting room.

Only then did he move. With as little fuss as possible, he gathered his belongings from the last seat of the passenger car and transferred them to the sweet-smelling straw piled high opposite his horse.

Through it all, he tried to convince himself that the change of seating arrangements had been a result of Everett's warnings and not the lithesome shape of Miss Felicity Pedigrue.

As he settled into the makeshift bed, he reassured himself that this evening had been something extraordinary, but such meetings could never happen again. *Would* never happen again.

Unfortunately, as the murmurs of the passengers returning to their places sifted up to greet him, he couldn't escape the sinking sensation that settled deep in his chest. As much as he might wish to ignore it, his instincts kept warning him that he would see her again. Sometime soon.

The notion was enough to plant the sharp tang of foreboding on his tongue. As well as the fleeting sweetness of hope.

* * *

He wasn't there.

Felicity Pedigrue ignored Miss Grimm's continuing diatribe on the dangers of being separated from one's chaperone—just as she had as they'd been allowed a few short minutes in one of the railway lavatories to wash and refresh themselves for the journey ahead. Quickly, she searched the benches of the car. The train had gathered a whole new set of travelers since stopping, and the seats had grown quite crowded. But even through the sea of people, she knew that one man was missing.

Logan Campbell.

Her stranger.

He was gone.

The sense of loss she experienced was so real, so overpowering, that she pressed a hand to her stomach. Again, she searched the dozens of faces, but even as she did so, she knew she wouldn't find him.

She would have cried if it wouldn't have provoked another of Miss Grimm's examinations. When Felicity had returned to the station, the woman had been beside herself with indignation. She'd scolded, then patted and fussed until Felicity had been clenching her jaw in frustration. She hadn't wanted to endure the woman's fretting. She'd wanted to think of Logan's kiss.

Her first kiss.

Her first beau.

Felicity's brow furrowed in a frown. Could the man really be considered a beau if Felicity had only known him a day?

A day. Was that all it had been? She felt as if they'd known each other for an eternity, as if they'd experienced some sort of lifetime together once before.

Shaking her head, she tried to rid it of such nonsense. He was a man, nothing more. Her emotions —these strange sensations pounding through her body—were the result of her first experience with desire. She would never see him again.

Not ever.

But even as the thought reverberated in her head, she thrust it aside. Providence had brought them together once. Surely it would see that they met again. Somehow. Some way.

Ignoring Miss Grimm, who was rambling on and on about "duty" and "discipline," Felicity reached beneath her seat, taking out the battered leather portfolio. Removing a stub of a pencil and a sheaf of papers, she balanced them on her knee and began to write.

This time, after so many aborted efforts to outline the stories of murder and mayhem and revenge she adored in the penny novels she read, she began to write about a woman. A woman and a man who met on a train.

Five

The train arrived in Saint Joseph to a gray and
overcast sky. Gathering his things, Logan tamped his
hat low over his brow and slid the ramp to the ground.
After leading his horse down the incline, he carefully
surveyed the area under the guise of checking his
cinch.

Just as he'd hoped, the usual crowd of travelers
made the platform and the surrounding area chaotic.
Wagons were being loaded with freight; carriages,
with debarking passengers. There were shouts of
recognition and instruction, children laughing, babies
crying.

Even so, Logan didn't miss the two men who leaned
indolently against one of the luggage carts. Sheriff
Grigsby and his long-time cohort, Nathaniel Moon,
had an office and a three-man jail adjacent to the
station. If their jail cells were empty, they invariably
spent their afternoons making their presence known
to any arriving "rabble-rousers." The two men were
open southern sympathizers and rabid enforcers of
the Fugitive Slave Act. Logan would do well to escape
their attention. Although neither man had ever given
him much heed, Logan didn't want to press his luck.

Because this would be his last run north, he seemed to be acquiring some of Brant Rassmussen's suspiciousness.

"Well, brother? Any last-minute advice?"

He glanced at Everett, who was about to take his place on the boxcar. The transformation from railway official to wandering vagabond was incredible. Everett had refrained from shaving, and a bristling shadow was already coating his sharp chin. His sandy-colored hair had been combed down over his forehead and augmented with a small amount of bacon grease, judging by the smell. He wore a dirty kerchief around his neck, a stained red gingham shirt, and patched woolen trousers.

"You look like hell, Everett."

He grinned. "Thank you very much."

"Where'd you find that getup?"

"I bought it."

"Oh, really?" Logan drawled.

"Yep. From a vagrant who hangs around the rail yards. I bet he'd been wearing it for at least a month."

"I don't doubt it, judging by the stench."

Everett took Logan's comments as a compliment, and his smile widened.

"So," he prompted. "Any last-minute instructions?"

"Yeah. Don't go. Let me do this."

Everett's good humor faded into a scowl, and Logan held up his hands in defeat. "All right, all right," he conceded. "But make sure you get the boys out as early Saturday evening as you can. That will give you all day Sunday to make a head start since the slaves won't be gathered for work until early Monday. See if you can't smuggle some liquor into the slave quarters to make those who might be inclined to spy on you drunk as hell."

Everett nodded even though Logan was sure that

Everett had relayed the same instructions to Logan dozens of times before he'd headed south.

"Once you've left the plantation, stick to the swamps as much as possible to throw off any bloodhounds that will follow. I put a map in your saddlebags outlining the route that Barker claimed was the safest one through Georgia, but don't be afraid to go off on your own if you think any of them have been compromised."

Logan slid his rifle from the scabbard, handing it to Everett.

"And for hell's sake, be careful. If anything happened to you . . ."

Everett gripped his shoulder. "Nothing will happen. I'll be back at Mother LaRee's Boarding House within ten days, and you can be on your way to Canada with the boys."

The sultry summer heat sank heavily upon his shoulders as Logan sought something else to say, something to make Everett stay where he could see him for just a moment longer. But the "All aboard!" of the conductor signaled the lack of time.

Slapping Everett on the back, he said again, "Be careful." Then he checked the rope securing his brother's mount in the boxcar and slid the ramp inside.

As soon as the huge doors were rolled shut, he considered staying at the station just until the train had left. But one glance in Grigsby's direction changed his mind. After all, Logan had work of his own to do. Once Everett had returned, Logan intended to take his brother and Ezekial's sons out of harm's way. He needed to get off the streets and away from Grigsby's eagle eye.

Keeping his back to the men by the luggage cart as much as possible, he made his way out of the rail yard and into the town of Saint Joseph.

The city's tender age was especially apparent here. Stacks of new lumber and freshly painted store facades crowded the rutted streets. Lines of canvas-topped wagons bound for California and Oregon jostled for space with buggies and men on horseback.

Logan welcomed the confusion, welcomed the namelessness it gave him. Here, where there were so many new faces, one more wasn't likely to be noticed nearly so much. Once again, he thanked some unknown printer named Raddison for helping him to maintain his anonymity by ruining the sketch he'd been given.

He made his way down the congested street to the gleaming Bluebird Saloon, which had been erected only a year before. Turning into an alley, he tied the reins to the rung of the staircase that hugged the outside corner of a narrow clapboard building tucked behind the gambling establishment.

Swatting at the simple placard reading Doctor Randall Wanger, he took the stairs two at a time and let himself inside.

A cramped parlor had been converted into a waiting room of sorts. Mismatched chairs lined all four walls, and a low bookcase holding a dozen dusty medical tomes served as a reception table.

This late in the day, there was no one there, a fact for which Logan was grateful. Crossing into the examining area, he found Doc Wanger leaning back in his chair, his dusty boots propped on the blotter of his desk, a handkerchief draped over his face, the fabric fluttering with each snoring breath.

Logan took great care in waking him, knowing Doc Wanger kept a loaded pistol in a side drawer and a rifle bolted to the bottom of his desk.

"Doc?" He tapped the man's foot. "Doc, wake up."

The man snorted, yawned, and drew the hankie from his face. Upon seeing that it was Logan and not some medical emergency, he stretched and rubbed his eyes with the heels of his hands.

"What time is it?"

"Past five."

He made another grumbling noise deep in his chest. "Gadfrey Moses, I only meant to take a ten-minute nap."

"How long have you been here?"

"At least an hour." His feet thumped to the floor, and he scooped his spectacles from a pile of papers, hooking them over his ears. "I spent the better part of the night delivering babies."

"How many?"

"Three. Can you believe it? Three! There must be a storm coming."

He leaned forward, bracing his arms on the desk. "So what in damnation are you doing back here so soon, Logan?"

Logan had to fight the urge to squirm beneath the man's intense scrutiny. If the truth were known, Doc Wanger, a retired army surgeon, had proven to be more of a father to him than any blood relative. It had been only natural for Logan to seek out the man's help when he and Everett had decided to pursue their abolitionist cause.

"Tarnation, boy. I thought I told you to stay in Canada for a while."

Without being asked, Logan went to a nearby medicine cabinet and withdrew a bottle and two glasses.

"I have a job to do."

Doc Wanger didn't look surprised. "Ezekial's boys." It wasn't a question. Logan had taken a bullet to the arm while he was in the army—a stupid accident caused when a new recruit had been cleaning his weapon. Doc Wanger had recognized Logan's fiery temper and had feared he would beat the recruit to a bloody pulp for his carelessness, so he'd confined Logan to the infirmary until the wound healed. During that time, the two men had become fast friends, and more than one secret had been shared. Except for Everett, Logan doubted any man knew him better than Doc Wanger.

"You know you can't go back to Georgia," Doc Wanger said. "You've been seen in Mississippi. It wouldn't be safe for you to go south again so soon."

"Everett told me." He grimaced. "Who in hell could have given them my sketch?"

Doc Wanger peered at him with narrowed eyes. "I'm afraid that's my fault. Since you put me in charge of Mother LaRee's, I've tried to change the girls every six weeks."

Logan was well aware of that fact. When it had become apparent that neither Logan nor Everett were in town enough to effectively run the bordello, they'd sold the establishment to Doc Wanger. Since then, the man had taken his role as proprietor quite seriously. Except for Clarice and Lena, who helped with the escaped slaves and oversaw the business aspect of the house, the girls who worked at Mother LaRee's were regularly dismissed and a new set hired.

Doc Wanger rubbed his tired eyes beneath his spectacles. "I made a mistake with the last batch. One of them—a Miss Boopsie Ruth—was responsible for going to the authorities."

"But why?"

Doc Wanger's expression grew grim. "I've always made sure that the girls had no southern roots, but it seems Miss Ruth lied about her background. Lena discovered that she was originally from Mississippi, and when she was let go from Mother LaRee's, she returned home. The minute Lena passed on that information, I tracked Boopsie to Natchez. After some . . . persuasion, she admitted she'd seen you sneaking a pair of slaves into the boarding house a few months ago. When she saw you riding through Natchez during your last run, she was down on her luck, looking for a job, and decided to turn you in to the authorities in the hopes of gathering a reward."

Logan sighed. He should have been more careful about disguising himself during his trips out of state.

"Where is Miss Ruth now?"

Doc Wanger's smile was slow and rich. "I sent her—along with some of the other girls—on a wagon train west to join up with a bordello in Denver. When she heard how much money could be earned out west, she went quite willingly."

Logan's breathing grew easier.

"So what will you do about Ezekial's boys?"

Logan filled Doc Wanger's glass, then his own, and downed the contents in one gulp before saying, "Everett's gone to fetch them."

"Ahh." Doc Wanger's chair squeaked as he leaned backward, staring into the whiskey he held as if it were a crystal ball. "That must have you fit to be tied."

Logan didn't bother to answer. Such a statement didn't need a comment—not when it was true.

"How long did you give him?"

"Ten days. Once he meets me at Mother LaRee's, I'll take the boys north."

Wanger took a sip, held it on his tongue, then swished it around his mouth before spitting it—with great finesse—into the spittoon at his feet, which was kept there for just such an occasion. A pistol ball to the gut during an army stint in the territories had caused his stomach to rebel against strong liquor, but that didn't mean he'd lost the taste for it.

"I wish you'd talked to me first, Logan."

Logan, who had been reaching for the bottle, paused in midmotion.

"What's wrong?"

Wanger dismissed his instant concern. "Nothing serious, I'm sure, but I would have liked more time to assess the situation."

"Situation?" Logan didn't enjoy the sound of that word.

"After the scare with Boopsie Ruth, I sent all of Mother LaRee's girls to Denver—except Clarice and Lena, of course."

"So what has you worried?"

"The property next to Mother LaRee's was sold a few weeks ago."

"Is that a problem?"

Wanger shrugged. "I'm not sure. The new owners are rumored to be arriving soon, but before we started using Mother LaRee's as a shelter again, I wanted a chance to meet them. You know how new neighbors can be—curious, even downright snoopy. Women are especially bad. They feel it necessary to 'pay calls' and introduce themselves."

"Surely the news that they've moved next to a whorehouse will put off any visitors."

Wanger chuckled. "Now that depends on the sort of neighbor moving in, doesn't it? It will also depend on how long it takes them to figure out that Mother LaRee's is not as respectable as it might appear from the outside. I thought that by cutting down the workforce at the boarding house, I could arrange a logical way to keep any pesky visitors away. But since you've returned, you'll have to play along with my little plan."

Logan stood, paced to the window, peered out at the street in a purely habitual manner, then turned.

"What did you have in mind?"

Wanger took another swig of whiskey and swirled it around his mouth. After absorbing the taste as much as possible, he spit it out. Instantly, his lips split in a wide grin.

"I thought I'd put the whole place under quarantine for some mysterious disease."

"What kind of disease?"

"I'll make something up. Something with a grand name and horrible symptoms. I'll spread the word through town that the illness is highly contagious, and those who catch it die in gruesome agony." He chortled. "I might even go so far as to say it will make a person's private parts rot and fall away."

Logan stared at him, then grinned. "That'll even keep Grigsby away—he's developed some sort of obsession with Lena the last few months. His feelings have allowed us to gather some interesting information, but I wouldn't relish having the man hanging around Mother LaRee's for the next ten days."

"I doubt the ruse will keep Grigsby completely away," Doc Wanger proclaimed. "As the local law officer, it's his duty to see the quarantine is being enforced. According to local statutes, he's to make an inspection of any quarantine site at least twice a week. Other than a doctor, he is the only person allowed to cross the designated boundaries. Nevertheless, the whole setup should keep him out of the house and scare the Pedigrues completely away to boot."

Logan froze. "Who?"

"The Pedigrues. Some fellow named Pedigrue bought the house next door to Mother LaRee's for his daughter. He's sending her here as a provision of his will, from what I understand." His brows ground together. "Now, what was her name? Happy? Folly? No, *Felicity* Pedigrue, I think it was."

This time Logan didn't even bother with a glass.

Reaching for the whiskey, he drank straight from the bottle.

She spent her days wondering when he would appear, when she would look out and see him . . . merely by chance.

The thought that she would meet her stranger again, somehow, some way, should have been a physical impossibility.

But she knew she would.

She must.

The dreams were the worst to bear. At night, asleep, she saw him with such clarity, tasted his lips on her own, felt his arms tightly surrounding her waist, that when she awoke, she experienced a bereavement she could not contain. On such evenings, when the sky was black and laden with stars, she often went to her window, where sometimes, sometimes, she thought she saw him there in the shadows of the trees across the lane.

Whether he was truly there, she did not know. Nevertheless, it made her feel safe, warm . . .

And incredibly impatient for their next encounter.

Felicity set her writing materials aside and peeked out of the lacy panel covering her new bedroom window.

For years, she'd dreamed of making her way into the world, searching out adventure, and becoming a famous novelist. But as she studied the sleepy residential street below her, she realized that her wishes were coming true one by one. All but her writing. Rather than dwelling in fiction, she found that the pages she'd finished so far were more autobiographical than she would have ever wished.

The fact was quite disturbing. She'd been taught that a woman's thoughts and emotions were to remain completely private. Once she'd been caught keeping a journal, and her father had thrown it into the fire for being far too "frank" for a woman of quality.

Nevertheless, Felicity couldn't seem to keep the words from pouring onto the paper. All her hopes and dreams . . .

Dreams.

Her fingers clenched around the curtain, and she stared down at the thick shadows gathered beneath the lilac bushes and oak trees crowded into the corner of the lot across the street. Last evening, she'd felt Logan Campbell's presence—she *knew* she'd felt it. She'd awakened from a dream that had been particularly vivid, one that had made her body thrum and her skin burn. Seeking some stray breeze, she'd leaned out the window.

He'd been there. He must have been. With barely a glimpse of moonlight, she couldn't be sure, but there had been a shape standing in the trees. A form. A man. Tall, lean, rugged. She'd been so sure he'd been watching her.

She'd been so sure it had been *Logan.*

But looking at that spot in the clear light of day, she chided herself for entertaining such foolishness. Logan Campbell had left the train somewhere in midroute—at whatever small town they'd stopped in that night she'd followed him into the station yard. To think he would trail her all the way to Saint Joseph would be the height of conceit.

No matter what her heart insisted might be true.

Logan Campbell couldn't possibly be in the same city. So she'd best get on with her own affairs.

Filling her lungs with the muggy heat of the afternoon, she took in the sights that surrounded her.

Saint Joseph, Missouri.

The Wild Wicked West.

The thoughts were enough to send a thrill of pleasure streaking from nerve to nerve, and she resisted the urge to pinch herself to ensure that she was truly here. If the truth were known, she'd already pinched herself black and blue in the last few days. Ever since arriving in Saint Joseph to discover that her father had arranged for more than a teaching position at the academy. He had also purchased a house for her to live in with the stipulation that the bottom floor be used as a part-time tea shop and reading room to help supplement her income.

Far from being dismayed by such a prospect, Felicity had been delighted. Because the arrangement had included a handsome allowance, she'd spent most of her time buying furniture for the shop and ordering books. She'd designed fliers to be distributed in the finer ladies' shops and had even arranged for discreet, elegant posters to be printed by a local newspaper office. All of the arrangements had been made with the highest sense of taste and decorum, because Felicity had known that any business success would depend on a sterling reputation. Because she was a stranger here, she would be judged quite critically by the cream of Saint Joseph's society, and her shop would rely upon the patronage of such women.

Opening the sash even wider, Felicity breathed deeply of smells she had never encountered in such variety in Boston. Again, she was assaulted by a sense of familiarity. As if she'd been here before. Or somewhere like it . . .

The images swam into her brain. A one-street town. A store. Jars full of penny candy. And a woman who had held her hand. Not her sisters, but someone older.

Her mother?

But no. It wasn't possible.

Her lips pressed tightly together as the familiar anger and betrayal burgeoned within her. She'd been a baby when her mother had abandoned the Pedigrue family, but her father had reminded her of that fact over and over again. He'd told her how Louise Pedigrue had left them all because she had been tempted by the devil. She'd never loved them. She'd never stopped to think how Alexander Pedigrue would punish his daughters for the rest of his life because they looked like her or talked like her.

Felicity huffed in indignation. Such thoughts were better left in the past. Her mother had never been a part of her life—and never would be. Why, if she were to walk through the door today, Felicity would . . .

Well, she didn't know what she would do. Heaven only knew she'd fantasized about Louise's return often enough when she was younger. But at that time, Felicity had also dreamed her mother had experienced a change of heart and meant to liberate her daughters from their father's strict household. Now that Alexander Pedigrue was dead and Felicity was embarking on a grand new adventure, she had no need of a mother.

None whatsoever.

She would be better off keeping her mind on the here and now. On the smells of dust and manure, the crisp scent of newly mown hay, a hint of flowers, and an encroaching storm. Mingled with it all was the illusive scent of personal success.

Yes, it was there. Just waiting for her. All she had to do was grasp the opportunities being handed to her by a father she'd never really known. One who actually knew her fondest wishes and had uncharacteristically allowed her to pursue them to a point where each new example had become eerie.

Such an idea was enough to tighten her throat with emotions. Why, in all these years, had she never known that her father cared for her in some small measure? He'd been so cold and unfeeling, wishing her to be a boy, wishing her to become a piece of furniture in his house. Silent, unseen, but useful to his needs.

How had he possibly guessed what she'd wanted of her future? She'd been so sure that the travel logs she'd borrowed had been carefully hidden, the notebooks with all her lists and plans and sketches buried beneath tomes of accounting and etiquette. Even this house . . .

Leaning out the window, she surveyed it again, feeling the same thrill of delight she'd experienced when the hired wagon loaded with her belongings had stopped at the carriage block out front.

The house was grand, a sprawling two-story brick affair settled like a comfortable old woman beneath huge stands of oak and pine trees. Two towering structures bordered her on either side. One spacious clapboard structure was the home of a large German family—if the number of blond-haired, gutturally speaking children were to be believed. On the other side, a pale peach-colored house of stone gleamed in the sunshine, a discreet hand-lettered sign, Mother LaRee's Boarding House, swinging from the porch awning.

"Perfect," Felicity had murmured to herself as she'd opened the gate on that first day, offering a curt nod as if to underscore the sentiment.

The inner trappings of the brick house had proven to be even more inspiring than the exterior, especially when she'd been informed of the future plans for a reading room. Rich woodwork, new woolen runners, walls papered in the distinctly feminine colors of rose and green and pink, as if whoever had owned the house previously had instinctively known what Felicity liked. It was quite unsettling to see how the house reflected her personal tastes even though her father couldn't have foreseen his demise. He couldn't have requested a place with simple, open rooms on the first floor where she would put the tearoom, the library, and the salon. Nor could he have arranged for a raised dais of sorts in the front parlor that would serve beautifully for guest lecturers and musicians should she care to do so.

Upstairs, the building was no less satisfactory. There were three small bedrooms, each with their own adjoining sitting room for Felicity's and Miss Grimm's personal needs. The older woman would be staying on as her companion, although Felicity would be more than willing to look for a replacement some time soon. Heaven only knew there was more than enough living space in the walk-up attic for anyone else she might employ.

Beginning this week, the furniture she'd ordered would be delivered, supplies purchased, curtains hung, linens aired, and fliers distributed. Then, in two weeks, the day after she began her teaching appointment at the academy, Milady's Reading Establishment would open at five in the evening for three hours each night and Felicity would be its proprietor. The very thought caused a tingling excitement to rush through her veins.

Reluctantly easing indoors again, Felicity closed the sash and discreetly rearranged the curtains. Sighing, she supposed she shouldn't have been so hasty, poking her head out-of-doors in such a precipitous fashion. Especially since she had not yet put her bonnet on.

But she hadn't been able to help herself. She'd spent so much time on trains and wagons and in carriages that she was dying to experience this place firsthand. Unfortunately, the journey had brought about a bout of ague for Miss Grimm, and Felicity had been allowed little more than two excursions into town.

She was sure, quite sure, that if she waited another moment, she would burst. Absolutely burst!

Tiptoeing to the smaller cot placed in the corner of the room and shielded from view by a privacy screen, she leaned around the corner, studying the angular outline made by her chaperone and companion.

The woman was a paragon of virtue, a symbol of strength, an unbending rod of righteousness. But at the moment, she was dead to the world, worn out by travel and worry and her devotion to duty as well as by the terrible cold she'd been fighting since her arrival in Saint Joseph.

Her chest rose and fell with each breath, the rattling of her lungs proclaiming to one and all that she was truly ill and in need of the rest she'd finally won, even though Felicity could not account for the way a distinct odor of rum hovered over the woman's body.

It was a pity, Felicity thought, retreating again lest she waken her. She'd begun to respect Miss Grimm's knowledge of etiquette, but Felicity *had* to get out. She had to explore. No matter what Miss Grimm might say to her when she discovered Felicity had ventured into the "American wilds" on her own. Not even the threat of having Miss Grimm notify Constance and Patience was enough to dissuade her.

Surveying her reflection in the mirror hung on the wall, Felicity donned her bonnet and took a deep breath to keep her excitement from being displayed on her features.

Although her life with her father might have been hard—and at times downright gloomy—at least she could thank Alexander Pedigrue for one thing. He had seen to it that his daughters were taught how behave. And if her attempts at teaching and business were to succeed, Felicity knew that she would have to tow a careful line. Her mode of dress, her manner, her speech, must be above reproach. She couldn't afford to appear too animated or too stern. She must adopt a careful mixture of serenity and poise even though she wanted to run into the street, whirl in a circle, and lift her hands high to the warmth of the sun.

Stifling a giggle at the thought of such an outlandish reaction here, in such a quiet neighborhood, she adjusted a fold of her skirt. Thank goodness, she'd been allowed to spend some money on her clothing so that she wouldn't have to tromp through Saint Joseph in threadbare gowns. Despite the heat of the day, she had dressed in her finest black wool visiting costume. A bonnet with only the tiniest hint of lace inside the brim had been perched squarely upon her head. Her hair had been savagely combed from a center part and persuaded to cover her ears just so. Beneath her chin, a single bow held the hat in place—the adornment neither too large to attract attention nor too small to serve as a firm anchor. Her basque jacket was tightly fitted to her torso, one that had been carefully restrained by the stiffest of corsets. Her skirts were a perfect bell, resting over her only indulgence for the trip west—the cane crinoline—instead of the masses of petticoats she normally wore. Black woolen hose and black kid boots finished the ensemble, leaving her quite prim and respectable. And if the whole costume itched like the dickens, she would bear it, just as she had borne it so many times before.

Snatching her shawl—despite the warmth of the morning—she crept out of the bedroom and down the steps to the tiny table situated by the front door. As she took the last few treads, she pinned the brooch-like anchor of her finest pince-nez spectacles to her chest, pinched the glasses onto the brim of her nose, and gathered the basket of home-baked goodies she'd prepared earlier that morning.

As she had been taught by Frau Goethe, who had originally served as Felicity's governess a dozen years ago, she was about to make her calls to the surrounding houses to introduce herself and to deliver a small token of friendship. Frau Goethe had once explained that a woman's first visit would often set the tone for many years to come. Therefore, Felicity had prepared carefully. She would step from the front door precisely at ten-thirty. Allowing herself fifteen minutes per household, she should be able to introduce herself to her immediate neighbors well before midday, when she would return home in order to keep from intruding upon anyone's luncheon as well as to keep from incurring Miss Grimm's ire.

A trifle irritated by the constant inner reminder that Miss Grimm feared they had journeyed to the edge of civilization, Felicity snatched her gloves from the table and tugged them over her hands so that not a bit of her bare wrists was left exposed.

Taking one last peek up the stairs, she whispered aloud, "I'll be back soon. There will be no harm done."

But as the door snapped shut behind her, she couldn't hush the voice in her head that urged her to go back. A voice that sounded too much like Miss Grimm's.

Six

Pausing on the far side of her gate, Felicity withdrew a list of the names of her neighbors that she'd tucked in her pocket. Names that had been neatly printed in her own hand and gathered from the mailboxes that lined the lane.

To her left was Mother LaRee's, to the right, the Kleinschmidts. Noting the gaggle of children on the lawn, their faces stained with strawberry jam, she decided that the boarding house would be the first stop. She would rather test the waters in a more genteel atmosphere. Besides which, if she went to the Kleinschmidts with a full basket of goodies, there was no telling if the children would let her leave with anything at all. So far, they had been quite persistent in visiting her, climbing over the fence, peering through her windows, and asking innumerable questions—only a few of which she could understand with their broken English. It made her wonder why they were so curious about her but had never once tiptoed into Mother LaRee's yard.

Employing a militarylike posture, Felicity turned on her heel and marched the short distance to the boarding house gate. As she made her way up the walk, she found it odd that the establishment should appear so quiet, so nearly . . . reverent. Since coming to Saint Joseph, Felicity had not seen a single guest coming or going from the building. She would have thought it empty if not for the blaze of lamplight and the faint tinkling of piano music she heard each night.

Squinting at the facade, which upon closer examination was in need of a fresh coat of paint around the eaves, she wondered if perhaps the owner had taken a holiday from her boarders during the summer as a sort of rest-cure.

But that would not explain the oddly exciting music that had drawn Felicity more than once to the windows in the hopes of seeing what social affair had inspired such unusual melodies. Tunes that were rowdy, raucous, and bold. A curious choice for such a simple establishment.

Unfortunately—or perhaps fortunately, considering her rabid curiosity—the shades and draperies had always been firmly drawn.

Prodded by another burst of impatience, Felicity didn't allow herself another moment's hesitation. Twisting the brass bell in the middle of the door, she leaned imperceptibly closer, waiting until she heard the faint corresponding ring from within.

There was no answering sound. Not even so much as the muted thud of footfalls.

Again she twisted the bell. But this time, cocking her head slightly to the side, she detected the mumble of voices coming from the rear.

Of course, she thought with a self-deprecating smile. Mother LaRee was probably in the kitchen or on the back porch where a cool breeze would temper the heat of the morning.

Picking her way over the warped boards of the porch, Felicity rounded the house, making her way past wicker rocking chairs and planters, braided rugs, and footstools. Midway along the side of the house, the shade became thicker and sweeter as she passed into the cooler confines of a walled garden. Trailing her fingers on the railing, she peered over the side. There, planted close to the foundation, she saw a neatly furrowed herb garden and tender starts of tomatoes, cucumbers, and squash. Beyond that were larger rows of vegetables, a cutting garden, and, farther beyond, a tangled orchard.

What a charming place. What an ideal place. If she hadn't already had a house for herself, Felicity might have been tempted to stay here. With other people. Westerners.

From the rooms overhead, the plinking melody of a music box sifted through the subtler noises of birds and riffling leaves. The farther she went along the wraparound porch, the more evidence of humanity she encountered. A murmured cough, a muffled exchange of words.

The back door stood wide, and she tiptoed to it so that she wouldn't startle anyone who might be working in the kitchen. Pausing at the threshold, she rapped her knuckles against the wooden frame. "Hello?"

Nothing but her own echo greeted her for a moment, and she resisted the urge to nibble on her lip at the quandary. Should she knock again and risk disturbing the quiet of the house? Perhaps she had unknowingly intruded upon some sort of midmorning napping practice performed here in the West, although she'd never read of the Spanish siesta extending this far north of the Mexican border.

"You there!"

She started, whirling to face the strident command. A hand automatically flew to the base of her throat to quiet the furious pounding of her heart, sure she was about to be accused of trespassing by some brawny servant.

Then she blinked, focusing on the petite shape of a woman standing by the discreet, whitewashed outhouse.

"You there!"

The female's voice was low, husky—so deep, in fact, that Felicity would have mistaken her for a young boy until she caught sight of her attire. She was dressed completely in black—black bonnet, black veil, black gown. If not for her tiny stature and the brazen way she stood with her hands on her hips, her gaze altogether too bold, Felicity might have been gazing at a mirror image of her own visiting costume.

The woman took the steps one at a time, slapping a slender quirt against her full skirts.

"I thought they got word to you not to come after all. You were supposed to stay in town until you were notified. If you're going to stay here and work, you've got to learn to follow instructions."

Felicity opened her mouth to disabuse the woman of such a fanciful notion, to correct her of the assumption that she'd been expected, but the woman continued without pause.

"Quite the fancy outfit you've got," she commented, her brown-black eyes narrowing, "but I'm the only one who wears black around here." She frowned in disgust. "Frankly, I don't know why we'll be needing another bit of fluff the likes of you, but nobody asked me." She drew near, tapping the end of the quirt against Felicity's chest. "Just stay clear of Hap Grigsby if he comes, you hear? He's mine. I'm the only one who can deal with his type."

"Yes, of course." The words burst from Felicity before she could prevent them.

Offering another scowl, the woman brushed past

her, making her way into the kitchen. She was nearly gone when Felicity dared ask, "Mother LaRee. Is she in?"

The woman made a noise that sounded suspiciously like a snort of disbelief. *"Mother* LaRee? It's the man in there you need to be talking to." Then she tipped her head to the right and disappeared down the hall to the left.

Felicity couldn't quite prevent the way she shuddered and grew limp—as if in relief.

Relief? Preposterous. Absolutely preposterous. Nevertheless, when she surveyed the doorway again, she couldn't help thinking that maybe she should have waited until Miss Grimm had accompanied her.

The starch returned to her posture. Nonsense. She was here on a call. A quick call. What could be the harm of that?

Again she knocked, calling, "Hello? Is anyone at home?"

To her delight, she heard a muffled, "Here . . . back here."

Felicity was not quite sure how to respond to such an invitation. Proper etiquette demanded that visitors were met at the door either in person or by a servant. She wasn't sure how she should respond to being summoned inside.

On the other hand, Mother LaRee could be an invalid of some sort and was unable to greet her on the porch; that would explain why the bell had not been answered. And Frau Goethe had been quite blunt about the dangers of offending new neighbors.

Felicity stepped over the lintel just as another call—more of a shout, really—identified the location of the house's occupant.

"I said . . . *here* . . ."

How she could refuse?

Making her way through a narrow sort of cloak-room, she entered the cooking area. A very untidy cooking area. In fact, she was horrified that such an establishment had mounds of dirty dishes in the sink. Pots and pans of every description littered the stove and tables. Flour had been dribbled across the floor and mingled there with splotches of other unidentifiable splashes and streaks.

My, oh, my, the voice in Felicity's head whispered again. Mother LaRee *must* be temporarily indisposed. There was no other explanation for the owner of a boarding house to engage in such chaos.

Hurrying from the kitchen, Felicity made her way down a hallway cramped with oversized furniture, bric-a-brac, and paintings. Every available surface had been covered in thick brocade, tassels, and gilt. So much so that the effect was stifling. One might even say gaudy.

With each step, Felicity knew she'd been right to come to Saint Joseph. Evidently, there were women in the West who were not privy to the tidbits of etiquette that Frau Goethe and Miss Grimm were so fond of delivering. Otherwise, she would have been greeted straightaway and not beckoned to like a stray puppy. Therefore, she would *not* have become a witness to Mother LaRee's less than tidy housekeeping practices.

It would be up to Felicity to help all of the women in the area, to bring a bright light of gentility and propriety to a place struggling out of its baser origins.

Hearing a high giggle from the room ahead, Felicity prayed that she would soon have the honor of addressing Mother LaRee in person. Then she could offer her a loaf of her applesauce walnut bread and a crock of her raspberry butter and be on her way. She wouldn't stop at the Kleinschmidts' today. She would wait for

Miss Grimm to accompany her as was proper. After all, she couldn't have it be said that the rougher practices of America were beginning to rub off on *her*.

Clearing her throat and smoothing the hair at her nape, she rounded the corner of the doorway, flashed her best lady-paying-a-call smile, and declared, "Hello! My name is Felicity Pedigrue. Do I have the honor of speaking to the . . . lady . . . of . . . the . . ."

The words trailed off, becoming stuck somewhere in the tightness of her throat as Felicity's eyes focused, then clung to the only occupants of the room. A bedroom. A very dim, intimate, layered-in-lace-and-reeking-of-cheap-perfume bedroom.

A giggle caused her gaze to bounce first to the woman who clung to one of the footboard posts, her corset gaping from her body, the strings dripping to the floor, half of her chemise draped so low over her shoulder that her left breast threatened to spring free.

"Clarice . . ."

At the low growl, Felicity's eyes wrenched from the woman to the man who lay sprawled on the bed, a pillow wrapped around his head, the corner of a rumpled sheet the only thing that saved him from complete immodesty.

The air whooshed from her lungs as if a giant hand had closed around her ribs. The air became suddenly hot—too hot—absolutely sultry, thick and muggy and impossible to breathe.

To her ultimate horror, the basket she held dropped from her fingers with a thud, the crocks rattling ominously.

At the noise, the man sprang to a sitting position.

Felicity gasped when the movement threatened to unveil him completely, revealing that he wasn't a complete stranger. It was the man from the train. Logan Campbell.

And he was naked. Completely and utterly naked.

When he would have sat bolt upright, she held out both hands in automatic restraint. "No!"

Her spectacles slipped from her nose and dangled from the end of their chain, quivering in far too telling a manner, demonstrating quite clearly how his bare body had startled her. Alarmed her. *Overwhelmed* her.

"Felicity?" Logan wiped a hand over his eyes and stared at her in utter amazement, as dismayed as she. He focused blearily on her face, making her believe that he must have been ill—or perhaps even addled. But as he cradled his head in his hands, she realized in disgust that he was not sick, but suffering from a night of overindulgence.

Felicity's gaze bounced from the gaudiness of the room to the untidy bed and the scantily clad woman. In an instant, she acknowledged inwardly that this was no boarding house. Not of the sort she had been led to believe it would be anyhow.

"How could you, Logan Campbell?" she demanded in a raw whisper. So he *had* been in Saint Joseph. He had followed her. Watched her.

"How could I what?"

It was obvious he was trying to figure out which end was up, so Felicity ignored his question. Pressing her lips together in disapproval, she knelt, swiftly gathering her parcels. She had to get out of this place. Now. Before anyone knew she'd entered a den of iniquity.

Before another peek at Logan Campbell tempted her to stay.

No. She couldn't even think of such things. She mustn't. She would gather what dignity she possessed and run back to her home. Back to Miss Grimm. Back to safety.

Adopting a ramrod stiffness, she was tucking a cloth

around her crocks when she exclaimed, "I apologize
for the"—she stared at the woman dressed in little
more than her briefest undergarments—"inconve-
nience. But I thought that someone had called to me,
instructing me to come in."

Logan squinted at her, his eyes the oddest shade of
blue in the light streaming through the window. A
clear, brilliant blue like the searing skies of an August
afternoon. His hair, a streaked wheat brown and gold,
tumbled over his face to his shoulders, all tousled and
wayward as if he'd run his fingers through it time and
again. Or rather, she thought, as if that *woman* had.

He squinted at her again, his gaze having the ability
to sear her even through the layers of wool she wore.
"You could have rung the doorbell," he complained
abruptly, his tone so disagreeable that it was obvious
that he thought *she* was somehow to blame for this
whole debacle. "I would have sent you home."

The words wounded Felicity much more than she
would have imagined. He would have sent her away?
Without so much as a how-do-you-do?

Felicity glanced at the other woman. Clarice. It
galled her to admit that she was much more beautiful
than Felicity could ever hope to be. With her doe-
brown eyes and curly blond hair, she was the sort that
could bring any man to his knees. Even Logan Campbell.

"How dare you?" Felicity said again, her voice
quivering in hurt.

"What? *What!*"

She was about to lambaste him for his emotional
cruelty when Felicity realized that she had no claim
on this man. None whatsoever. They had kissed once
in the shadows of a railway station. Since Logan
obviously frequented houses of ill repute, he'd probably seen Felicity as only a taste of what awaited him

once he had the opportunity to truly indulge in corporal pleasure.

Stamping toward him, Felicity brought her hand back, then swung it with all her might, slapping him on the cheek.

His head reared, and he stared at her as if she'd sprouted wings.

"That," she said with as much calm as she could muster, "is for all the other women you've been chasing around train stations in this portion of the country."

He caught her hand when she would have left him. The imprint of her fingers grew red on his cheek.

"If you'd rung the bell," he said slowly, distinctly, "I would have met you at the door and—"

"I *did* ring the blasted bell," she said through clenched teeth, not about to be held responsible for this man's peccadilloes.

"I didn't hear you." Again, his eyes flashed; his jaw beneath its dark stubble adopted a square, stubborn line.

"Obviously." She shot a glance at the girl. "When no one responded, I also knocked at the back door. You called out and directed me to come here."

He sighed. "I wasn't talking to you. I was calling to Clarice."

"That, sir, is painfully obvious."

She stared at the woman who was watching their exchange with wide, unblinking eyes. Even Logan had the decency to appear somewhat disconcerted when he noted the way the sunlight had pierced the woman's silk chemise, leaving her body all but bare to examination.

Yanking her arm free, Felicity fumbled to put her glasses back on the tip of her nose. She didn't really need them, only when her eyes were tired or she did a good deal of book work, but she had always felt that she was more intimidating with them on. Felicity had never minded obtaining results from intimidation.

But the ploy had its disadvantages as well. When she turned her attention to Logan and off the nymph standing by the foot of the bed, the outlines of his body were much crisper. She could see the etched planes of his features, the strong throat, and a chest broader and harder than any she'd ever witnessed before.

Of course, she had never seen a man's chest so intimately exposed. So naked. So intriguing, so—

"I will take my leave of you, sir," she blurted, knowing that she had to escape right now, this moment, before she became a spineless, babbling fool. Spinning on her toe, she marched into the hall, bumping into a coat rack, then a chaise in her haste to leave.

"No. No, damn it!"

She heard the squeak of springs and hastened her step, knowing instinctively that Logan had taken it into his head to follow her. If he caught her in his state of undress . . .

The thought sent such a shot of sheer panic through her system that she nearly tumbled headlong into the kitchen. She could see the door a few feet away, the sunshine gleaming against the whitewashed porch supports. Only a few steps more. Just a few.

"Stop!"

A firm, masculine hand grasped her elbow, spinning her to face him. Then Logan pushed her bodily against the wall, imprisoning her with his arms and the width of his chest.

For several seconds, she glared at him, her heart pounding, her mouth growing dry when the oh-so-familiar heat of his body seeped through her clothing to blister her skin just as it had in her dreams.

Once again, the basket dropped, the crocks spilling free from their nest of linens and rolling across the floor. Felicity was stunned by the fierceness of Logan's expression, by the near anger that flared in his blue eyes.

Anger? She was flooded by indignation. If anyone had a right to be angry, it was she. She'd come to this house, lured by its harmless sign intimating there were rooms to let, believing she would find a grandmotherly woman who had been forced to take boarders in order to make ends meet. Instead, she discovered that this was a house of . . . an establishment of . . .

Drat it all, it was a bordello!

Logan grasped her shoulders, shaking her slightly, and she fought him, the import of her actions hitting her full in the face. She had to get out of here! She had to leave this place before anyone discovered she was here. Otherwise her reputation would be in ruins, her teaching post rescinded, and all her business arrangements in tatters before they'd even begun.

"Damn it all to hell, woman!" Logan shouted, twisting her in his grip so that her back was planted firmly against his chest and wrapping his arm around her throat in a choke hold. "Will you settle down? I just want to talk to you!"

"Talk to me. *Talk!* I'll have nothing to do with your sort, sir."

"My *sort?*"

"A man who is obviously inclined to cheating and sneaking and . . . dallying!"

"Dallying?" he echoed in disbelief.

"To seducing innocent travelers—"

"Seducing, hell."

"Yes! Seducing! Now, if you'll unhand me . . ." Her face flamed when she realized that he was without a stitch of clothing and seemed inclined to hold her as tightly as possible. She forced herself to say more calmly, "If you'll unhand me, I'll take my leave and you'll never need to fear of hearing from me again."

"Oh, dear," a gruff, unfamiliar voice sighed behind them. "I'm afraid that's quite impossible. Quite, quite impossible."

The statement came from the porch, and Felicity jerked away like a guilty child. To her ultimate surprise, Logan responded in much the same manner.

A tall, bearded gentleman holding a black leather bag stepped into the kitchen from the porch, offered another sigh, and set his valise on the table. Frowning in obvious disappointment and frustration, he said gravely, "You see, miss, this house is under quarantine." He looked at Logan, frowned, then shrugged. "I'm afraid none of you will be going anywhere."

Seven

~

Quarantine. Quarantine?

Felicity offered a gay laugh, sure that this was some sort of joke. But when the men didn't respond to her humor, alarm skittered through her. Even Clarice, who had followed them into the kitchen and stood leaning against the counter, offered her nothing but a sad shrug.

"What—" Felicity couldn't even force the words out to inquire what she was being quarantined for, but the doctor apparently read her concern.

"Myslexia coreopsis nervosa."

The breath squeezed from her lungs. "What is that?"

"A rare, highly contagious disease that, if left untreated, can result in skin lesions, shortness of breath, seizures, and possibly death."

Her eyes closed, and she weaved on her feet ever so slightly. The disease sounded positively hideous.

"Why haven't I heard of such an illness before?"

"It's . . . er . . . some new strain. From the medical journals I've read, it is believed the disease was brought here by some immigrants from the Ukraine.

There have been only a few cases in the United States, but one flare-up about a year ago . . ." He shook his head. "What a horrible business. Sixty-four people in the western territories died."

Felicity's stomach lurched. "What are the symptoms?"

"Ahh. Symptoms."

In Felicity's opinion, the man took an inordinate amount of time to summon his thoughts. "The first stage of the illness includes a high fever, a rash on the legs, arms, and . . . delicate areas of one's body."

Despite herself, she flushed at such frank speech.

"This is followed by vomiting and lung congestion. If the patient isn't treated by the second stage, well . . ."

A cloud of doom seemed to settle over the room.

Felicity swallowed against the fear gripping her throat. When would she learn to stop being so impulsive, to stop gallivanting into places where she had no business going? But even as she chided herself for her foolishness, another part of her insisted that this must be a joke. A horrible, horrible joke.

"I think you've made a mistake. Such a rare disease couldn't possibly break out here. Right here. In this very house."

The words sounded faint to her own ears and she was not surprised when the doctor shook his head. "No mistake. One of my current myslexia cases spent several nights here just last week for . . . entertainment purposes. We have to assume that everyone here was exposed." The doctor's expression grew positively glum. "I'm afraid you are considered a risk at this point too."

Felicity shook her head. "No. No, I can't possibly be required to remain in quarantine. I've only been here a few minutes."

"That's all it takes to become a carrier—or worse yet, a patient."

"No. No!" She pushed Logan away from her, hoping to appeal to the doctor's better judgment. "Don't you see? I can't stay *here*. I can't!" She scrambled to think and said, "What about that other woman? The one in black. She was outside when I arrived."

Doc Wanger's gaze met Logan's, but his answer was smooth. "I have allowed short walks to the privy and through the orchard as long as no one has shown any symptoms. The disease is believed to be carried by contact with an infected person's skin, not by sharing the same air."

"That's preposterous," Felicity grumbled. "I haven't touched anyone."

"You slapped *me,*" Logan reminded her.

She glared at him. "I still don't see why I have to stay here. If it is permissible to walk in the yard, I should be able to go to my own house."

But the doctor wasn't paying attention. He was regarding Logan over her head and scowling.

"Considering the circumstances, my boy, don't you think you should put some clothes on?"

Logan dragged a tablecloth from a nearby pile and wrapped it around his hips, tucking the ends at his waist. It eased Felicity's nerves. But only a bit.

"Please, please let me go. I won't tell anyone I've been here; I'll stay in my own house for however long you want."

The doctor patted her on the head as if she were a recalcitrant child—or worse yet, some annoying sort of pet.

"No, dear. There are rules, I'm afraid. We must abide by the rules. According to city ordinances, quarantines are to be confined in areas of contagion whenever possible."

As if that was all that needed to be said, he turned his attention to Logan.

"Now," he continued. "Suppose *you* explain to me how this happened. Damn it, Logan, I thought I left you with strict orders that the house was to be closed up. That no one was to leave or enter. I even left you a sign to post on the front door."

"There was no sign—" Felicity began heatedly, but the doctor patted her again. She supposed it was his way of trying to calm her, but if the truth were known, its only effect was to infuriate her even more.

"I didn't *let* her in; she barged in." Logan's voice fairly dripped with disapproval. "Of her own accord."

"You called to me!"

"I did not call to you. I called to Clarice."

Setting her basket on the table with a bang, Felicity folded her arms tightly beneath her breasts. "It amazes me how a man could be so dense, especially when it is *my* reputation and word of honor that's at stake. Why won't you admit the truth? That you heard a voice—*my* voice—and you instructed me— and I quote—to 'come here . . . back here,' end of quote."

The doctor's gaze bounced from Felicity to Logan and back again. "I take it you two know each other."

The remark was made with such smug certainty that Felicity could have quite happily slapped him. But she didn't. She wouldn't. She was a lady and, as such, had been taught to reserve such methods of retaliation for those who were truly in need of it. She glared at Logan. Like *that* man.

"Well?" the doctor prompted. "Am I right?"

"No," Felicity said quickly.

But Logan responded just as swiftly. "Yes."

"Which is the correct answer?" the doctor asked wearily.

Thinking the truth would be far clearer and far less damaging to her reputation if it came from her own lips, Felicity said, "I met Mr. Campbell on a train— *briefly*—as I journeyed to Missouri from Boston. It was a less than memorable encounter." She threw Logan a scathing glance, hoping that he'd catch her subtle double entendre. "One that offered little more than an exchange of names."

A white lie at best, but it seemed better than admitting she'd kissed a total stranger.

Kissed him and enjoyed it. But she wasn't about to admit *that* fact either.

"Our meeting today is an unhappy accident, I assure you," she insisted. "I have recently moved into the house next door, and I was making some calls in the neighborhood to introduce myself."

The doctor's gaze connected with Logan's, and she did not miss the slight rolling of his eyes as if he'd been expecting such a statement.

Eager to prove her innocence, she insisted, "Had I known Mr. Campbell was in residence here, wild horses couldn't have dragged me inside."

This lie was far from white. If the truth were told, she'd done a great deal of thinking about Logan Campbell since he'd disappeared. *Obsessed* might prove an even better description, considering the state of her dreams, but she didn't believe the doctor would be interested in such wanton behavior. She didn't even wish to admit to herself that if she'd known Logan was here, she might have forced a chance encounter, might even have put herself in the position of garnering another kiss.

Of course, that had been before today when she'd still been suffering from the misconception that Logan Campbell was a man worthy of attention. One with a character to match the width of his shoulders.

One who had convinced her that beneath his rough-and-tumble exterior was a gentleman. A man who understood the vagaries of a woman's heart.

How could she have been so wrong?

"That, sir," she said, addressing the doctor, "is how I was put into this most precarious position. I assure you that if I'd had any idea—any *clue*—about the true nature of this . . . *boarding* house, I would have passed it by without a thought. Moreover, I would have made serious inquiries into changing my current residence."

She finished her speech with a tiny stamp of her feet, hoping that it would give weight to her argument. Unfortunately, when she looked at the doctor, his only real emotion seemed to be one of relief.

"You aren't from around here."

It didn't sound like much of a question to her, more of a statement of fact.

"No. My name is Felicity Pedigrue. I've come to take a teaching position at the academy as well as to set up my own business of sorts. A tea shop and reading room. Might I inquire your name, sir?"

"Dr. Randall Wanger, resident physician and owner of this establishment."

Her mouth dropped. She couldn't help it. *This* man owned the brothel? A doctor? The idea was positively indecent!

The doctor peered at her from beneath his bushy brows, examining her with an interest beyond that of mere curiosity. Indeed, he appeared to be measuring up her form as carefully as her character.

"Have you begun teaching yet?"

"No."

It was only after she'd told the man the truth that she reazlied she probably should have prevaricated more. Perhaps if she had important business to conduct, her argument might be given the attention it deserved. But since the response had been uttered, she felt obligated to finish. "I haven't met with the superintendent."

"I see." The doctor took a pair of spectacles from his pocket, then a handkerchief. "Is your family with you? Did they journey with you on the train?"

In Felicity's opinion, his questions were becoming increasingly more personal and far less medically oriented, but she didn't think she was in a position to quibble.

"No. Why?"

The doctor began to clean his lenses, the deliberate wipe, wipe, wipe, doing little to calm her. In fact, it put Felicity on edge.

"No real reason other than we should let someone know what has happened here."

Let someone know . . . Her eyes squeezed shut, and she felt a wave of faintness bloom inside her. For the first time in years, she found herself wishing she hadn't succumbed to vanity and laced her corset so tightly she couldn't take a proper breath. "There are my sisters . . ."

They would die if they heard what had happened. They would scold her no end for her carelessness. "But surely they don't need to be told!" Her lashes sprang open, and she sent a silent appeal to Logan. "They would be so upset, and there's nothing they could do about the situation. They both left Boston soon after I did."

The doctor and Logan exchanged quick furtive glances. Felicity couldn't help feeling as if they were conferring silently with one another about something she did not understand.

"What about the man who purchased your house?" She frowned. "Purchased my house? The one next door? I—I suppose that would be my recently departed father. He made arrangements in his will for me to come to Saint Joseph."

Again, the two men seemed to confer silently.

"What about the woman who was with you on the train?" Logan inquired.

Miss Grimm.

A sick dread gripped Felicity's heart. It was amazing how quickly Felicity had been able to wipe the woman's existence from her memory. After walking out the door into the sunshine of Saint Joseph, Felicity had banished her chaperone to the outer reaches of her mind.

The wooziness she'd only recently conquered returned again threefold. Thunderation, Miss Grimm would never let Felicity hear the end of this. Not in this lifetime. She would lecture her from morning to night, then probably fasten a bell to Felicity's neck so that she could be herded about like some lap dog with a penchant for straying.

Her eyes squeezed closed, and she began to pray. Quite earnestly. But when she received no impulse from on high, she was forced to explain. "Miss Elmira Grimm. After we arrived in Saint Joseph, she became . . . indisposed. I left her sleeping next door."

"I see," the doctor mumbled. "I'll make sure that she's contacted."

He patted her on the head for the umpteenth time, bonnet and all, and Felicity resisted the urge to scream. She was not a woman to be patronized, not when every decision about to be made would affect her so deeply.

"Clarice?" the doctor asked. "Will you escort our . . . guest to the Blue Room? I'd like to have a private word with Mr. Campbell."

"The Blue Room?" the girl echoed. "Is she going to work here?"

"No!" The very idea was enough to scald Felicity's cheeks, and she glared at Logan in response. With all the blushes she'd suffered since meeting him, she was lucky she hadn't melted into a puddle of mortification.

"Go with her," Logan urged.

Felicity dug her heels into the floor. "I will not! I refuse to wait in some sort of . . . concubinal chamber."

"Concubinal?" Logan repeated. Then he asked of the doctor, "Do you think there really is such a word?"

The doctor shrugged. "She said she's from Boston. If anyone should know . . ."

Felicity could not prevent the low growl of fury that rose from her throat. Snatching her basket from the table, she clutched it against her stomach.

"I'm so pleased that this situation—this dire, horrible situation—has proven to be a source of amusement for you both. Nevertheless, I insist you listen to me now and listen well. I am a woman of high manners and morals. I have spent my life developing a name for myself, a sterling reputation. I have done my best to appear honest, loyal, and above all chaste, and I will not—*will not*—be taken to your blasted blue room or any other of your . . . *rooms.*"

She would have continued her tirade, but the men had begun to regard her as if she were about to have a fit, so she took a deep breath, composed herself, and said as calmly as she could, "Since it is apparent that the two of you feel the need to have some sort of private conference about this whole affair, I will give you a minute alone—*a minute.* Then I expect you to do the honorable thing and let me go so that we can all pretend that this whole unfortunate incident had never occurred. I assure you that I can take sufficient quarantine measures in my own home."

Summoning as much dignity as she could possibly muster, she crossed to the door leading to the hall. "I'll wait in the front parlor—if there is one—until the two of you sort this mess out."

Holding her head high, she sailed from the room, praying all the while that her cheeks didn't look as hot as they felt.

Neither Logan nor Doc Wanger moved a muscle as the woman sashayed past. But when the doctor began staring at the twitching of Felicity's skirts too intently for Logan's comfort, he stepped in the man's field of vision, crossing his arms over his chest.

"Clarice?" It took all the will Logan possessed to keep his voice low and matter-of-fact. "Would you be so kind as to join our guest?"

Clarice's brows furrowed in confusion. "She's a guest? I thought we weren't supposed to let any guests into the house."

Logan resisted the urge to swear. Clarice was a sweet kid, the perfect sensual companion, and a beautiful woman. But if the truth were told, she was about as bright as a box of hair.

"Go sit with her in the parlor, Clarice."

"Why?"

This time he had to clench his jaw to keep calm. "To keep her company, to keep her from leaving, to keep her from stealing the knickknacks, I don't care! Just do it, please."

Rather than being offended by his curt command, Clarice grinned and offered a kittenish "All right." Brushing past him in a manner that was far too intimate to be necessary, she disappeared down the hall.

Only then did Logan turn his attention to the good doctor. "Damnation, man. What possessed you to ask all those questions?" Logan whipped the door shut behind him, but because it was mounted on a pair of swinging hinges, there was no satisfactory slam, only a puff of air as it *whooshed* into place.

Doc Wanger opened his mouth to talk, but Logan held up his hands in a bid for silence. "Never mind. I don't want to hear an explanation."

Making his way to the larder, Logan stepped into the cool, dark confines and retrieved a bottle of whiskey from where it had been hidden behind a crock of flour. Without even bothering to look for a glass, he removed the top and took a healthy swallow.

"It's early for that, isn't it?" Doc Wanger propped his shoulder against the lintel.

"Doubt it," Logan muttered abruptly before taking another sip. Then he replaced the top and leaned back against the cool stone wall. It didn't matter that the rough edges dug into his shoulder blades or that the temperature of the rock was a shock to his system. He needed to think—think, damn it!

Unfortunately, Doc Wanger wasn't inclined to give him that sort of time.

"Would you care to explain the real reason why that Pedigrue woman is here?"

Logan replaced the whiskey in its hiding place and ground the heels of his hands into his eyes. "You've already heard the real reasons. She came barging in all by herself. She was in my bedroom before I knew she was even here."

"Oh, really." Doc clearly didn't believe his explanation. "Yet you seem to know each other rather well. Why didn't you tell me you knew who was moving in next door?"

Logan's hands dropped. "She told you the truth about that too. We met on the train coming into Saint Joseph. That's it. End of story."

"You're sure?"

"Yes." But even as he spoke, Logan was reminded of a stolen kiss, of Felicity's body held close to his own. Worse yet, he remembered how he'd stood in the bushes across the street, seeking a glimpse of his new neighbor, only to see her silhouetted in her window wearing nothing but a flimsy nightshift.

"You must have made some impression on the woman for her to risk breaking quarantine to meet you again."

Logan sighed. "I forgot to hang up the sign."

"What?"

"I left the placard on the step until I could find a hammer. Miss Pedigrue was probably making casual calls like she said. She must have come here looking for Mother LaRee."

"Which was the precise reason we set up this quarantine in the first place."

"*You* know it and *I* know it, but *she* doesn't know that—and where in hell did you come up with that name? Myslexia core—watcha-ma-call-it?"

Doc Wanger grinned. "I made it up. I've been spreading rumors and information leaflets all over town, extolling the dangers and warning about quarantine sites. Too bad Miss Pedigrue didn't get a flyer."

At the reminder of their current problem, Doc Wanger huffed in irritation and lifted his spectacles to the light, squinting at them as if they held the answers to the universe. "Since the two of you have already met, just how much *does* she know about you and what's going on here?"

"Nothing. Absolutely nothing."

"You're sure?"

"Of course, I'm sure." Logan pushed himself upright and forced his way past the doctor. "How many times do I have to tell you? For all intents and purposes, she's a stranger."

Doc carefully hooked his spectacles over his ears, causing his eyes to become that much larger and more expressive from Logan's point of view, and there was no hiding the fact that he was worried.

"You keep insisting she's a stranger, Logan, but you fail to acknowledge the problem we have here. This woman has seen your face; she knows your name. If she were ever to discover your real reason for being in the city, she could tell the law where to find you. According to the Fugitive Slave Act, you are guilty of some very serious crimes."

Logan braced his palms on the table and stared down at the clutter of dirty plates and pans. Damn. He'd been so rattled at having Felicity appear in his bedroom he hadn't really thought of the consequences. She could identify him later on. If that information were given—however unwittingly—to the wrong sorts of people, he could be put in a very dangerous position. It would take only a casual word to the butcher or a passing remark to the pastor's wife. It didn't really matter that the quarantine was a hoax that he and Doc Wanger had developed or that she was at no risk of contracting myslexia whatever-it-was. The fact remained: Felicity was a danger to him.

"She can't leave, Logan."

"Shit."

"She can't leave," Doc said again. "We mustn't take that chance. Not until Everett returns with those boys."

A dull ache was beginning to form behind Logan's eyes. He wished suddenly that he hadn't tried to drown his boredom and concern in a bottle of liquor the night before. Maybe then he would be able to construct some sort of logical plan.

"How am I supposed to keep her here against her will? It would be wrong." He whirled, making a wide gesture. "Out there, in the world she comes from, a week spent in a bordello—no matter the reason—would be enough to ruin her. By keeping her here, we will be sentencing her to social ostracism."

"I don't see that you have a choice. It's her reputation, true. But it's also a matter of *your* life. Everett's life. The future of those boys he'll bring back with him."

Logan sighed. Doc Wanger was right. He couldn't let Felicity go free. He couldn't chance having her unwittingly disclose the location of the best stop for the Underground Railroad in this district.

"She'll try to escape," Logan said wearily.

Doc's eyes twinkled. "I thought you said you didn't know her very well."

"I'd have to be stupid to think otherwise."

"Just keep her as quiet as you can."

"Fine, fine." But even as Logan reassured the doctor, he had no doubts that Miss Pedigrue would prove far more difficult to handle than the older man would ever dream possible. Doc Wanger hadn't witnessed the way she'd followed Logan into a deserted portion of a railway station. Nor had he seen the way she could act so sweet and defenseless. He hadn't kissed her, held her, tasted her as Logan had.

Jerking upright, Logan abandoned that line of thinking, bringing himself back to the matter at hand. "I'll take care of her," he said again. "But in the meantime, you'll have to do something about her chaperone. I've had a good look at Miss Grimm. She won't take kindly to having her charge holed up in a cathouse."

Doc Wanger glanced at his watch. "Don't you worry about that. I'll make the Pedigrue house my next stop."

"What do you intend to tell the woman?"

"No more than she needs to know." Doc Wanger collected his bag. "Do you need anything?"

Logan shrugged. "The usual. We've got enough foodstuffs, but we could use some fresh eggs, butter, and the like."

"Fine. I'll bring it with me in the next couple of days."

It wasn't until Doc Wanger had reached the door that Logan asked the question that had needled him since the older man had appeared so unexpectedly. "Any word from Everett?"

"Not yet. But I'm sure there's nothing to worry about."

Nothing to worry about.

But there was. Logan, more than anyone, knew the kinds of risks his brother was taking. Everett was alone in a hostile environment with nothing but his wits to keep him out of trouble. Even so, Logan would have done anything to change places with his brother. It was so much easier to do something than to sit and wait.

But events had already snowballed and Logan was stuck where he was—by duty, common sense, and a sense of sibling pride. To go in search of Everett and try to take over his job now would be the ultimate betrayal.

"He's got to be here by the end of the week," Logan said quietly, more to himself than to Doc Wanger. "Otherwise, I'm going after him. He might need help."

Doc shook his head. "I'm afraid you'll have to give him more time than that. There was a mud slide on one of the railway spurs he took; it delayed him for the better part of three days. He couldn't have arrived in Georgia until early this morning."

Logan frowned and planted his hands on his hips, resisting the urge to swear a blue streak. He'd been counting on getting out of Saint Joseph as soon as possible. Each hour that had passed had been mentally ticked off in his head. He didn't know how much more of this he could take—the waiting, the wondering, the worrying. It made him appreciate what Everett must have experienced each time Logan had disappeared to make a run north. The uncertainty was excruciating.

"You'll let me know the minute you hear anything?"

Doc Wanger nodded. "You have my word." Slapping Logan on the back, he offered the younger man a cheeky grin. "In the meantime, you have yourself a nice day, you hear?"

Nice day? Logan thought as the door closed behind Doc Wanger. The man had to be kidding.

Logan was astute enough to know that he was about to have an afternoon straight out of hell.

Eight

Doc Wanger chuckled to himself as he pounded the quarantine sign onto the front gate, then made his way next door. If the truth were known, he wasn't too worried about Miss Felicity Pedigrue. As long as she stayed at Mother LaRee's until Everett returned, he didn't think she could prove to be much of a risk—and she might serve as a diversion for Logan. He chortled again—especially if the sparks he'd witnessed between them continued.

Climbing the stoop to the old Butler place, he rapped his knuckles on the door and waited.

Nothing.

Sighing, he tested the knob and found it to be unlocked. Because time was of the essence and Felicity had already mentioned her chaperone was indisposed, he felt no compunction about entering the house. He was, after all, a doctor.

Pausing in the foyer, he listened carefully. When he heard a faint, resonant snore, he snickered again and made his way upstairs, holding his bag in plain view should he chance to surprise the woman.

But upon entering the rear bedroom, he saw that

the lanky figure was snugly ensconced in bed, the covers drawn up to her pointy chin, her head swathed in a mob cap and a scarf drenched in the scents of menthol and eucalyptus wound around her neck. Even so, there was no disguising the scent of rum on her breath.

Randall grinned. If he were a betting man, he'd bet it wasn't so much a cold that ailed the woman but a good, old-fashioned hangover.

Sensing that sleep was the only cure for Miss Grimm, he backed out of the room. Once downstairs again, he scrawled a note on one of his cards and tucked it between the window and frame of the door, then let himself out.

As soon as the woman roused and came to fetch him, he'd see to removing this last complication. Until then, he'd have plenty of time to think of something suitable to say.

Once Doc Wanger had left Mother LaRee's, Logan knew he should join Miss Felicity Pedigrue immediately. Each second she spent in the parlor was merely one moment more for her to fret and stew and fuss, and judging by the display of temper he'd seen already, that was something he wanted to avoid.

But he also had enough common sense to take the time to put his clothes on. As far as he was concerned, he'd had plenty of surprises for one day. Although he was not averse to running around in the same state God had brought him into the world, he didn't want the disadvantage of trying to reason with that woman while he was wearing nothing more than a red-checkered tablecloth.

As soon as Logan entered the parlor, he was glad that he'd taken such precautions. Judging by the fire in Felicity's eyes, her mood hadn't improved. He wouldn't be surprised if she snatched the same hat pin she'd tried to wield on him once before and did her best to stab him with it.

The mantel clock filled a silence that was deafening with its insistent tick, tick, tick, and if Logan wasn't mistaken, a tiny muscle in Felicity's jaw kept time with the rhythm. The basket of goodies was on her lap as if she feared it might somehow be soiled by the very atmosphere of the room. She sat perched on the edge of a scarlet tufted chair, balancing in such a way that if she moved so much as a muscle, she would probably drop to the floor, thereby becoming even more tainted by the sensual surroundings.

If he hadn't been so tense himself, Logan might have laughed. Instead, he made his way into the parlor, stopping in the center, mere feet from where Felicity sat.

"You can go now, Clarice."

He didn't even look at the girl. He was watching Felicity, noting how out of place she looked in a room overflowing with objets d'art, red satin, and gilt. Idly, he wondered if she knew that she'd positioned herself directly beneath a sketch of a nude woman rising from her bath. Did Felicity realize that the line of the model's shoulders echoed her own, that her hair spilled down her back in the same way Felicity's might if it were left free?

"Are you sure you don't want me to stay, Logan?"

He started when Clarice spoke to him long after he'd assumed she'd left the room. For a man who had grown accustomed to knowing every detail surrounding him, the realization was unsettling.

"Yes, Clarice. I'm sure."

She touched his arm. "I could stay."

He glanced at her briefly, saw her earnestness, her childlike faith, and relented. No matter how sticky this situation might grow, he couldn't take his ire out on Clarice. He would never do anything to hurt her.

Offering her a warm smile, he stroked the top of her head, smoothing the riotous hair back into place. Clarice stretched and preened under the caress like a satisfied tabby cat.

"No, sweetheart," he said softly, knowing that Felicity had stiffened at the warm tone he employed with the girl. "I'll be fine in here with Miss Pedigrue. We're going to have a friendly chat. Why don't you go finish putting your clothes on in the meantime, hmm?"

Her expression immediately brightened, as if he'd offered her the secret to happiness.

"Yes. Yes, I'll do that."

Standing on tiptoe, she kissed him on the cheek. Then turning to Felicity, she wiggled her fingers in a brief farewell before skipping from the parlor with the giddy effervescence of a young child.

It was Felicity's snort of disapproval that brought his head around again. He saw the way her brow creased in a frown and her lips folded primly together.

"What's the matter, Miss Pedigrue?" he asked, purposely goading her.

"Not a thing." But the tone of her voice was similar to one she might have adopted if she'd sucked on a lemon.

"You don't like Clarice, do you?" he asked.

"It is not my place to like or dislike the woman."

"But you've formed an opinion."

"One that I'm sure you would not care to hear."

"Oh, but I would."

She didn't immediately speak. Instead she weighed her options carefully, as if she were afraid Logan would not welcome the truth.

"Honestly?"

He nodded. "Honestly."

"There's nothing but fluff between her ears."

Her response surprised him. He'd been anticipating

some scathing remark about Clarice's character or her means of employment but never a comment on her intelligence. It was nearly enough to make him smile.

Nearly.

"I suppose that would explain her willingness to live in this house," she added.

"You don't approve?"

"I neither approve or disapprove. It isn't my place." When he would have inserted a comment, she held up a hand in a gesture of silence. "However, if she'd been given a proper education, I'm sure even she would have chosen some other means of housing."

"Why would you say that?"

"She could have been taught skills to help her provide a better future for herself."

This time, Logan couldn't help but grin. "What makes you think she doesn't already possess talents of that nature?"

By the flaming of her cheeks, he supposed she'd caught his meaning, that Clarice had a distinct skill for seeing to a man's more carnal needs.

"Mr. Campbell—"

Her disgruntled tone pleased him no end. "Yes, Miss Pedigrue."

"I hardly think that we should be discussing Clarice's education or lack thereof. The fact remains that she is a bit simpleminded—"

"Perhaps," he drawled. "But she's got a great pair of—"

Felicity stood with such abruptness that the settee she'd been sitting on toppled over backward. "I do not wish to be given an inventory of her charms, thank you kindly!"

Logan laughed out loud. He couldn't help it. Felicity's cheeks were blazing in that manner he'd grown accustomed to seeing during their exchanges.

"Tell me, Miss Pedigrue, is your skin always this red?"

She offered a choked gasp. "I do not wish to discuss my . . . color."

Logan began to move toward her, astounded by the way this slip of a woman could bring out so many emotions in such a short amount of time. Since encountering her in his bedroom, he'd traversed an emotional scale from shock to anger to dread to amusement to . . . To what?

Desire?

Heaven only knew he shouldn't be feeling anything of the sort. He should be regarding her as an enemy to his well-being or, at the very least, a nuisance. Instead, he discovered that he wanted to see how far that blush extended over her body. Was it confined to her face alone, or did it move down her chest as well? To her breasts? Lower?

He took another step closer, then another, seeing the way her eyes widened as if he were a cougar about to pounce. "If your coloring is so inappropriate a subject, Miss Pedigrue, then what, pray tell, would you like to discuss?"

His blunt comments bothered her no end. Her breaths were irregular, and she retreated an inch for every step he took. Unfortunately, she was running out of room to escape. She tried to twist sideways, to move away from the barrier of the settee, but only managed to pin herself between a chair and a hassock.

He could all but see the gears working in her head as she mentally prepared for battle.

"If you would be so kind as to tell me when I'll be leaving this place, I won't trouble you any further."

Knowing she would not be content with his silence, Logan quickly calculated the time Everett would need, then added a few more days for safety's sake. "At least two weeks."

Her skin lost all tint. "You can't be serious."

"Two weeks, Felicity."

She swallowed visibly, her gaze darting about the room as if searching for some avenue of escape. "B-but I can't stay here that long."

"You don't have a choice."

That remark brought her chin up to a defiant angle. "We'll see about that!"

When she would have stormed by him, he caught her by the waist, hauling her close to his body. In an instant, he was inundated by all the details he had tried to strike from his memory. The way she'd felt against him when he'd took her weight. The way she'd smelled. Tasted.

Her eyelashes flickered as if she too remembered. As if the slow heat turning his blood to fire had settled into her bones.

He brought her closer still, bending around the ridiculous bonnet she wore to whisper in her ear, "Don't act this way, Felicity. You'll only make things worse for yourself if you fight me."

"Fight you?"

He nodded. "I've been put in charge while the doctor is gone. As the only physician in town with experience in handling this disease, the city council has given him the power to detain anyone he sees fit. If you try to leave, he'll have you arrested and brought right back."

"How many more people has he imprisoned here?"

"Just the four of us."

"Four of us?"

"You, me, Clarice, and Lena."

Lena must have been the woman in black.

"Don't buck me, Felicity. I've been ordered to see to it that you comply with the quarantine."

"Ordered?" she echoed faintly, then more strongly, *"Ordered?"*

Immediately, he knew he'd said the wrong thing. Instead of calming her, he'd managed to make her more angry.

"Ordered!" Felicity shouted.

Bracing her palms against his chest, she freed herself, but not before the imprint of her hips had been made on his. Even through the layers of clothing, he'd caught a hint of what lay beneath.

"I will not be ordered about like one of your . . . one of your . . . *doxies.*"

He caught her around the waist when she would have twisted toward the window. "Damn it, Felicity, I won't have you insulting anyone here."

"Insulting them. Insulting *them?* What about me? What about how this situation will affect my standing in Saint Joseph? I'm a newcomer here. Everything I do will be studied with a jaundiced eye from this moment on. No one will ever believe that I was never part of this . . . this *house.*"

"You are a part of it whether you like it or not. By walking through that door"—he pointed in the general direction of the kitchen—"with your basket of goodies, you joined something you don't understand, that you probably don't want to understand. But there's no going back."

"No. No, no, no!" She pried his arm from around her waist and grabbed her basket.

Logan automatically reached for her, planning to tie her down if need be until she saw reason. But his hand accidentally hit the bottom of the basket, throwing the contents toward Felicity's chest. To her obvious horror, the lids to the crocks jiggled free, and in an instant, she was covered from chest to ankle in sticky preserves and globs of freshly churned butter. Then her belongings plunged to the ground and scattered with a noisy crash.

The stamp of boot heels caused them both to look

at the doorway, where a tall, slender redhead had entered the room. In a wry twist, Logan saw that Lena's attire resembled the same ladylike attire Felicity wore, but the quirt at her side was anything but dainty.

"Food," she murmured wryly. "Now there's a new gimmick if I've ever heard one. But tell me, Logan, isn't she supposed to take her clothes off first?"

Felicity gave a squeal of outrage, and it was Logan who stepped between the two women to keep the redhead from being charged.

"You've misunderstood, Lena. This is Miss Felicity Pedigrue from next door."

"Next door?" Lena's brow furrowed. "She's not some new girl who didn't get the message?"

"New girl?" Felicity shouted.

"Yeah. The boarding house prides itself on changing most of its girls at least eight times a year. I see to that myself. The previous batch left here a week ago."

Felicity was trying her best to push Logan aside, but he held her fast.

"No, Lena. Doc Wanger managed to warn the last of our new employees to stay away for a few weeks. Miss Pedigrue has come on a . . . social call. Since she's broken our quarantine, she'll now be required to stay."

Lena eyed the broken crocks, the preserves, and the way Logan kept his body between them. "I see."

Lena wanted to ask more, Logan could see it in the way her lips parted as if to form a question. But she reconsidered, tipped her head to the side, and said instead, "She looks too starched to last a fortnight here in this house, don't you think?"

Logan eyed Felicity, seeing anew how out of place she was here. How prim. How fussy. How self-righteous.

"Perhaps you're right," Logan said slowly, thinking

that it was time Miss Felicity saw more of the real world that lay beyond Boston. *His* world. A place where things were rarely pretty and hardly ever proper. Where the niceties were often smothered by the will to survive.

He took Felicity's wrist and pulled her forward.

"Take her to the Blue Room, Lena, and help her clean up. Then see that she has something more . . . comfortable to wear while she's with us. It will be a while before someone can get that black monstrosity laundered."

"The Blue Room?" Lena's brows rose. "Really?"

"Yes. We want to make her as comfortable as we can." He paused, waiting for Felicity's full attention before adding, "Then, after she's finished washing, lock her in."

Nine

Felicity heard the key grind in the latch and groaned, sinking onto a silk-covered bed. Never in her life had she been so humiliated, so abused.

Her arms crossed her body, and she hugged herself as if chilled, which she was in a way. Upon arriving in this chamber, she had been forced to remove her jacket, blouse, skirt, and top petticoat. Even her hoops had been packed away.

Felicity damned herself for meekly stripping and handing over her clothes. She should have refused, put up some sort of a fight, or at least insisted she be given the opportunity to clean them herself. But that Lena woman scared her. She kept expecting to feel the lash of Lena's quirt if she didn't follow orders.

Only when the woman had been about to leave did Felicity summon enough courage to remind the redhead that she was supposed to find Felicity something else to wear. Expecting some sort of dress, a skirt, or a shirtwaist, she'd been horrified when Lena, adding salt to the wounds of her severely damaged dignity, had taken a flimsy sort of wrapper from one of the armoires and thrown it at her.

"Use this. I'll be back for your underwear later. Meanwhile, there's some things in the wardrobe—most of it new—that you can use."

When Felicity had been unable to hide her shock, Lena had said, "You'll have to be taking them off sometime in the next two weeks for washing. If you don't give them to me now, I'll get your underthings then."

Then Felicity had been left alone. At this point, Felicity wasn't sure if that was a blessing or a curse.

Holding the silk wrapper up to the afternoon light, Felicity blanched. She was expected to wear this—*this?* The garment was all but transparent. Without something to wear beneath it, Felicity wouldn't be leaving this room and certainly wouldn't be taking any constitutionals out-of-doors. Which was probably why it had been given to her in the first place, she supposed. She was going to be forced to stay in this house for two weeks.

Two long, interminable weeks. Perhaps even more if someone became ill.

Huffing in dismay and irritation, she threw the wrapper on the bed and strode to the door. But even before she tested it, she knew it was firmly locked.

Blast it.

She couldn't stay here; she *mustn't* stay here. Tarnation, how had she managed to get herself into such a terrible fix? One that, as far as she could see, had no real solution.

She gazed around the room that was to be her prison. She supposed that she should count her blessings that its windows looked out on the back orchard and not the front of the house. Maybe, because the blinds were always drawn, she could keep hidden from view, and the good people of Saint Joseph would never have to know she'd been here at all. She would only have to explain her disappearance to Miss Grimm.

And the superintendent at the academy.

Her sisters.

The lawyer in charge of her inheritance.

Blast it all! What was she going to do?

Her bare skin prickled, reminding her that it had been relieved of its layer of wool, and she dodged to the armoire in the corner. Surely, if there were new sets of underthings for her to wear, there would be some sort of dress she could borrow as well.

But when she opened the oak wardrobe, she was horrified by the array of garments left at her disposal. There were lacy garters and garishly clocked hose, scanty silk camisoles, indecently short petticoats, corsets of every color and description, feather stoles, lace wrappers, and brightly colored shoes.

She slammed the doors closed, leaning against them, suddenly short of breath.

No. She couldn't borrow anything that indecent, that shocking, that . . . that . . .

Her eyes squeezed closed as she struggled for calm. If she had been exposed to myslexia coreopsis nervosa, she could be a responsible adult and maintain her own quarantine, but she had no choice. She would have to find a way to leave.

Soon.

Tonight.

She waited until it had grown pitch black outside and the moon had climbed high enough so that its light was obscured by a stand of trees. Then she rose from where she had been sitting on the extreme outer edge of the bed and gathered the tools she needed for her escape.

Only once since she'd been interred in the Blue

Room had anyone bothered to check on her. Clarice had slipped inside, left a tray and a lantern on the bureau, felt her forehead for evidence of a fever, then waggled her fingers in that odd sort of greeting Felicity had become to associate with the blonde before she tiptoed out again.

Although her temper had not entirely cooled, Felicity had actually been glad to see the girl, especially since it had not been Lena who'd been sent to help her. Moreover, she'd been grateful for the meager source of light the lantern provided—that was to say, she'd been grateful until darkness had fallen and buttery warmth had revealed to her that a very erotic pattern had been incorporated into the lace bed curtains. Indecent. Positively indecent.

Ignoring the fact that she was beginning to adopt Miss Grimm's favorite phrase, Felicity turned a blind eye to the shadowy figures of heavily endowed women and posturing men that had been thrown onto the walls about her. Firmly grasping the lantern, she crept to the door.

For hours now, there had been some sort of merriment taking place downstairs. If not for the fact that the house was under quarantine, she would have assumed it had been opened for business.

The idea was enough to squeeze the air from her lungs. She mustn't think of such things. She mustn't dwell on the activities that took place in this establishment. She must keep her mind on the matter at hand and her wits firmly gathered.

Placing her ear to the wood, she listened to the distant *plinkety-plank* of a piano. Above that, she could hear singing, even the stomp of feet as someone danced, and her fingers curled into tight fists.

How dare they? How dare the three of them carry on with their pleasures as if nothing had happened? As if they weren't all under the threat of disease? As if there weren't a *real* lady in the house? One who didn't want to be locked in some blasted place called the Blue Room where she wouldn't be able to escape whatever sounds would fill the house later.

After the revelry.

When they decided to go to bed.

Together.

Dear sweet Mary and all the saints, she had to escape. Now. This instant. But even as the thought flashed into her head, the cacophony from below grew louder. In fact, the more of their carousing she heard, the more the story about a quarantine was beginning to rankle. There was something wrong about the whole affair. Something decidedly fishy, as Constance would say.

She didn't know when she'd first begun to suspect the quarantine's validity. Probably upon meeting the doctor. If the members of this house were in such dire straits and were in danger of infection, why hadn't he bothered to examine anyone? As far as she could remember, he'd done little more than step into the kitchen, where he'd confronted her and Logan. Soon after she'd gone to the parlor, she'd seen him striding down the walk.

Yes, something was amiss here. Most definitely. And Felicity didn't intend to wait around to find out what.

Kneeling on the floor next to the door, she peered through the hole beneath the knob, grinning to herself when she saw that the key had been left there. Careless. Very careless. But very fortuitous for her.

Taking the remains of a playbill she'd found in one of the drawers—a very risqué playbill with pictures on the cover that never should have been allowed to be printed—she slid the paper beneath the door, directly under the knob. Then she retrieved her hat pin from where she'd kicked it under the bed. It had been quite brilliant of her to hide it from Lena, she thought. Quite brilliant indeed.

Returning to her original place, she knelt and squinted through the aperture. The tip of her tongue eased out of her mouth as she carefully inserted the pin through the slender opening and then through the hollow tip of the brass key. Bit by bit, she lifted it up and out of the lock until it dropped to the ground with a muffled clang.

Her heart pounded as she waited for some sort of response. She kept expecting Logan to begin shouting or Lena to thump on the door with the butt of her quirt.

But nothing happened. Nothing at all.

Allowing herself a single self-congratulatory moment, she slid the paper back to her side, nearly crowing aloud when the key came into view.

Yes. Yes! She would show Logan Campbell that she was not to be trifled with, was not to be treated so rudely.

Her fingers closed around the cool metal, and she sprang to her feet. From that instant she was in a rush, knowing that her time was limited. She couldn't take a chance that someone might pass down the hall and see the empty lock. She had to get out of this room before anyone decided to check on her again. More than that, she had to get out of this place before the women took any more of her clothes than they already had, thereby forcing her to choose something to wear from that iniquitous supply to be found in the armoire.

Tugging a blanket from the top of the bed, she wrapped it around her body toga fashion and prayed that the noise from below would cover any sounds she might make in escaping. She mourned the loss of her clothes—most especially her new crinoline—but there was no helping that. Perhaps Miss Grimm would agree to come fetch them at a later date.

Grimacing at the image that thought brought into her head, Felicity retrieved her hat pin and used it to keep the bed linens in position. In a final bid of defiance, she tossed the key into a potted plant. Let them find it there after she'd gone and wonder how on earth she'd managed to obtain it.

Listening intently for anyone who might be lurking on the other side of the wall, she wrapped her fingers around the porcelain knob and twisted it sideways. It moved easily in her hands, relieving her of the notion that a horrible joke might have been played on her and a different key had been put in the lock as bait.

The hinges squeaked as she opened the door, and she winced. But when she peered around the frame, she discovered the hall was dark and empty.

Good. Good!

Tiptoeing into the corridor, she paused, her heart pounding. But the noise from below continued unabated. Lifting her petticoats, she rushed as quickly as she could to the ornate landing, anticipating the scolding Miss Grimm would give her once she returned. But Felicity wouldn't mind. She would listen quite attentively, then indulge herself with a hearty meal, a hot bath, and the comfort of her own soft bed.

She would be free.

"Good evening, Felicity."

Felicity jumped and whirled, pressing a hand to her chest to still the furious pounding of her heart.

A form stepped away from the wall. A shape. A man.

"Logan," she whispered, feeling a wave of helplessness, then a tide of indignation. "How dare you sneak up on me like that!"

"You weren't supposed to be here, remember?"

"That is neither here nor there," she insisted heatedly.

"Isn't it?"

"No. You had no right to lock me up that way. No right at all."

"I told you before: Doc Wanger put me in charge while he was gone. I thought it was best to keep you in your room."

"Why?"

"To prevent what appears to be occurring right now." He stepped closer, and enough lamplight spilled into the hall from the Blue Room for her to see the ironic quirk of his brow. "For if I'm not mistaken, you are trying to escape."

His mocking expression was clear. Drat it all, she'd forgotten to extinguish the light. If she had, she could have run for freedom.

But even as the idea bounced into her head, she knew such an attempt would be preposterous. This man could probably see through the blackness. Like a hunter, a predator.

"How did you get loose, Felicity?"

He'd caught her in the wrong, but she didn't intend to give him the satisfaction of discovering how she'd done it. Let him worry; let him wonder. Tipping her chin in a defiant angle, she challenged him with a haughty stare. "Loose? Whatever can you mean? I merely thought I'd join the party."

He didn't believe her, not that she'd thought he would.

"You meant to spend your evening with us?"

"Oh, yes."

"For what possible reason?"

She offered her best careless shrug, then regretted the action when the coverlet she'd draped across her shoulders threatened to fall. "It sounded like such fun. It was cruel of you to exclude me."

"Cruel, huh?" He edged closer, so big, so tall, so lean. So infinitely male. "Do you really expect me to believe such a fairy tale?"

"What else could my reason be?"

"Come now, Felicity. Enough games. You're trying to break the quarantine."

"What quarantine?" she demanded hotly, dropping all attempt at coquettish charm. "I don't believe there really is one. I've never heard of mylexia coreopsis nervosa. *Never.* I think this is some sort of twisted campaign to put me in my place."

"Your *place.* And what might that be?"

"You resent me and my position."

"Resent you?" he echoed. "Whatever for?"

"I don't know yet, but you do. It was in the tone of voice you used when you talked about Boston. It was there in the way you ogled me on the railway platform."

"You surprised me. That's why I . . . ogled you, as you so daintily call it. I didn't expect someone like you to be scrutinizing me so intimately."

"Scrutinizing you!"

"Come now, Felicity. You started staring the minute I came into view. You had the hungry look on your face of a woman who's been without a man far too long."

"What?"

"How could I help but take a closer look? Especially when you conveniently trapped yourself on that nail—"

"I did not."

"—doused my arm with water—"

"An accident."

"Slid your hand under my shirt."

She was livid now, positively livid. How could he think that such innocent happenstances could be linked to an ulterior motive on her part?

She assumed the best dignified posture she could maintain and still keep hold of the blanket. "I assure you, Mr. Campbell, that I have never had, nor will I *ever* have, any ulterior designs concerning your company."

"Is that a fact? Then why did you follow me later that night? Why did you abandon your chaperone and come looking for me in the rail yard?"

He snagged her elbow, jerking her close, his features becoming harsh and somehow frightening in the dim light. "Or was it something else? Tell me, Felicity, are we really the strangers I thought we were, or have you seen me somewhere before? Did you already know me?"

"Know you?" she gasped. "I'd never set eyes upon you until you joined our train."

"Why should I believe you?"

"Why shouldn't you?"

"Because I think you're hiding something."

"Like what?"

"Information. Information that you'd best be telling me here and now."

She stamped her foot in indignation. "Botheration! You are the most suspicious, most ornery, most *nerve-wracking* person I've ever met. You parade about the country wearing dusty trousers and a shirt unbuttoned to your navel and expect a woman—a delicately bred woman—to be able to look away as if nothing is out of place. Then you accost her—"

"I kissed you!"

"—promise to commit bodily harm—"

"When?"

"—and threaten her very livelihood. Which brings me full circle to my original accusation. You resent me. You resent me horribly and for no real reason. No reason at all other than the fact that—unlike you—I am acquainted with such habits as bathing and tidying my hair."

Her accusation stunned him momentarily, then his eyes grew dark, sparkling with some sort of inner energy that she was not sure she wanted to fathom.

He still held her at the elbow, and his grip tightened—not enough to bruise, but more than enough to convince her that he had grown completely serious in his attempt to control her. She started when his free hand tipped her head even higher to the light, nudging her this way and that as if to study her quite thoroughly. In fact, he gave every appearance of searching for some sign of deceit, although Felicity could think of no reason why he would be convinced of such a thing.

The infinite silence of the hall swept around them; its emptiness made more powerful by the faraway music drifting up from the parlor. But the raucous tunes seemed to be coming from another world. As if Felicity had been marooned upon an island of sensation with this hard, angry man.

Logan's finger moved to her cheek, stroking, caressing, and she started at the abrupt change of emotions that came with such a casual exploration. At the gentleness. Gooseflesh raced from that point of contact, down her neck and lower, so much lower, until she became distinctly aware of standing before Logan in her underwear and a silk coverlet.

"Oh, no, Felicity." His voice was low, compelling, rich. "There are many things you inspire in me, but resentment isn't one of them."

As much as she despised the sensation, Felicity's knees trembled. A molten languor stole through her body, threatening to eradicate her will to do what was right. "Please," she whispered, "let me go. You don't really need me to stay here."

His lips quirked. His eyes gleamed in a way that she could only describe as wicked. "I assure you, my . . . need for your presence, as you put it, is quite genuine."

Felicity flushed, wondering how such an innocent phrase could have a bawdy ring to it. But this was neither the time nor the place to be analyzing such a thing. She had to put some space between them. Otherwise, she would be clinging to him in much the same manner she had at the train station.

"I don't believe you need me to stay here."

"But I do."

"What I meant by my statement," she began again, "was that if this quarantine is so dad-blasted important, then I could continue my seclusion in my own house among my own things."

But her attempts at logic fell on deaf ears.

"Doc Wanger is the man in charge of this situation, and he insists on having only one quarantine location. Besides, I want you here myself."

"Why?" She clasped his wrist to keep him from touching her again, to keep him from muddling her thoughts so completely.

He shrugged. "I'm not sure."

She tried to jerk away in anger, but he held her fast.

"You're being very obtuse, Mr. Campbell."

"I don't mean to be."

He edged closer, so much so that the coverlet gracing her breasts rubbed against the buttons of his shirt.

"You know, Felicity, you look very fetching in blue."

Felicity wished she had the nerve to slap him for reminding her of her indelicate state of undress.

"Isn't that the coverlet from your bedroom?"

She pursed her lips in disapproval for his inappropriate reminder. "Since you've taken my clothing, I had no other recourse."

"Lena said she supplied you with something to wear."

"Something of hers, I suppose."

He shook his head. "Doubtful. She tends to collect articles of clothing that are rather distinct and . . . uncomfortable for the average woman. She has a fondness for leather."

Felicity didn't even *want* an explanation of that remark. Scrambling to regroup her defenses, she retorted, "Nevertheless, what I was given will never do."

"But why?" Again, he followed so near to her now that her hips were pushed against the railing of the landing, reminding her that there was no space to retreat.

"It is rather . . . sheer."

"Ahh."

She didn't like the sound of that reply. Nor did she like the way he watched her as he spoke. There was something altogether intimate about it, causing an effervescence to enter her veins. Especially when, to her utter mortification, the edge of the blanket slipped, taking the strap of her camisole with it and exposing her bare shoulder.

An immediate change came over Logan, one that even in her meager experience she recognized as a flash of desire.

"Get back in the bedroom, Felicity."

His low moan was so unexpected, she actually shivered.

"No."

He grasped her arm, all but lifting her on tiptoes. "Get in there. Now. And lock yourself in."

Suddenly, she realized that he was no longer talking

strictly about the quarantine. His statement had been personal. Very, very personal.

To her astonishment, however, it didn't frighten her. It only made her more bold.

"Why?" The word was a breathy whisper.

He took her other elbow, lifting her against him, into him. "I think you know why."

"No, I don't. Tell me."

But he didn't speak. Growling low in his throat, he bent, his lips closing over hers.

Their first kiss had been a series of gentle, teasing advances. This embrace was an explosion of pure, masculine need. He crushed her to him, his mouth slanting over hers, his tongue plunging inside to rob her of the sweetness he found there. His arms became bands of iron, wrapping around her so firmly she couldn't breathe.

Not that she wanted to. Somehow, in the storm of ensuing passion, she forgot all mortal ties. She became something else, someone else. A woman who reached, who caressed, who held, who tasted. A wildness entered her body. So much so that she abandoned herself to the sensations, forgetting all training, all dictates of propriety. She had only one goal: to satisfy the hunger that raged within her.

Logan yanked away from her.

"No."

When she would have pulled him back, he clasped her wrists together.

"No," he said again, more forcefully this time. His voice was thick with some untold emotion, and she wondered halfheartedly if she looked as dazed and as rumpled as he did.

She couldn't. She mustn't.

Reality rushed into her head like an icy wind, and Felicity tried to pull free. But even after ordering her to leave, he wouldn't let her go. She could neither retreat nor advance.

"Damn you."

His curse was a blow to her heart.

"Why did you have to make me feel like this? Why now?"

The hurt dissolved, followed immediately by shock. Then wonder. Had she touched this man? Emotionally? In a way that was unsettling to one so rugged and in control?

But as soon as she thought such a thing, she thrust it away as silly, idealistic nonsense. Logan had no use for her. None but as an outlet for a bit of kiss and cuddle.

When he opened his mouth to explain further, she said quickly, "Don't. Don't say anything. Don't offer me platitudes you don't really feel. Don't cheapen me that way."

His eyes narrowed. "Cheapen? Is that what you think happens when a man and a woman—"

"Stop!" This time she was able to jerk free. "Just . . . stop!"

Then she couldn't say a thing. If she tried, she was sure that only a squeak would emerge past the lump in her throat. A lump that felt disturbingly like rising tears.

Running past him, she dodged into the Blue Room.

As Logan stood in the hall, shaken, still radiating a passion like he'd never experienced before, he heard the lock slip into place—this time, from Felicity's side of the door.

"Damn," he whispered to no one in particular. Then, struck by something she'd said, he sniffed his hands, his shirt. "And I do bathe, damn you!"

He received no answer. Which was probably just as

well. Because, whether he wanted to admit she'd pricked his conscience or not, he was probably going to be spending most of his evening bathing.

Sighing, he made his way downstairs to the narrow room he used whenever he was in Saint Joseph. He'd been awarded the chamber when Doc Wanger had taken over the business, and the girls who worked here were told that as a friend of the owner, he was to be given special consideration.

But Logan had made it a rule never to mix business with pleasure, no matter what assumptions Felicity had made of Clarice's asking his help with her corset. In his state that morning, he had been in no condition for anything of that nature. He did not avail himself of whatever women were working here. Because Mother LaRee's success as a safe house depended on its being used as an actual bordello, he hadn't wanted anyone growing too fond of him or too aware of his movements. He came and went as he pleased, as if he were the saddle bum Everett had described him as being. He'd developed numerous ways of getting slaves in and out of the cellar under the cover of raucous music and laughter. In all his years he'd never been caught.

He had been caught. By Boopsie Ruth. A girl he couldn't even remember.

Hell. He'd better make damned sure he didn't get caught again.

Ten

He wasn't the man she'd thought him to be. He was neither noble nor gentle nor honest. He was a cad of the highest degree. The sort who preyed upon defenseless women, who drew them into a sensual lair as surely as a spider spun a magnificent web to attract an innocent fly.

They were ensconced in the same house—if house *was the term one should use for such a place. Things had occurred in this residence, carnal acts that a lady should not dwell upon.*

Even if she were curious.

So curious that in the dead of night, when the old house began to creak and groan, she lay awake wondering what carnal *meant, why she wasn't supposed to think about such activities, let alone indulge in them . . .*

And why the mere thought of it caused her body to burn.

Something woke Felicity. Not a noise, not a flash of light. More of a presence. As if she were being . . . watched.

Her lashes flickered open, and she reached for the

covers, fearing that it was Logan who stood at the foot of her bed, studying her so carefully that the hairs on her arms prickled in warning.

But when she focused, it was to see that it wasn't Logan who waited for her to rise, but Clarice and Lena. The early morning sunlight streamed over their features and gilded their delicate forms.

"We've been told to come and get you."

It was Lena who spoke. She'd wound her arms around one of the bedposts and leaned forward in such a way that a good deal of her "charms" showed above the leather-bound edge of her corset.

"I see."

It was a stupid reply, but at the moment, it was the only coherent thing Felicity was capable of saying.

"Do you have a fever?" Lena asked.

Felicity felt her cheeks. "No."

"Have you had any trouble breathing? Evidence of a rash?"

"No."

"Then get up."

Felicity dragged the linens more tightly against her chin, glaring at the redhead who had apparently elected herself spokeswoman.

"Why?"

One of Lena's brows rose at the open rebellion.

"Because Logan wants to see you."

Felicity didn't miss the bite of temper in the woman's tone. Nor did she miss the way the tip of Lena's quirt appeared from between the folds of her petticoats. Tarnation, did that woman carry a whip with her everywhere she went?

"Mr. Campbell is not my master. I do not have to kowtow to him whenever he calls."

"Maybe, maybe not. But you won't be fed until you do. Doc Wanger put him in charge."

Felicity was growing tired of that particular phrase.

Hoping to divert the conversation, she sniffed in disdain. "Judging by the cooking I sampled yesterday, such a fact would not be a misfortune."

Lena glared at her. "Then why don't you do the meals, Little-Miss-High-and-Mighty? If you're going to be here for two weeks or more, you might as well make yourself useful."

"I will not be here for two weeks," Felicity insisted. But this time, it wasn't her reputation that served as her motivation, it was the memories of the kiss she and Logan had shared.

"I will *not!*" she said again even more forcefully, throwing back the covers and swinging her feet to the floor.

She'd worn all of her undergarments to bed and had augmented them with an old blouse and an extra layer of petticoats from the gaudy pieces of clothing she'd managed to find deep in the armoire. They were less than satisfactory, the bright red shirtwaist cut much too low, the orange flounced skirts hemmed much too high, but at least they managed to help her preserve some sense of modesty. Not much. But some.

"Where is he?"

It was Clarice who offered, "In his bedroom."

"Fine."

Felicity marched out of the room and down the stairs. But some of her bravado left her when she took two steps into Logan's bedroom, arriving as Logan was shrugging into his shirt.

He must have heard her enter, because he turned, his blue eyes raking down her form. One of his brows rose with mocking insolence. "You look like a cat that's been dragged through a knothole backward."

The insult, having come so close on the heels of her doing everything in her power to protect her sense of decorum, was like a match to dried timber.

"How dare you?" she hissed.

He sighed. "That seems to be one of your more favorite responses. Have you noticed?"

Her hands balled into fists. "I would like a word with you, please," she said, barely able to get the request out because of her temper.

"Have as many words as you'd like. We're going to be together for some time."

"Not here. In the parlor."

She marched stiffly to the front of the house, then whirled to confront him.

Drawing to full height, she demanded, "I want you to make some sort of arrangement to protect me from the sort of women living in this household."

His eyes narrowed. "The 'sort' of women living here? What is that supposed to mean?"

"Mr. Campbell, until meeting you, I led a very sheltered existence."

"Hardly my fault."

She continued as if he hadn't spoken. "I was taught quite clearly the difference between right and wrong."

He fastened two of his shirt buttons, then abandoned the rest of the discs, staring at her in such a way that she felt suddenly small and mean.

"Is that a fact?"

"Yes. My father was a very strict man."

"How strict?"

She hadn't expected him to interrupt her again, and his question momentarily diverted her.

"Well . . . I was allowed no outside company. I was to complete my lessons and my chores, then spend the rest of the day in my invalid father's bedroom reading to him."

"What did you read?"

She huffed at the way he kept sidetracking her. "Plato, Socrates."

"Pity."

"Why?"

"There are other more entertaining authors."

"I was only given permission to read from the classics."

"So what about Shakespeare, Sheridan, Molière?"

"My father did not care for theater."

"Why?"

"Because he felt it was too frivolous a subject for a young lady. Far too suggestive."

"Ahh. What about your mother?"

She stiffened. "I have no mother. She abandoned us when I was a baby."

It was clear that Logan wished to ask more, but she glared at him, making it apparent that she would not talk about her mother. Not now. Not ever.

He began moving toward her, his eyes gleaming in the way she felt sure a stalking cat would employ just before pouncing on its lunch. "I suppose that's your problem then."

"Problem?" she gasped in disbelief. "I have no *problem,* as you call it."

"Haven't you?" He stroked the skin exposed by her low neckline. When she reared away, he wrapped his hand around her nape, drawing her closer. "You're a very disturbing woman, Miss Pedigrue. Inside that pretty head of yours, you're a mass of contradictions. Maybe that father of yours is to blame. He kept you too long at his bed*side* and away from the bed*room* of any other man who might have tempted you."

Her gasp of outrage choked her as he drew nearer and nearer, his free arm sliding around her waist to pull her against his hips.

"You must have hated those afternoons spent reading to your father. You must have longed for freedom, adventure. Yet now that you've been given your first taste of such a thing, it frightens you to the core.

You're suddenly confronted with the fact that the man who raised you may have been wrong. Maybe what he told you doesn't really bring happiness. Maybe you don't want to be good. Maybe . . . ," he whispered close to her ear, "you want to be very, very bad."

"No." She tried to free herself, but he held her fast.

"So quick to refuse the idea, hmmm? Why is that? Because you truly believe that you were born to spend your life dressed in wool, surrounded by starched doilies and even stiffer morals? Or is it because you're afraid to see any other possibility? That there might be another kind of life waiting for you? One that's closer to those being led by Lena and Clarice."

She swung her hand back to slap him, but he caught her wrist and held it in midair.

"Do you even know what you want, Felicity?"

"I want to leave this place," she said between stiff jaws.

"Are you sure? Are you *really* sure? Or is it your head telling you that's what you should say?"

He twisted her arm behind her back, effectively trapping her. "Why don't you step off that high horse of yours and take a look—a good look—at what's going on around you? Not here in this house, but in that world out there, the one you were so eager to join? It's not all roses and peppermint drops. But it's not all manure and thistles either."

He released her little by little, and Felicity was astounded by the way she felt so . . .

Disappointed?

Empty?

Alone?

Ashamed.

"You'll be here for two weeks, Felicity."

She looked up to find him studying her quite closely.

"This isn't a hotel, Miss Pedigrue."

He ignored the rude snort she made at that comment.

"Since our quarantine began, all of us here have had to pull our own weight. You'll be expected to do the same."

She folded her arms tightly beneath her breasts. "What does that mean?"

"It means you have your choice of chores: cooking, ironing, or washing."

"What about you?"

He grinned, not put out by her bald intimation that he was the drone in this particular hive. "Even though you may not believe it, I have my own jobs to do, one of them being that I make sure you don't leave."

"How lucky for me," she muttered sarcastically, turning on her heel to leave the room.

But she didn't hurry fast enough to escape Logan Campbell's throaty chuckle.

Elmira Grimm rose from her bed feeling as if she'd been kicked in the head by a mule.

She'd never taken well to traveling. There was something about the worry, the strain, and the bother that inevitably sent her to her bed once she arrived at the assigned destination. Of course, the fact that a bottle of rum, taken for medicinal purposes, had accompanied her confinement was not to be examined.

Taking her wrapper from the end of the bed, she slid her arms into the voluminous sleeves, sniffed, and belted the garment around her waist. It was fortunate for her that Miss Felicity had finally learned to tow the line. True, Elmira had encountered a few problems on the way here, but she'd nipped that sort of behavior in the bud.

Humming softly to herself, she made her way into the hall. "Felicity!" she called brightly, deciding that today they would venture into town for some shopping. Elmira had decided that Miss Pedigrue's wardrobe was too limited. The girl had taken it upon herself to buy three new gowns for the trip, and although they were black, Miss Grimm felt the designs contained too many furbelows for a girl who had recently lost her father. It wouldn't do for her to attract a gaggle of beaux. Not for a while.

Poking her head around the privacy screen and into Felicity's room, Elmira frowned when she saw that the chamber was empty and the bed was rumpled as if it had been hastily made.

Bless the child. She'd probably gone downstairs to begin cooking some sort of meal for them both. But halfway down the staircase, Elmira became aware of a potent silence. If it were not for the bonging of the grandmother clock hung on the parlor wall, the stillness would have been ominous.

She shook such nonsense away, hurrying back to the rear of the house. There was no one there.

"Miss Pedigrue?" When Miss Grimm received no response, a sharp taint of panic filled her mouth. "Felicity!"

Then she saw it, the small card resting on the polished foyer floor. It left the name and address of a local doctor and instructed Elmira to come as soon as she could in order to receive information concerning her charge.

Spurred into action, Elmira whirled and raced up the steps, moving faster than her lanky frame had in years. She must find Miss Pedigrue immediately. If anything had happened to her . . . Elmira Grimm will have lost her meal ticket.

But an hour later, she had still not found the doctor,

who had left the city on some medical emergency. With each minute that passed, she grew more frantic.

She had to find Miss Pedigrue. Now.

The kitchen was no less the scene of disaster than it had been the day before. Every space had been covered with dirty crockery, soiled towels, linens, and glassware. As soon as Felicity entered the room, she debated changing her mind and assigning herself another set of chores.

But upon taking a look at the inadequacies of the laundry system of this household and the amount of clothing and bed linens needing attention, she decided that the kitchen was probably the safest place to be. Especially if she didn't wish to starve to death in the next few days.

Finding a batch of tablecloths in the bottom of a cupboard, she draped one around her body and pinned it in place as a makeshift apron, vowing that by the end of the day, she would have her own garments back or know the reason why.

After hauling bucket after bucket of water to the stove, she brought it to a boil, dropped the first batch of dishes into its depths, and began to scrub.

Hours. It took positively hours to uncover the true surfaces of the tables and cabinetry from the mounds of crockery. And once she'd washed the dishes, there were towels to boil and the floor and woodwork to clean. But Felicity felt a grim sense of satisfaction at having accomplished at least this much. In fact, there was something comforting about the familiar routine. Although their father had insisted upon hiring the finest tutors he could find, he'd felt his daughters should learn to care for the house themselves.

Felicity generally balked at the time involved in performing such chores, but today, the physical effort settled her nerves and calmed her fears. Day by day. She would take this situation day by day. Then she would deal with whatever consequences resulted even though she didn't want to think about what the future would bring. She would probably lose her job over this, her standing in Saint Joseph, her inheritance, her means to live comfortably . . . *Stop it.*

Sinking onto one of the chairs, she allowed herself a brief respite from her work. Five minutes. Maybe ten. Then she would begin on the next layer of grime.

"Hello."

The soft greeting came from the doorway, and she found Clarice smiling tentatively, her fragile face framed by the horrible bric-a-brac mounted on the wall behind her.

Felicity wasn't quite sure how she should respond to the woman. Only a few hours ago, she probably would have ignored her, but some of what Logan had said earlier had returned to haunt her as she worked. In essence, he'd accused her of being intolerant, and she supposed that was true. She'd frowned upon these women for the role they played in this house. But Felicity's father—no matter how strict and severe he may have been—had provided for her needs. She'd had food, shelter, warmth.

With her own future looming so uncertainly before her, Felicity had to acknowledge that should her inheritance be withheld, she would be forced into much the same dire straits as these women must have been when faced with earning a living. Modes of employment available to women were limited to serving as teachers, governesses, traveling companions, housekeepers . . . or prostitutes.

"Should I go away?"

Felicity jumped to her feet. "No, no. I was . . ."

"Daydreaming?"

"Yes." She gestured to one of the chairs at the table. "Won't you join me?"

"Well, I . . ." Clarice bit her lip as if debating a weighty decision. "I don't know if I should. Logan doesn't want us to frater . . . flater . . . fatern—"

"Fraternize?"

"Yes! Logan doesn't want us to fraternize with you."

Despite her own change of heart, Felicity felt a slow-burning fury. It didn't matter that she'd asked him to keep the women out of her way. It was one thing to provide some emotional breathing room and quite another to forbid them to visit with her. "I see."

"What does . . . *fraternizing* mean?"

"It means you shouldn't talk to me."

"Oh." Clarice was clearly disappointed.

"Did Mr. Logan offer a reason for his edict?"

"His what?"

"His order."

"Oh." Clarice smiled, making her expression that much more guileless. "He says you would be a bad influence on us."

Felicity's anger was so sudden that she was fairly sputtering, but before she could say anything, Clarice had begun speaking again.

"I suppose I shouldn't really be here—and I don't want to interrupt your work—but I brought you something."

She held out her hands, revealing the bundle she'd previously hidden behind her back. "Those don't fit you," she said, gesturing to Felicity's haphazard ensemble. "So I sneaked you some of mine. We're about the same size."

Felicity accepted the carefully laundered gown, noting in an instant the expensive Indian cotton with its hand-printed design. Her father had never allowed

Felicity to own such a thing, although she'd read all about them in *Godey's,* which Constance secreted home from the market on occasion.

"What happened to my own things?" she asked softly.

"Lena has them. She's been put in charge of the laundry since Topaz is gone."

"Topaz?"

"She and the rest of the girls moved away before the quarantine."

"Moved away? But why?"

Clarice started to respond, then snapped her jaw shut. "I'm not supposed to tell you," she finally said.

"I see." But Felicity didn't really. Vaguely, she remembered Lena saying the house prided itself on having new girls every few weeks, but Felicity thought such measures must grow incredibly complicated.

Deciding that if she were to have any answers, they would probably have to come from this woman, Felicity offered her a bright smile. "Sit. Please. I'll go change into this quickly, then we'll talk. I could even put a kettle on for tea."

Clarice's face visibly brightened. "I'd like that. It's been such a long time since I had tea."

Judging by the state of the kitchen, Felicity could very well believe it.

Moving into the larder, she closed the door all but a crack. Quickly, she tore off her apron and the horrible clothes she'd borrowed. Then, seeing that Clarice had been kind enough to supply a fresh petticoat, pantalets, and a camisole, she stripped to the skin and dressed again. In silk scanties. Feather-soft, stroke-against-her-skin scanties. Struggling into her corset, she then donned the cotton dress and fastened the ivory buttons.

Once she'd finished, she stood for several long minutes in awe, absolute awe. So this was what it felt like to wear something other than wool, to don something made for the hot summer weather. It was so cool, so light, so delicate, she felt as if she weren't wearing much of anything at all.

Touching the pagoda sleeves, the tight bodice, and full skirt, she frowned. The dress was entirely modest, completely feminine, and decidedly form covering. So why had her father detested the use of such a "frivolous" fabric? In her opinion, it was far more suitable than being forced to confine one's movements during hotter weather to keep from swooning. Why, if the fabric weren't so fine, this dress would be ideal for housework, gardening, a veritable host of activities.

Stepping into the kitchen again, she met Clarice's worried stare.

"Do you like it?"

"Like it!" Felicity couldn't help rushing to give the girl an impulsive hug. "It's beautiful. Thank you."

Uncomfortable with the spontaneous show of affection, the girl wrapped her arms around the ladder-shaped back of her chair. "Keep it as long as you like."

"You're sure you don't need it?"

"I don't have much call for clothes."

The remark brought a shuddering, self-conscious silence to the room, one that Felicity regretted. Busying herself at the stove, she sought to break the tension.

"I'll be making our tea. There's only a tiny bit in the tin I found in the larder. Would you have any more somewhere else?"

"Only a week's supply is kept in the larder due to the fact that sometimes the customers come snooping and help themselves. The rest of the foodstuffs are kept in the—"

The girl stopped dead in midsentence, the color

fading from her cheeks. "No. Oh, no, I don't think I would care for any tea after all," she said hurriedly. Then she bounded from the room, leaving Felicity to wonder what she'd done wrong. Or what sort of forbidden information she'd nearly uncovered.

As soon as the thought flashed through her head, she pushed it away. Nonsense. How could the location of a new tin of tea possibly be considered "forbidden"?

Nevertheless, even though she was ready to resume her cleaning, she found herself moving the teakettle from the stove, wiping her hands, and going in search of Logan. She would see how he reacted when she asked about more stores—a perfectly logical request since she had volunteered to fix meals.

She found him in much the same place she'd left him. Logan sat on the brocade settee—a rather delicate piece of furniture for his large frame. What gave her pause was not that his shirt still hung loose, but what he was doing.

On his lap, he cradled a pistol that had been taken apart for cleaning. Around him on the floor were other weapons in similar states of disrepair.

Felicity paused, wondering when he would look up, if he would notice her new dress, if he would approve.

Approve?

Poppycock. She didn't care what he thought. That was the least of her concerns.

Nevertheless, she couldn't help standing taller, smoothing her hair with her palm.

"Was there something you wanted?"

She jumped. The blasted man hadn't even looked up, yet somehow, he'd known that she was there.

"I thought we should have a chat."

"About what?"

"You asked me to fix a few of the meals."

"All of them, if I'm not mistaken."

"All of them, then."

"So what's the problem?"

He still hadn't met her eyes, and the fact rankled.

"I've discovered that your stores of food are insufficient."

"*My* stores?" He finally looked at her. "What makes you think I have anything to do with supplying this place?"

"I naturally assumed that since Doc Wanger put you in charge, you would know where everything was kept."

"Why?"

"Clarice said something about—"

"Clarice," he interrupted her, standing and setting the revolver on the table in front of him. There was something about the way he was watching her, so carefully, so intensely, as if she'd done something wrong. "What did you say to Clarice?"

Felicity became instantly defensive even though she didn't know why. "Nothing. She brought me a dress." She waited pointedly for some kind of comment. When it was not forthcoming, she sighed and continued. "I was going to make us some tea."

"You mean you were going to grill her."

"I had no intention of doing any such thing." But she couldn't ignore the warmth she felt creeping up her neck. "Anyway, when I mentioned we were out of tea—"

"Drink something else."

"That isn't the point."

"Sure it is. You want tea. We don't have any more. Drink something else."

She huffed in indignation, folding her arms under her breasts. "Clarice intimated that there was a stash of supplies somewhere. Then she grew startled and left."

"I don't know anything about that."

149

But he did. She knew he did. Dash it all, why was this particular subject so darned touchy? "You're sure?" she asked.

"Why wouldn't I be?"

"I'm not certain, but for a man who seems to be shouting at me every hour of the day, you've become rather reticent." This time it was she who advanced, she who was suspicious. "What is it you and your women are trying to hide from me, Mr. Campbell?"

Eleven

~

Felicity stood her ground, determined that nothing would persuade her to leave this room until she'd been given her answers.

"Well, Mr. Campbell?" she prompted when he appeared to be weighing the matter.

But even as she watched, his gaze strayed to the window, his brow furrowed, and he swore.

"Damnation! Lena, get in here! I need your help!"

Felicity twisted to see what had upset him so much. She'd caught little more than a figure clad in dusty trousers before she was yanked out of the room and into a small coat closet. "What in the wo—"

She wasn't allowed to finish her question. Logan's hand clamped over her mouth, and his body pressed her into the corner, crushing the coats and jackets and umbrellas being stored in the small space and bringing with them the smell of tobacco and cheap perfume.

Felicity tried to wriggle free, even going so far as to kick her captor in the shins. But the proximity of the man in the small closet allowed no such luxury. She only managed to convince him to crush closer, his body pressing so intimately against hers that she could feel each button, each buckle, each ridge.

He bent low, whispering in her ear, "Do not speak, do not squeak, do not squirm, or so help me, I'll—" He didn't have time to finish his threat before it was interrupted by the harsh ring of the front bell.

Felicity was amazed by the way Logan grew even more tense. It was enough to silence her automatic objections and cause her to listen carefully to what was occurring outside the door.

She heard the rustle of skirts—Lena's, most likely. Although she strained to hear, she caught snatches of conversation.

". . . doing here, Grigsby?"

". . . come to check on the quarantine . . . Open the door . . ."

"No one is supposed to come in . . ."

"I'll be the one exception . . ."

"You know Doc Wanger will have a fit of apoplexy if you . . ."

". . . hell with him . . . You've been locked up for . . . no signs . . . doubt you have anything . . ."

To Felicity's ultimate surprise, Logan began to release her bit by bit. She saw the way he reached for his side, then, after realizing his gun was still in the other room, he went lower to slide the knife from his boot.

Felicity wondered if he knew how much such an automatic action revealed to her. That this man was so accustomed to wearing a revolver, that it had become second nature to him, something he expected to be there. Moreover, the fact the knife was already in place, hidden and honed, explained that he would be ready for any contingency.

He had completely released her now. Indeed, he seemed to have forgotten that she was even there. Turning away from her, he pressed his ear against the panels of the door. The conversation on the other side had grown more intimate and that much more difficult to ascertain.

". . . come on, Lena . . . ," the deeper, obviously masculine voice cajoled.

". . . no . . ."

". . . just want to touch your . . ."

". . . said no!"

". . . let me in and I'll . . . like a real man . . ."

". . . go away or I'll . . ."

". . . What's this . . . arming yourselves . . ."

". . . Doc Wanger . . . away . . . at all costs . . ."

There was a low groan from the porch, then a string of intimate, bawdy innuendoes that made Felicity's cheeks burn. When Lena answered the suggestions in turn, Felicity felt she would faint on the spot. The woman—Lena—was "entertaining" someone using little more than words alone. Right through the door. And the sheriff was obvious responding, judging by his response; the man was enjoying the unusual encounter.

Felicity closed her eyes, doing her best to banish the ideas from her head, to keep from brooding about the way that woman was pressed against the door, murmuring her instructions, while the man on the other side . . .

No. She couldn't think about such things. She wouldn't.

The encounter lasted for hours and hours, Felicity was quite sure of the fact. That was the only thing that could account for the way the air in the closet became close and thick and fraught with tension. It was the only possible explanation for how she became unaccountably aware of Logan and the way they were wrapped together in a dark cocoon of woolens.

Finally, when she feared she would faint and fall to the floor in an ignominious heap, the porch floorboards squeaked, and low footsteps disappeared down the walkway.

". . . later, my dear . . ."

The words came from the direction of the gate.

Then nothing.

Closing her eyes, Felicity wilted against the coats, breathing as deeply as she could, hoping to disband the lightheadedness that persisted long after the whine of the hinges signaled that the visitor had left.

When the closet door abruptly opened, flooding the cubicle with light, she shielded her face, more to hide her embarrassment than to protect herself from the sudden illumination. She was so concerned about her own reaction, she almost missed the fact that no one was paying attention to her.

Almost.

Blinking, she saw the way Logan rushed to the window and pushed the lace panels aside with the tip of his knife.

"What did Grigsby want?" he was asking.

Felicity was able to catch Lena's grimace. "What do you think?"

The tilt to Logan's lips was wry. "Other than that."

"Who knows?"

"Did he offer any tidbits we should know?"

She shook her head. "He seemed more intent upon getting inside. I don't think he'll be dissuaded by the quarantine sign for much longer."

As soon as she'd spoken, she glanced in Felicity's direction, but Logan continued. "Then we haven't much time. He'll be back again. I'm sure of it."

"Wait a minute."

Felicity hadn't realized that she'd spoken the words aloud until the two of them stared at her in annoyance. But since she'd already broken into their conversation, she wasn't about to back out now.

"That man said the quarantine was almost over."

Saying the words aloud made them stick even more firmly in her brain. "He said it was almost *over,* yet you informed me I would have to stay here for two weeks."

"So?"

Logan's flippant reply caused her fingers to ball into fists.

"So as a law officer in charge of maintaining the quarantine, he ought to know. He said the quarantine was almost over and no one had shown any signs of the disease."

"Yes."

"If the blasted time is nearly finished, I should be allowed to leave. No one here has any signs of fever or rashes or anything else!"

"But you broke the quarantine," Logan stated. "Because of the infraction, the waiting period was extended another two weeks."

She supposed that she should be content to leave the subject alone, but she couldn't do that. Not yet. Not when she knew there was some hidden agenda at work here.

Before she could question Logan, she was caught by another flash of movement. This time, the person approaching the front door was a woman, judging by the voluminous black skirts.

Miss Grimm. Miss Grimm!

The woman had come to save her. She would whisk Felicity away and insist she be taken to a more appropriate location. Felicity knew she would. Dear, dear Miss Grimm.

For the second time in a quarter hour, the bell rang. But this time, it was followed by the rapping of knuckles against wood.

"Miss Pedigrue? Are you in there? I thought I saw you through the window. Felicity, it is I, Miss Elmira Grimm. I've been searching high and low for you and some fool doctor who's supposed to explain your absence."

"I'm here. I'm here!"

Logan whirled, whipping an arm around Felicity's waist and hauling her against him, once again planting his hand over her mouth. But this time, she was prepared for him, and she bit the fleshy part of his palm.

He jumped, his grip loosening ever so slightly. It was all Felicity needed to bring her heel crashing down on his instep. For a split second, she was loose. Long enough for her to reach the doorknob, twist it, and throw the portal open. Then she was being wrenched into Logan's embrace.

Miss Grimm, her hand lifted to knock yet again, saw the picture presented before her. Moving with a swiftness that belied her obvious gentility, she rushed inside, brandished her parasol like a saber in front of her, then began whacking Logan over the head.

For some time, Felicity could piece together little more than the slam of the front door, the bang of Miss Grimm's parasol, and the flash of petticoats. Then there was a sharp, piercing whistle, and everyone froze, turning to face Lena, who stood with her thumb and middle finger still poised by her mouth.

"Stop this at once! This is a bordello, not a railroad station."

The ensuing silence crashed into the room. Miss Grimm turned a deathly shade of gray.

"Bor . . . dello?" she gulped.

Then, uttering a slight mewling sound, she crashed to the floor in a dead faint.

"Don't tell me the old bat hasn't roused yet?"

Felicity glared at Logan and held a finger to her lips. "Shh."

"Why?" Logan asked angrily, striding into the Blue Room. "My questions aren't likely to disturb her."

Unfortunately that was true. Twice Miss Grimm had shown signs of regaining consciousness. Both times, her eyelids had flickered, opened, and she'd focused on the lace of the Blue Room's bed coverings. Then she'd made an odd sort of strangling sound and fallen back into her stupor.

"I think you should let us leave," Felicity said bluntly.

Logan only shrugged. "I don't share your opinion."

"We've both broken quarantine. Why can't we return to our own home to wait out the next few weeks?"

"No."

"But why?" She jumped to her feet, forgetting that Miss Grimm's head had been cradled next to her lap. The older woman moaned, opened her eyes, then slumped again, and Felicity had to resist the urge to stamp her foot in impatience. Drat it all, Miss Grimm was proving less than satisfactory as any sort of deterrent to evil.

"I've given you all the reasons I plan to give," Logan said tersely. "You will stay here because I've told you to stay here. Nothing more needs to be said on the matter, and I don't want to hear the argument again."

When he would have strode to the door, she stopped him in her tracks with "I don't think your quarantine scheme is real, Mr. Campbell."

His gaze was so piercing, so sudden, she had to steel herself to keep from stepping backward. Her remark had been a gamble, but to her surprise, it paid off.

From the start, she'd felt that there was something suspicious about the whole arrangement—a mysterious, unheard-of disease, a doctor who didn't examine his patients, people with an obvious disregard for their own health. Except for a few inquiries about rashes and fevers, Felicity's well-being had given them no more concern than if she'd been a bothersome visitor. But through it all, Felicity had continued to believe the quarantine was genuine because she had seen no reason to enact such an intricate ruse.

Until now, when she'd seen Logan's reaction to Sheriff Grigsby. It was obvious that he would do anything to avoid meeting the man face to face.

But why?

"This quarantine is a hoax," she repeated again.

"Oh?" It was an idle retort, but there was nothing idle about Logan's stance, about the way he was staring at her.

"I think this is some sort of ruse."

"For what reason?"

"I don't know. You've shown a distinct aversion to Sheriff Grigsby."

"I dislike the man. I always have. Why would I invent some disease to keep him away?"

Why indeed? But Felicity was not ready to let the matter drop. "Perhaps you have some reason for wanting to keep me here."

"And why would I want to do that?"

"I—I . . ." She couldn't think of an answer quick enough so she said instead, "I think you have designs upon my person."

His chortle was less than flattering. "Designs upon your person," he repeated.

"Yes."

"Miss Pedigrue," he drawled mockingly, "you seem to have a very high opinion of yourself."

She ignored the less than subtle barb. "It's true. Why else would you be so hard pressed to keep me here against my will?"

He considered that idea, considered it for so long

that the atmosphere of the room became decidedly uncomfortable. Prickly. Tense.

"Perhaps you're right, Miss Pedigrue."

He prowled toward her in a way that stole the breath from her lungs. "I must confess that I'm quite confused."

"Confused?" Now she was the one repeating things.

"Your manner has changed since coming to this house."

"How so?"

"The woman I met on the train was decidedly different from the one I'm seeing here now."

"I don't know what you mean."

"Don't you?"

He was close now, very close, crowding her against the bed in such a way that if she tried to escape him, she would collapse on top of the supine Miss Grimm.

"The woman I encountered on the train was ripe for adventure. She was a flirt—"

"I was not!"

"A tease—"

"Oh!"

"A veritable temptation." He touched her cheek, and she started as if burned. "But now"—he shook his head from side to side in infinite regret—"I discover you've become something of a prude."

Her huff of indignation caught in her chest when his thumb strayed to her lips. It dallied there, brushing back and forth, exploring, seeking, tormenting.

"Why do you think that is, Miss Pedigrue?"

But she couldn't speak. Not with him stroking her lips so intimately, as if . . . as if preparing her for a kiss.

"Don't you know, Felicity, that evolving into a prissy miss is the worst thing you could do?"

He eased nearer, one of his arms sliding around her back.

"There is nothing that a man finds more of a challenge than a woman who needs rumpling."

She swallowed, hoping to ease the dryness of her throat enough to speak. But it was a vain attempt, especially when he leaned toward her, his own lips parted, his hair, thick and wavy, falling around his face in such a way that she longed to push it back. To feel its weight. Its warmth.

"Shall I . . . rumple you, Miss Pedigrue?"

She tried to shake her head, she truly did. But at the moment, she couldn't think that far, couldn't do anything but watch him bend closer and closer.

Then his lips were covering her own, and she was lost completely. Lost in a maelstrom of emotion and sensation. Want and need. Hunger and fulfillment.

Dear heaven above, why had she never known that a man's embrace could be like this? Even her novels hadn't prepared her for such a swirl of intense desire.

"Is this what you think I want, Miss Pedigrue?"

His hands were circling her waist, lifting her, carrying her, until she felt the wardrobe being pressed against her back. One of his palms shifted low on her stomach and began to inch up, up, up. She gasped when it spread wide over one breast, burning her there, instilling her body with an unsettling heat.

"Don't . . ." It was the only word she could manage to gasp.

Rather than dissuading him, it only caused a smile. "Don't what?" He leaned close to her ear, causing a rash of gooseflesh to race down her neck. "Don't touch you?"

"Yes. Let me loose."

He shifted so that his thumb could circle the hard bud of her nipple.

"Are you sure that's what you really want?"

"Yes, oh, yes," she moaned. Her eyes were growing

so heavy, all of her attention centering on that tantalizing point of contact.

"What if I thought there was something else you would like me to do instead?"

She couldn't speak. She knew she should order him to release her—from his arms, from this room, from this house. But when he bent even further, nipping at her breast through the layers of her blouse, she gasped, shuddering, her fingers gripping clumpfuls of his shirt. All coherent thought scattered. She could only concentrate on the storm of feeling radiating from her body in ways she never would have believed possible.

Only once did he relent in his seduction and draw back.

"Do you want me to let you go?"

The question shuddered in the air around them. Felicity was not sure how she was supposed to respond to that query. Did he mean to ask if she wanted to be released from his embrace? Or from this house?

But as her own hands slid up his chest and around his shoulders, she realized there was only one answer she could give. "No. Don't let me go."

Her answer brought a mix of emotions into Logan's eyes that was painful to witness: disbelief, tenderness, regret.

"You never should have come here."

"No."

"You never should have let me touch you the first time."

"No."

"I should lock you up with Miss Grimm and keep you out of my sight."

"Yes."

"But I won't."

Her body sagged into his. She had been expecting

him to do the noble thing, the gentlemanly thing. The *wrong* thing.

Wrong?

The word stuck in her head, and she could not dislodge it. Wrong. It truly would feel wrong for her to be kept from this man's company, to be denied his warmth, his embrace, even though society and its rules would dictate otherwise. Something was happening between them, something she did not understand and didn't really want to have explained away. All she knew was that at this moment in time what she was doing felt right, so very right.

This time it was Felicity who reached for him, Felicity who drew his head down to hers. When they kissed, it was she who reached, caressed, explored, her hands trailing over the firm musculature of his body, slipping beneath his shirt to absorb the heat of his skin.

His body was as beautiful as any Roman statue, as vibrant and heady as any hero in her novels. But best of all, it was real.

She clung to him, reaching on tiptoe so that she could kiss him again and again. Then, not understanding why, only knowing that she must meld even nearer to him, she began to reach for the buttons of her gown.

"No." He retreated suddenly.

She tried to hold him tightly to her, but he stepped back.

"Not yet. Not so fast."

She stared at him in confusion, her mind still dazed by all that had occurred. "Why?"

He uttered a short bark of laughter. "Why? Because I'm not the sort of man you should even talk to, let alone—"

Felicity cast a quick glance at Miss Grimm, who was still unconscious on the bed.

"Let alone what? Kiss? Hold? Caress?"

"Stop it, Felicity."

Her brows rose ever so slightly. "So it's acceptable to do it, but we mustn't talk about it?"

He grabbed her arms, hauling her onto her toes. "Just stop it. Stop forcing things between us into places they shouldn't go."

"Why?"

His eyes narrowed, and he shook her. "Why? *Why?*"

"Don't you like me?" It took all the strength she possessed to ask him, to bare her soul so completely.

"Hell, Felicity—" He bit off whatever else he'd been about to say. Then, as if unable to resist the urge, he scooped her close, kissing her with a passion that stole her very breath.

But before she could bask in his desire, he released her and stormed from the room, banging the door closed behind him.

From the bed, Miss Grimm, who must have roused sometime during their interchange, gasped and collapsed against the pillows yet again.

Twelve

~

She wasn't the same woman who had been drawn into this house only days before. She wasn't sure how such a change could occur so swiftly, but the differences were noticeable. She wasn't nearly so ready to judge. Nor was she so quick to use propriety as a shield. She was beginning to learn that in the world around her black and white were tempered by thousands of shades of gray—most of which she had only begun to explore.

She supposed that was why it was becoming increasingly more difficult to sleep at night. Her body had become attuned to the fact that the man she'd sworn to ignore had caught her fancy in a way she didn't entirely understand. He had awakened her body to passion, but there was much more to it than that. He'd also awakened untold corners of her heart that she'd never known existed. He'd taught her that she was a sensual creature, and no matter what she'd been schooled to believe, she not only liked such a role . . . she craved it.

But life was not so easy as that. She might want something, but that didn't mean she would have it.

If such were the case, she would have spent most of her days in his arms.

Instead, she was confronted with a man's will to prevent such a thing from happening. For two days she didn't see him, and considering the size of the house they shared, such a feat was amazing. Even on those times when she managed to slip away from her chaperone, he didn't approach her.

Soon the days melded together. After the first week, she began to see him now and again. But never alone.

Never alone.

After their encounter in the Blue Room, Logan tried his utmost to ignore Felicity Pedigrue. For almost a week, he avoided her, and with each day that passed, he told himself it was for the best. He wasn't in a position to dally with any sort of woman—least of all a respectable one from Boston. Maybe after this last run to Canada, he could find a way to court her properly and show her that he might be a bit of a heathen but he wasn't entirely beyond civilized behavior.

However, even as he told himself to wait for some distant point in time when things would be "right" for wooing, he knew he wasn't the sort who could ever do such a thing with any flair. He'd never entertained a woman's interest with candy and flowers and long talks on the porch swing, and he didn't think he'd care to try. He would be better off forgetting Miss Pedigrue, forgetting her strange allure. They were fire and ice, sugar and vinegar. Their worlds were too far apart for any sort of a relationship to grow to fruition, and he would not be responsible for involving this woman in a brief, heated affair. Not when his own future was so uncertain.

So he did his best to avoid her. It wasn't as easy as

he thought it might be. He might have found a way to circumvent her physical presence, but he couldn't avoid touches of her personality. Hers and Miss Grimm's.

The moment that fussy old woman had appeared on their doorstep, he should have warned her off—as if it would have done any good. The woman hadn't contacted the doctor as she'd been instructed, she hadn't even noted the quarantine sign on the gate. Seeing Felicity's form in the window, she'd marched right up to the boarding house, sure that her charge had crossed the lines of decency somehow.

But it had been Miss Grimm who had received the worst shock as soon as she'd entered and discovered she was to be quarantined in a bordello. After she'd recovered from her initial fit of swooning—a feat that had required nearly a day in bed and a half pint of whiskey "for medicinal purposes"—she'd become a mothering old hen guarding her chick from the big, bad, evil wolves. She seemed intent on making this house more respectable and its occupants more genteel.

"Mr. Campbell."

Logan's eyes closed, and the razor he'd been using paused in midstroke. When he glanced in the mirror again, it was to find Miss Grimm glaring sternly at him. It gave him the willies. He'd caught that sort of look often enough from his mother whenever he'd been caught doing something he shouldn't.

"Yes, Elmira."

Her lips folded tightly together in annoyance. Since her arrival, he'd been addressing the woman by her first name, and it was apparent that such a fact was not appreciated.

Behind her, he saw a ghost of movement, the sway of skirts, then Felicity appeared in the doorway. Seeing her again, this time dressed in a gown of her own, he was struck to the core. When Doc Wanger had stopped to check on his "patients," Miss Grimm had insisted the man fetch some of Felicity's things.

How could anyone be so lovely? So heart-wrenchingly alluring? Especially when clothed in a prim cotton housedress and a voluminous apron. He was infinitely glad that she had never mentioned the possibility of the quarantine's being a hoax. He knew she still suspected the truth, but his own reactions to her questions had offered her enough doubt on the subject to waylay her fears for a time. In addition, Logan had seen to it that the threat of mylexia became more real. Doc Wanger had given everyone a complete physical. Lena had applied rouge to her hand and had fretted about having a rash. Even Clarice had spent a day pretending to suffer from a fever.

"*Mr.* Campbell," Miss Grimm began again, emphasizing the title, the formal address.

He pretended not to notice as he tore his gaze back to a safer spot: his own neck exposed to the straight-edged razor. "Yes, *Elmira?*" he drawled.

A flush settled into her cheeks, making him wonder if all gentlewomen were prone to the same reaction. Gripping her hands in front of her, she asked in a voice that betrayed only the slightest quaver of temper, "I would like your permission to make some changes to the Blue Room."

He shot a glance at Felicity to see if this was her idea, but it was obvious that she was embarrassed by the request.

"Changes? What sort of changes?"

He finished swiping away the last swathe of shaving cream and stubble, rinsed the blade, then dabbed his face with a towel. The whole time, he felt Felicity watching him with more care than was necessary. One that caused a slow fire to begin in his stomach, making him remember everything he'd been so determined to forget: how she smelled, how she felt, how she tasted.

"*Mr.* Campbell," Miss Grimm droned.

But he wasn't paying much attention to the spinster. Not when Felicity was studying him so intently, so completely. It was obvious that he unnerved her. He could see it in the trembling of her body, the way she retreated half a step.

"Mr. Campbell—"

He yanked his attention back with some difficulty. "Elmira."

Again, the elderly woman pressed her lips together for control. She shifted to plant herself more firmly between him and Felicity. "You must agree with me that this situation with my charge is entirely untenable."

"Oh?" he propped a hip on the dresser. "How so?"

Again, her mouth puckered. "Miss Felicity is a chaste, innocent maid." She didn't pause long enough for him to comment, making him wonder if she knew how guilty Felicity was looking at that moment. "The fact that she has been kidnapped—"

"She was never kidnapped, Elmira."

"—and held here against her will—"

"That might be true."

"—is completely reprehensible."

"But necessary considering the quarantine."

Elmira held up a trembling hand to stop him before he could go on. "Nevertheless," she continued as if he hadn't spoken, "I am resigned to helping her make the best of the situation."

"How wonderful."

She must have sensed his sarcasm, but other than another frosty glare, she didn't bother to chide. "Since this whole debacle is entirely your fault—"

"*My* fault?"

"I think that you should help to rectify matters."

"In what way?"

"That room you've assigned for her use, for one thing. There are certain . . . objectionable adornments that I would like your permission to remove."

"Such as?"

"I believe that decision should be left up to my own discretion."

Because he was curious to see how the woman would change things, he nodded. "It's Doc Wanger's house."

"But he left you in charge."

Logan shrugged. "Very well. I don't think he'd mind."

"Also . . ."

One of his brows lifted. She wasn't finished?

"I would like you to speak to your women."

The other brow rose as well. He couldn't help it. *"My* women?"

"Yes. Because you have developed a certain . . . rapport with them, I think you should explain to them that their modes of dress are entirely unacceptable."

"I see."

"Especially the one named Lena." Elmira huffed. "Is it necessary for her to . . . prowl around the house with that blasted whip of hers?"

"It's not a whip; it's a quirt."

The fact seemed far from reassuring to Miss Grimm. "Even so, I expect you to urge them to be on their best behavior for our stay."

"What would you consider best behavior?"

"They should indulge themselves in ladylike pursuits such as handwork, sketching, reading, and household chores."

"What if they've had no experience in those sorts of activities?"

The concept obviously stunned her because she stood before him, her mouth working like a fish out of water. Then she straightened her shoulders, wiped her hands down her skirts, and said, "We'll see about that, won't we? Come along, Felicity."

She stormed from the room, but Felicity was not as quick to follow. Instead, she stood uncertainly inside the threshold.

"You've been avoiding me," she finally said.

He saw the emotions she tried to hide: disappointment, anticipation, awareness. Seeing that, he could not help but be honest. "Yes."

"Why?"

"It's better if I do."

"In what way?"

He threw her a chiding gaze. "Come now, Felicity. You know why."

"You think you're bad for me."

"Bad?" He shrugged. "Wrong? Most definitely."

"Ah." It was a forlorn sort of answer. "So is this how men are taught to treat women? They bring them to the edge of seduction, entreat them to reveal their innermost desires, then walk away, leaving their subjects . . . curious?"

He could not stay still. Logan had to move toward her. Had to. "What are you curious about, Felicity?"

Her lashes flickered, showing him that she was not quite as brazen as she would care to appear.

"I—" But she didn't finish her statement. She had no opportunity.

"Fe-li-city!" Miss Grimm called from the end of the hall.

"Your watchdog is calling," Logan teased.

"Yes. I suppose." She grimaced. "Sometimes I wish her concern wasn't so dependent on her salary. Maybe then she wouldn't be so vehement about protecting me from the world."

"Who would you rather have as your chaperone?"

She shrugged. "A family member. My sisters."

"Your mother?"

Her lips pursed together in obvious displeasure. "My mother abandoned me. Even Miss Grimm is preferable to such open contempt."

"Maybe she had her reasons for leaving you."

"Selfish reasons."

Sensing now was not the time for such a discussion, Logan said, "You'd better be going."

"Yes."

"I believe she plans to have you redecorate the Blue Room."

"Mmm-hmm." But even as she turned to leave, she could not resist reaching out to touch his chest and trail her fingers down his abdomen.

Long after she'd disappeared, Logan stood stunned, amazed at the rush of passion such a simple gesture had inspired.

"Damn it," he muttered to himself as a voice in his head whispered, *Ignore her, just ignore her.* But somehow, he knew that voice of conscience would be denied its wish. She was the forbidden fruit.

And now that he'd had a taste of her sweetness, even a chaperone like Miss Grimm wouldn't dissuade him.

Much later, Felicity sighed, arching her aching back and pushing the sash to her bedroom window high in an effort to catch a slight breeze. She and Miss Grimm had been hard at work since early that morning. Since she'd seen Logan. His chest bare.

His chin recently shaved.

The mere memory was enough to cause her belly to warm and her breath to quicken. True, she'd caught him without a shirt before, had indeed seen him without *any* clothing.

That memory nearly choked the air from her body and she squeezed her eyes shut, leaning her head against the warm wood, wishing it were softer, more tensile. Firm. Masculine.

A sigh pushed from her throat.

"So pensive."

She jumped at the low male voice, wondering how on earth she'd conjured the sound from thin air. But when her lashes fluttered open, it was to find him sitting on the shingles of the roof beside her.

Felicity blinked, sure he wasn't there, that her mind had taken a turn for the worse.

Then he reached for her, wrapping his broad hand around her neck, pulling her off balance and toward him. She could not resist. Did not want to resist. His lips met hers passionately, hungrily, quickly. Then he was letting her go so swiftly she had to grip the sill to keep from tumbling forward.

She saw the way he glared into the gathering darkness, his jaw tight, a muscle working.

Weak-kneed and unsure what she was supposed to do or say, Felicity sat in the window aperture, one hand gripping the opposite side. Around them the evening deepened, a symphony of night noises intensified. But even the lulling sounds of the crickets and cicadas could not divert her enough to forget the man who sat so close to her. So close but, oh, so far away.

"What are you doing on the roof, Logan?" she finally asked when the silence between them threatened to smother her.

Logan didn't face at her. Instead, he drew a flask from his pocket, removed the top, and took a deep swallow. "I don't know."

"It's dangerous out there."

She was speaking of the height and the pitch of the roof, but when he met her gaze, fiercely, intently, she knew he had taken the statement in an entirely different way.

"Yes, it is. More than you know."

She leaned her head back against the wooden frame. "Why?"

To her surprise, he answered her directly, speaking not of the distance to the ground below, but of the attraction they shared.

"You've led a sheltered life, haven't you?"

She wanted to deny it but could only nod.

"I wish I could claim the same sort of background," he admitted lowly.

It was the first time she'd heard him speak of his past.

"I was born in Georgia."

Her brows raised at that tidbit of information, but she didn't want to interrupt.

"I was the bastard son of a plantation owner."

He looked at her then, and it was obvious that he expected her to be shocked. Felicity supposed that a mere week ago, she would have been. But she'd been in this man's company enough to know that the state of his birth had nothing to do with his code of values.

"Tell me more," she prompted.

"I have an older brother. Everett." His smile was grim. "Everett has always been the sensible one, the level-headed one."

"And what are you?"

His grin was quick and sad. "The hellion."

She answered him with a smile. "I can very well believe that." She waited a few beats of silence before asking, "What about your mother?"

The humor he'd displayed disappeared as quickly as it had come. "She died."

"I'm sorry."

He shrugged, but she knew that his mother's passing still had the power to hurt him. "What about you, Felicity? What has your life been like?"

"This is the first time I've been outside of Boston. As a matter of fact, it is one of the first times I've been allowed any place other than my father's house, the market, and the local chapel."

"Why was that?"

"My father was a . . . severely religious man. He believed that the root of evil was excess." She sighed, wondering why in the space of a few short weeks— days even—all the unpleasantness had faded away.

"Go on."

She was sure he was merely humoring her, but his face radiated a sincere interest, so much so that she found she couldn't resist.

"There are three of us children, all girls. My father didn't care for us. At least I always thought so."

"Why would you say that?"

"He was not a kind man."

"Oh?"

"He wanted nothing more than to close himself away from the evils of the world and to keep us with him."

"Was he always that way?"

Her finger traced a lazy circle on her knee. "I don't know. Around us, he was. Especially after I confronted him once and asked why our mother abandoned us." She squinted up at the stars. "I was about fourteen when I demanded an explanation. He refused to answer me, and I sensed she'd angered him somehow long ago. I don't think she was ever happy with him." She shrugged. "I don't remember anything about her myself. I was only a baby when she left us."

"Perhaps they argued," he stated as if understanding the situation completely.

"Yes, but there was more to it than that." She peeked at him under his lashes. "I found a packet of letters hidden in the attic where her wedding gown was stored. They were held together with a satin ribbon, each one creased and well read. Although the dates were older than I, the language was so filled with love and longing . . ." She sighed, realizing she'd never told anyone else about her discovery. "I always wondered who sent them."

"You're sure it wasn't your father?"

She shook her head. "The script was not the same."

"You found no signature?"

"Not a name. They were all closed with 'Your Beloved.'" What Felicity didn't say was that she'd feared her mother had once had a lover and that she had abandoned her family to live with him and begin a new family.

Now, after her own brush with passion, she understood how such a thing could happen. She finally understood.

But she still couldn't forgive.

Logan wiped his thumb over the top of the flask and sought to dispel the heaviness that had settled around them. "So you're the eldest sister?"

She shook her head. "The youngest."

"The others are married?"

"No. As I told you once before, my father did not allow us the company of men."

"Ahhh."

She wasn't sure what to make of that response, so she ignored it. "I don't want to give the impression that our lives were entirely grim. My father brought tutors into our home. We learned to read and add figures; we even studied art and languages. When we were small, we had nannies and governesses. But with each year, my father became increasingly more taciturn and brooding. Then his health began to fail." Her fingers pleated her skirt, and she regarded Logan shamefaced. "That's an awful way to describe one's father, isn't it?"

Logan didn't appear shocked by her lack of sentiment. Indeed, there was a wealth of sympathy in his gaze that she could not credit from such a stern man.

"I would say you were commenting on a fact, not judging him."

Felicity considered that point. "I suppose. Anyway, when he was confined to his bed, it became my responsibility to read to him." She shuddered. "He had a horrible taste in literature. Most of it agricultural tomes or volumes on shipbuilding and weather. It was all I could do to stay awake."

Logan chuckled. "I suppose that would explain the novels you've chosen for your own entertainment. I saw one of them in the bags Miss Grimm insisted be brought over."

A flush stole up her cheeks.

"The Ruffian's Revenge," he drawled.

The heat in her cheeks intensified; though what she had to be ashamed of, she wasn't sure. "I assure you, that despite the title, the novel is very expertly written."

"I'm sure it is."

"I intend to write something of my own one day," she informed him archly. "I plan to be an author—after I've suffered sufficiently."

He frowned. "What does suffering have to do with it?"

"It develops character."

"I would have thought it would be more important to build an extensive vocabulary rather than character."

"Words aren't as important as the ability to convey emotions."

"But don't you think that being locked up in an invalid's house, forced to read shipping volumes and treatises on weather, would have been a source of suffering for about anyone?"

She'd never thought about that before. Nevertheless, she shook her head. "I don't think that counts."

"Why not?"

"It just doesn't," she insisted.

He watched her for some time, and she was disturbed by the way his eyes gradually lost their humor, becoming dark and angry. He took another swig of the liquid in the flask and eased onto the balls of his feet.

"I suppose being quarantined in a bordello for two weeks, withstanding the resulting repercussions, ought to be enough suffering for any would-be author." Then he was moving across the roof, climbing down the trellis, and swinging into his own bedroom window.

As Felicity watched him go, she wondered what had happened to change his mood so quickly. There was much more to his reaction than a bit of guilt at having disrupted her new, adventurous life. No, there was something else, something he would never tell her, something so dark and intrusive that it dampened his very spirit.

Thunderation, she thought as she straightened and wrenched the curtains closed against the evening. What was this man hiding? What did he consider so awful about himself that he felt he couldn't confide in her? That he thought himself yet another burden for her to bear?

A man who was beginning to wriggle into her heart as much as her head.

What in the hell was he doing? Logan railed silently as he swung into his own bedroom window and stomped to the inner door. He was a bastard. A total bastard—literally and figuratively. Women like Felicity Pedigrue didn't associate with men like him. Not knowingly. Not willingly. It didn't matter that he might find some way to explain his less than ordinary occupation. There was no escaping what he was.

A man without a name. Without a heritage.

Without breeding, and education, and eloquent manners.

"Damn, damn, damn."

A soft tap interrupted his tirade, and he threw the door open, sure that he would find Felicity waiting on the other side. But it wasn't Felicity. It was Clarice.

She jumped, and he softened his expression, sure that he'd frightened her with his manner.

"What do you need, Clarice?" He was pleased when the demand held only a trace of tension.

She hesitated a split second before saying, "It's Doc Wanger. He sent a message saying that he needs to talk to you. Something about . . . Everett."

"Hell," Logan rasped, an icy dread sinking into his stomach.

Something had happened to his brother. He knew it. He could feel it to the bone.

Even so, Logan had to wait until after sundown before he could go in search of the doctor, and the fact that the man hadn't come to find him in the interim filled him with worry. If Doc Wanger was willing to have Logan chance breaking the quarantine scheme they'd cooked up, he must be in some sort of trouble himself.

It took all the will Logan possessed to stay within the confines of Mother LaRee's until the sky outside was dark and black. The moon, thank heaven, was obscured behind a bank of clouds, allowing him the opportunity to move through the streets virtually undetected, shifting from shadow to shadow, alley to alley, until he'd managed to reach the burned-out wreckage of the Methodist church that had been destroyed years ago when a heating stove had exploded.

The trap doors to the cellar were located only a few yards from the trees, and he ran to them, holding them up long enough to slip into the cool, musty depths.

Patting the wall beside him, he located the lantern, lit it, and held it aloft. But the cellar was empty. He would have to wait until Doc Wanger could come here himself.

He took the creaking steps one by one, his free hand resting on the butt of his revolver in a way that was far from casual. Automatically, his gaze roamed the narrow area, looking for anything amiss. Only after he'd reassured himself that all was as it should be, did he ease the light back down to his side.

Then he began to pace. He didn't like waiting. He'd never been a patient man. Yet tonight it was even worse, wondering what had happened to Everett, why he'd had to send a message through the doctor.

When the overhead trap whined, Logan whirled, setting the lantern on a crate and whipping his revolver free. Only after Doc Wanger's familiar face appeared in the dim light did he relax ever so slightly.

The man quickly joined him, brushing the dust from his shoulders as he descended the stairs. "I got a telegram from one of our contacts," he said without preamble. "There's been some trouble in Georgia."

Logan immediately stiffened. "What's gone wrong?"

"I'm not sure exactly. Here's the telegram."

He held out a scrap of paper, which Logan held up to the light. *Boys freed. Shots fired. Blood found.*

"Blood," Logan said, looking up. "Whose blood?"

Doc Wanger shook his head, obviously worried by the development. "That's all the information I've received, but someone must have been wounded or they wouldn't have felt it necessary to warn us."

"Who all has given chase?"

"According to what I've been able to piece together from other contacts along the way, a posse of local plantation owners and a bounty hunter are hot on Everett's tail. They've also notified Sheriff Grigsby to be on his guard since his trail seems to be heading this way."

"Damn."

There was no way to warn Everett. No way to tell him to take another route.

"Everett must have been seen during the escape," he said slowly.

"I think so."

Logan slid his revolver back into its sheath. "I'm going after them."

But as he started to leave, Doc Wanger grabbed his arm and held him fast. "You can't do that."

"He's my brother, damn it!"

"I know that." Doc Wanger shook his arm. "But if Everett is wounded, he and the boys won't follow the usual route, especially with a posse on his tail. Unless you know the direction he's taken, it would be impossible to find him."

Logan knew he was right, but that didn't mean he had to like it.

"You've got to stay here, get everything ready from this end on," Doc Wanger insisted quickly. "As soon as they arrive, you'll need to be heading for Canada. Double time."

Logan took a deep breath, acknowledging the sense of Doc's instructions even though they didn't make him feel any less helpless or guilty.

"I've got another piece of bad news for you as well, Logan."

What more could there be?

"Sheriff Grigsby has been asked to discover what happened to a pair of newcomers who are supposed to be setting up house next door to Mother LaRee's. It appears they've been reported missing by the superintendent of Saint Joseph's Academy. He had word his new teacher arrived in town, but she disappeared before reporting to work."

"Damn." If Grigsby started poking around the area, Mother LaRee's was no longer safe, especially if the sheriff entered the house for an official search. It wouldn't require too much effort for him to find the women. If he found the latch to the cellar, a thorough search could even uncover evidence of an Underground Railroad stop.

"If push comes to shove, you might have to take the women north with you—at least part of the way," Doc Wanger said quietly. "They can't remain here to spread rumors about your involvement in the quarantine. They can't talk to Grigsby at all. One mention of your identity, and there would be wanted posters in every lawman's office from here to the border. I want you out of the country before anyone even mentions having seen you."

"I know." The agreement was made without relish or enthusiasm. But it was the only way. "But I can't afford to take the chaperone too. You're in charge of her. A bottle of rum should keep her quiet."

"Fine, fine."

"I've got to have some more horses, Doc," Logan said slowly, the course of action he would take already sinking into his brain.

"I'll get whatever you need."

"Good"—Logan was already on his way to the trap door—"because I want you to get word to Brant Rassmussen. He was supposed to be at the crossroads this weekend. Inform him of the delay, and tell him to meet me at the Rosses' in Addington. They have a safe house on their property, and I may be forced to use it. Then I want you to head to the mortuary." He was already heading toward the door. "I'll also be needing a coffin."

"A coffin!" Doc Wanger exclaimed.

"Yes. Here's hoping we don't have to use it."

Thirteen

~

Felicity woke with a start, her heart thudding painfully against her ribs. A hand had been clamped over her mouth. Even so, she screamed deep in her throat and grappled with her unknown assailant.

"Hush. Hush!"

Although she could not see him in the blackness, she recognized Logan's voice immediately. Her wriggling ceased, and she tried to pull his hand away from her face.

"Shh."

Sweeping the covers from her body, he tugged her upright, still covering her mouth. When they stood—and she remained quiet—he released his grip, took her hand, and drew her forward.

"Come with me."

"Where?"

"Just come."

She managed to grasp her wrapper from the foot of her bed. Clutching it in front of her, she allowed him to lead her blindly through the house, down the stairs, and out the back door.

"What—"

"Shh . . ." Then he was running across the grass.

The dew-covered blades tickled her feet and moistened the hem of her gown, but he didn't pause nor did she want him to. Not with his fingers intimately twined with hers.

The sky hung dark and luminous above their heads, filled with a thousand bits of starlight. The moon was shrouded in wisps of clouds, but a gentle breeze was already pushing the horsetail shapes away.

Not for the first time since coming west, Felicity felt a familiarity tug at her heart. As far as she could remember, she'd never taken a midnight walk such as this, but the action filled her with such nostalgia, she could barely breathe.

Logan moved into the orchard, far away from the house. When she stumbled and gasped at the nip of twigs and rocks, he paused only an instant to lift her into his arms.

"What are you doing?" she asked, the breathiness caused partly by amusement, partly by the sensual storm seeping through her body. Even in her novels, no man would dare to steal a woman from her bed in the middle of the night.

"I thought we'd count the falling stars."

She gazed at him in astonishment, her mouth agape. Stars? This rash, angry man had brought her outside to count stars?

"What about the quarantine?"

"We're only going as far as the backyard. None of us have shown signs of developing full-blown myslexia." His grin was wry. "I figured this was the only way to get you away from Miss Grimm."

She breathed a none-too-silent sigh of relief and linked her hands behind his neck. "And here I thought something awful had happened."

He didn't immediately reply. Indeed, his eyes took on a faraway stare, the sort that warned Felicity that no matter what she might want to think to the contrary, something *had* happened. Something that had shaken this man to the core.

As he set her on a quilt spread out on the grass, she resisted the urge to keep her arms around his neck and draw his head to her breast so that she might soothe the pain radiating from his eyes.

As much as she wanted to, she didn't think that Logan would repond to such treatment. Instead, she lay back, her arms stretched over her head, and stared up at the night sky, hoping that somewhere in its depths she would find the peace she sought.

Logan took his own place at the opposite corner of the quilt, lifting her legs into his lap. He began to stroke them with firm, circular motions. She sighed in delight.

"What are you doing?" she sighed.

"Nothing. Nothing at all."

It didn't feel like nothing. Not when his caress caused her skin to grow hot and her muscles to become languorous and heavy.

"You shouldn't have brought me here," she said more as a means to fill the silence than as any sort of a rebuke.

When she looked at him, his lips twitched in amusement. "Then you shouldn't have come so willingly."

"Did I have a choice?"

What was meant as a teasing rejoinder was taken quite seriously. "No."

Setting her legs back on the quilt, he leaned forward. The stroking becoming longer, heavier, reaching far past her feet, to her calves, and up, up, up to her thighs.

She shuddered. Never in her life had a man touched her in such intimate places. And never would she have believed how a man's caress in those secret spots could have offered her so much pleasure.

He lay down beside her, his chin hovering above her breasts, his hand skimming over her hip and up to her navel, where it easily found its way beneath the fabric of her underthings to encounter the smooth, bare flesh.

"You should run from me, Felicity."

There was such depth of emotion in that simple phrase, a self-deprecating anger. But rather than pushing her away, it merely made her want to draw him closer.

"I don't think so."

He eyed her questioningly.

"Do you know that I came out west seeking some sort of adventure?" She brushed a lock of hair from his brow. "You have been my adventure, Logan Campbell."

"Some risks shouldn't be taken no matter what pleasures they bring."

"I think that's my choice."

"What if you make a mistake?"

"Then I make it with my eyes open, my conscience clear."

He dropped his head between her breasts, and this time she could not help holding him there, pressing him into her flesh, feeling his resistance as well as his reluctance.

"Tell me," she whispered, surprised when she found the courage to actually utter the words aloud. "Tell me what's wrong."

He didn't speak. Not that she'd thought he would.

Seeking some way to ease the tension building between them, Felicity said, "Months ago, I never would have dreamed that I would spend an evening lying in the grass, gazing up at the moon."

"If anyone discovers where you've spent all this time, you will never be able to take your teaching position," Logan said abruptly. "Not here in Saint

Joseph. They have rules about how often a woman must be seen in church. Two weeks in a bordello will make you completely unemployable here."

She shrugged. "I know. Such a fact will also prevent my tearoom from succeeding. No woman of quality will dare to darken my door." She sighed, but the sound held no pain or regret. "Frankly, I don't care anymore."

"You should care."

"Why?"

He stared at her in amazement. "Because it's what you came here to do."

She shook her head. "I came here to fulfill the requirements of my father's will so that I could claim my inheritance." She shrugged. "I've since learned that I don't wish to have my life dictated to me in any fashion—even if the medicine I'm to take is sweetened with a bit of honey."

"So what will you do once you're free to leave this place?"

She regarded him carefully, intently, wondering what he would say if she told him the truth: that she wanted to stay with him.

But he had not asked her such a thing. Nor would he, she realized. He was a man accustomed to being alone. He valued that independence and the freedom it gave him. He would never allow himself to be trapped by a mere woman.

"I don't know," she said slowly. "I don't think I can fulfill the will's requirements. Just as you stated, I doubt the school board will let me teach once they discover where I've been staying this past week, and because my tearoom is doomed to fail as well, I suppose I'll have to find some sort of position that will allow me to fend for myself."

"Like what?"

She shrugged. "I would like to travel, see more of

the world. There are hundreds of places yet to visit and at least as many interesting people to meet." She looked at him then. "What about you, Logan? What will you do when this is over and you're free to leave?"

But he didn't reply. Instead, he looked at her so intently, so intimately, she could scarcely believe that any man could ever watch her that way. Then he was sliding up beside her, framing her face with his hands, and leaning down for a fierce, passionate kiss.

She returned the embrace full measure, needing to feel this man, to absorb his essence into her own so that no matter what the future brought, he would be a part of her. Her arms swept around his shoulders and he shifted so that his body stretched over her own, his legs straddling her on either side. Then he bent to suckle her neck, moving lower and lower until he grazed the curve of her breast.

She shivered beneath him, the sensations so startling, so powerful, that she could barely manage to lie still beneath him. Her hands worked feverishly at the buttons of his shirt before finally ripping them free so that she could explore the firm contours of his chest.

His skin was hot to the touch, feverish. A slight film of perspiration made his muscles slick and, oh, so inviting. When he took her nipple into his mouth, nightshift and all, she could not keep from digging her nails into him in reflex.

Dear sweet heaven above, how could this man arouse so many emotions in her at once? Desire, confusion, and regret. Not regret for what was happening now, but for the fact that he might stop wanting her one day, leaving her alone and bereft.

Twining her fingers in his hair, she lifted him up to her then, taking his lips with her own, hungrily exploring the tongue that had so recently laved her nipple. When he took her hand, bringing it down to touch the part of him that remained a mystery to her, she gasped but did not move away.

So this was why women were so closely chaperoned and guarded? To prevent them from falling victim to such a passion, such a wanton need? To keep them ignorant of the way men were fashioned and what drove them to the brink of utter madness?

Knowing that she had the power to bring a man such as Logan to his knees was a heady sensation. She wanted to make him moan against her ear, her neck, her breasts. If she strained to hear what he was saying, she thought it might even be a litany of endearments.

"Make love with me," she said, the plea coming from her very soul.

But when he looked up at her questioningly, she knew that this might be all she was ever given. His body. His passion. Never his heart. Even so, it was enough. For now, it was enough. So she took him in her arms, reassuring him that this was what she truly wanted.

There was no awkwardness, which surprised her. Instead, her body followed his lead as effortlessly as if this were an elaborate dance and Logan served as her teacher.

Lifting herself slightly, she allowed him to strip the nightgown from her body, then watched him eagerly as he tore his own clothing away.

Then he lay beside her, their arms and legs entwined. She was allowed to kiss him, caress him, lovingly trace each hollow and swell of his body. Rolling on top of him, she allowed him to unbind her hair and comb the strands over them both. She gasped as he explored the tender line of her neck and nibbled on the lobe of her ear. Then she did the same for him, relishing the way it made him tremble.

Even so, she could not escape the heat building within her, the tension, the yearning. She began to grow less patient, more demanding, until she was gripping his shoulders and writhing against him.

Only then did he roll over, pressing her into the quilt. For a time, his heat, his weight, were enough to satisfy her, to allow him more time to kiss and caress her until she could no longer contain her impatience.

"Please," she panted, not sure if she'd spoken aloud. But he must have heard her, because he smiled sadly.

"If we do this, there will be no going back."

"I don't want to go back. I have no regrets for anything that has already occurred."

"But you will."

"No. I will never regret anything done with you."

He squeezed his eyes closed, and she could see that he was about to allow the warnings of his brain to intrude upon what his heart was telling him was true. So she wrapped her fingers around him.

"Make love with me," she commanded again.

It was all she needed to do to shatter his resistance. Growling, he ran one hand down her body, releasing her hold on his manhood. Then he was reaching low between them to ready her, to position himself. She moaned in pleasure and pain as he began to push inside her inch by inch.

He was aware of her distress, aware of the precise instant when her body became accustomed to him and at long last he could delve into her to the hilt.

She cried out, wrapping her arms around his neck, sinking her teeth into his shoulder. But when she was about to gain her equilibrium, he began to move again, thrusting in and out, rocking, straining.

Her body began to quiver, growing taut with some reaction that she did not understand. She only knew that she couldn't stop, couldn't get close enough, couldn't breathe. Her body was trembling with the need for . . . what? What?

And then, when she feared she would not be able to endure another second, a fantastic implosion began deep in her body, radiating outward. She cried out, closing her eyes as the shuddering burst came again and again. Vaguely she heard Logan cry out, felt him strain against her one last time, and felt a warmth and wetness spill into her body.

Then all was still.

Quiet.

Peaceful.

Her lips lifted in a smile, but she did not open her eyes even when Logan kissed her there.

"Are you all right?" he asked against her ear.

"Oh, yes," she sighed.

He rolled away from her, then drew her into the hollow of his shoulder.

"Cold?"

"No."

Even so, she snuggled more tightly against him.

"Sorry?"

She knew how much it cost him to ask such a question. Rubbing his side, she finally opened her eyes, meeting his careful regard.

"Not at all."

He smiled at her then. A boyish sort of smile that warmed her very soul.

"Good."

"What about you, Logan? Are you sorry?"

He shook his head. "I could never regret anything I've ever done with you. Not now. Not ever."

His words echoed those she had offered him only a few minutes earlier.

"I'm glad." It was the only response she could utter even though the words lacked the breadth and depth of the emotions she was feeling at that moment.

Looking up, Felicity saw a star streaking through the heavens, and she laughed in delight, automatically closing her eyes to make a wish.

"What are you doing?" Logan asked in amusement.

"I caught a glimpse of a falling star so I'm making a wish."

She expected some sort of teasing rejoinder. When he didn't speak for some time, she looked at him.

Felicity was startled to see Logan staring up at the blackness as if he'd seen a ghost passing through his line of sight. It was only then that she remembered that a shooting star had another, more somber interpretation. One that wasn't a harbinger of hope but rather a symbol of a soul who would soon be forced to surrender to death.

"Logan, what is it?"

He didn't speak. He merely gathered her tightly against him.

"Hold me, Felicity. Hold me like there is no tomorrow."

So she did, cradling his head between her breasts and stroking his hair. Wondering the whole time why such a strong man had chosen to turn to her to ease some unknown torment.

Fourteen

~

After that night, a change occurred at Mother LaRee's. Felicity had been in the house for nearly two weeks, but because of Miss Grimm's arrival, Dr. Wanger had insisted on another fortnight of quarantine. Felicity was still guarded over by Miss Grimm during the older woman's every waking moment. But at night . . .

At night, Felicity learned how to creep through her window to the arbor, then climb down to Logan's room without making a sound, how to offer hidden caresses and heartfelt glances without anyone growing suspicious.

Nevertheless, she could not escape the fact that there was a tentativeness, a cautiousness to Logan's responses. At first, it hurt to think that her affection was so much more pronounced than his. Then she began to understand that each of her overtures was being returned, but through it all, he was somewhat guarded, and she sensed there was something else weighing heavily on Logan's mind. Something so dark and brooding and private that Felicity was not allowed to share that corner of his soul. She could

193

only watch and wait and hope that one day he would trust her enough to confide in her. To tell her what was wrong.

The fact that she needed such confidences from him astounded her. Except for her sisters, she'd never craved anyone's attention. She'd kept her own company and had been quite happy doing so. But now she needed more. So much more. From a man. Logan. She wanted to know more about his childhood, where he'd been raised, and what his family was like, especially Everett. It was clear that Logan loved his brother and that part of his current worry stemmed from that relationship. She longed to be privy to his hopes and dreams. Moreover, she prayed that when she had the answers to such questions, there might be some sign that he needed her too. Just as intensely.

As the days wore on, however, there was no lightening to Logan's mood. He became more brooding, more solemn, even as his passion grew brighter and his need for her deepened.

What disturbed Felicity more was that his concern was becoming contagious. Clarice and even Lena had taken to standing by the window, pushing the curtain aside ever so slightly, and watching—who knew what? Only once did Felicity see any sort of response to what they saw. Doc Wanger had crossed the road a half a block away. As soon as Lena had seen him, she'd made some sort of odd wave, then disappeared into the orchard where Logan had been sitting under a tree. They'd conversed, and Logan had raked his hands through his hair and stared up at the sky, shaking his head as he spoke.

Soon Felicity was forced to come to the conclusion that there was something happening all around her in this house, some sort of secret drama to which she was not privy. As she'd suspected, this was no normal "quarantine." There was something wrong here. Something horribly, horribly wrong.

It was while she was scrubbing the kitchen floor that she discovered her first hint that all was not as it appeared to be at Mother LaRee's. The wooden slabs had been carefully laid, sanded, and polished. But in the pantry, on the other side of the threshold, the workmanship was not quite as fine. Indeed, although some attempt had been made to keep the floor shiny, it appeared quite scuffed, the scratches making an odd half-moon shape away from the east wall. As if . . .

No. It couldn't be.

Setting her buckets aside, Felicity wiped her hands down the length of her apron and stood, tiptoeing into the storage room. Looking carefully to the left and the right—as if someone were crouched in one of the cupboards—she gripped the edge and tugged.

Nothing.

Huffing in disappointment, she shrugged. Had she really expected the heavy shelves to slide back and reveal some sort of secret passageway? Such things were the stuff of novels, not real life.

But then again, Clarice had said something about hiding the stores of food and liquor from the paying customers. What better way to do that than to put it behind this wall, behind this room?

Leaning closer, she began to examine the area more closely, running her fingers over the paper-covered shelves that were crowded with crocks and tins and bags of potatoes. The minutes crawled by, reminding her that if she was right about this hunch of hers and she were caught looking for such a hinged door, she would probably be locked in the Blue Room for good—whether or not she and Logan had become lovers.

For at least twenty minutes she searched, until finally, with a huff of irritation, she was forced to concede that if such a place existed, she had been unable to find it. Bending, she grasped the handle of her buckets in order to dump them in the backyard. She was about to rise when her eyes caught a gleam of brass under one of the lower shelves. From here, the metal had the distinct shape of a garden latch.

The instant the thought seeped into her head, Felicity became quite still, her heart thudding in her chest, her mouth growing dry in excitement.

"Felicity!"

She jumped, knocking one of the buckets over, when Logan called out to her from the next room.

"What?" Her reply was filled with a measure of pique that she couldn't control.

His broad shape filled the doorway, blocking the light.

They were alone. If only for a minute.

Felicity stood motionless, her breath coming faster, her skin tingling from the memories of the night before. From the way he'd stroked every inch of her body, caressed it, kissed it.

"What are you doing, Felicity?"

She didn't know how the sound of his voice could affect her so completely, but it did. The heat of it, the timbre, slid through her body like hot honey, making it nearly impossible to stand.

"You made me spill my bucket," she accused, but there was no sting to the words. Not when he was looking at her as if he wanted to strip her clothes away. Here. Now.

"Why are you mopping in the larder?"

Felicity vaguely remembered the door she suspected lay on the other side. Instinctively, she knew that she shouldn't speak to Logan about it. Not yet.

"I dropped some sugar."

"Ahh."

"*I* had it nearly cleaned up until you spilled all this water." She put her hands on her hips, hoping she could buffalo her way out of this situation. Logan mustn't know that she'd been snooping about or he would lock her up sure as not.

"*I* made you do it?" he asked with a grin.

"Yes." She extended the mop toward him. "Clean it up."

"Yes, ma'am."

He bent to swipe at the puddle, and she took the opportunity to study his shoulders, his back, the golden brown hair spilling to his shoulders. Her fingers twitched with the effort it took to refrain from touching him.

"Is that satisfactory?"

He straightened, catching her ogling him, but she didn't care. His own eyes burned with a sensual light that she couldn't ignore.

"You missed a spot."

She pointed at the floor, not sure if he'd missed something or not. She couldn't pull her gaze away from his.

He pushed the mop over the planks. "There." Then he leaned the handle against the wall quite determinedly. "That's enough."

"I think I'm supposed to be the judge of that."

"It's enough." His hand cupped her cheek. "Where's the old woman?"

"Napping."

"She does that a great deal."

"Most elderly people do."

He shrugged. "Personally, I think it's the stash of liquor she keeps under her cot."

"She does not!" Felicity gasped in mock affront, but

they both knew it was true. How else could Felicity slip away so easily each night if not for the fact that her chaperone was often unconscious from her nightly "medicinal tonics."

Logan exerted a slight pressure, pulling her to him. "Your chaperone isn't proving to be the best deterrent to sin."

"I—I suppose not." Her response was too breathless, too needy, for her own comfort.

"Wherever did you find her?" He was so close now that the question whispered across her lips.

"In the personal advertisements."

"I see."

Then it didn't seem to matter where she'd found Miss Grimm, what the woman drank, or how she failed in her duties a little more each day. All that mattered was this moment. Together. Touching. Kissing.

Their movements were feverish, hungry. Felicity grasped at his clothing, his muscles, his hair, seeking a point of anchor as her senses began to whirl and her heart to pound. When he responded in much the same fashion, hungrily reaching beneath her skirts, she didn't have the power to dissuade him, didn't want to dissuade him. So when he braced her against the wall and lifted her, she wound her legs around his hips. When he thrust into her, she kissed him to muffle her cries. And when he brought her to a shuddering climax, she could not help but weep.

It was some time before she opened her eyes to see that they were both sprawled on the now-dry floor, her head cradled over his thumping heart.

"I never knew it would be like this," she whispered.

"What?"

"Falling in love."

The silence thundered in the room, and Logan's

withdrawal was immediate. Not physically, but emotionally—a fact that hurt her more than she would ever admit.

"I never should have touched you," he growled, the anger turned inward toward himself.

"But you did."

The words hung in the air around them.

"What do you want me to do, Felicity?"

An iciness eased into her veins. She didn't want to *tell* him to do anything. If any promises were to be made, any futures considered, she wanted it to be something that he *wanted* to do, not something he'd been ordered to do.

"Nothing. Not a damned thing," she said quickly, rising to her feet and repairing her clothing as much as she could. With a degree of haste that was not really necessary, she grabbed the bucket, her scrub brush, and mop, and stormed out of the larder. Marching to the back portico, she set her things in a patch of sunshine to dry.

When she turned again, Logan was right behind her.

"Will you kindly stop doing that?" she snapped.

"Doing what?"

"Sneaking up on me."

His eyes narrowed. "You're awfully jumpy today, Felicity."

And how was she supposed to respond to that? "Jumpy? Jumpy? Yes, I'm jumpy." She poked him in the chest with a finger. "I've been locked in this house with the lot of you, and I'm ready to dart from my skin."

"Why?"

Why.

"Because I don't know who I am anymore. I don't know how I'm supposed to act or what I'm supposed to think. Everywhere I turn, there's some sort of reminder that I'm in a bordello—and even though I've been taught to resist the baser instincts of human nature, I've succumbed to them."

"What would you like me to do?"

She smacked him in the chest. "Stop asking that! There's nothing you can do. Nothing. I'm out of sorts, that's all. I've only been here a few weeks, but I've forgotten what I used to devote my attention to— good things, noble things."

"And how are you accustomed to spending your time?"

"I . . ." Drat it all, why did her mind invariably turn to mush in this man's presence? "In activities of gentility and refinement."

"Such as?"

"Such as . . . music, literature."

"Literature?"

"Yes. I told you once before how I was looking forward to opening a reading club for the ladies of the community. I relish the discussions such groups invariably generate."

His brows furrowed, and his eyes darkened. Not in anger. No, it was something deeper, darker, more solemn than that.

"What a wonderful idea," he growled. Snagging her wrist, he dragged her into the house.

Felicity followed him, more from astonishment than a sense of docility, but when he stopped in front of an ornate oak secretary stuffed with dime-store novels, she began to resist, sensing instinctively what he meant for her to do.

"Choose one."

"What?"

"Choose one. You aren't the only woman in this house who would relish the opportunity to indulge in such 'ladylike' pursuits. Choose one of these novels, and I will see to it that Clarice and Lena have the first chapter read by the end of the evening. Then you can give us a demonstration of those well-bred Bostonian values you hold so dear."

She opened her mouth to refuse, but no sound came out. Not once did she catch the glint in his eye. Logan expected her to refuse, to become the prissy miss he'd once accused her of being.

Well, she wouldn't do it. She wouldn't give him the satisfaction.

"Fine."

She reached blindly into the case, removing a book. "But see to it that they read *two* chapters instead of one."

"Logan?"

When Lena came to find him nearly an hour later, Logan didn't move. He was sure that someone would be sent out to the orchard to fetch him sooner or later. Sometime each day, Doc Wanger managed to cross in front of the boarding house and flash a hand signal. Fist open to show that he'd received some sort of news about Everett, closed to convey that nothing had been heard yet.

"What did Doc Wanger have to say?" he asked when she'd closed the distance.

"He sent this with the supplies."

Logan perused the crumpled note. "'Grigsby received word that Felicity Pedigrue was seen riding north,'" Logan read. He looked up at Lena. "What's this about Felicity being seen riding north?"

Her grin was coy. "Doc Wanger told him one of his patients had seen her. He thought it would keep Grigsby busy and out of the way should Everett try to return."

"What about Doc Wanger himself? Any sign of him?"

"Nothing yet. Clarice is keeping watch." She sank into the cool grass. "Why do you keep coming out here?"

"I don't like being stuck indoors."

She made a tsking sound with her tongue. "She's giving you fits, isn't she?"

He looked at her then, meeting her open amusement.

"Who?"

"Come now, Logan. It's not like you to be coy." She tipped her head in the direction of the house. "Felicity."

He focused on the distant trees that marked the boundary of the orchard. "I wouldn't think you'd care one way or another."

She plucked a piece of grass from beneath her skirts. "Why would you say that? I've always cared about you, Logan."

"I thought it was one of the customers—Dauber Baker, wasn't it?—who'd captured your attention."

"He's nice to me. There aren't many men I can say that about. But you, Logan . . . I think you know I've always considered you a friend."

He was uncomfortable hearing the words aloud even though he shared the sentiment.

"You and the doc were the first men to really respect me, you know? Always before, I was a body. But you, you saw I had a mind as well. You let Clarice and I help with the escapes. By doing that, you made us see that our futures didn't have to be spent on our backs."

He wasn't sure how he was supposed to respond to such comments, but Lena didn't seem to need an answer. "As much as we've enjoyed helping with the Underground Railroad, after this is all over, Clarice and I have decided to move on if that's OK."

His brows rose.

"We figure Mother LaRee's won't be a safe station for much longer, and neither of us wants to go back to being mere whores."

Logan winced at the crude word.

"We've got money put aside, and we'd like to go someplace where nobody knows us. Start over. Do something respectable, maybe even make a niche for ourselves in the community."

"I think that's a wonderful idea." Logan couldn't keep the words from emerging all gruff and tight.

"What about you, Logan?"

"Me?"

"What will you be doing when this is all over?"

He shrugged. "I thought I'd stay in Canada. Find a piece of land. Settle down."

"Alone?"

He couldn't answer that. He didn't want to answer it.

"What have you told her about yourself?"

Logan didn't even bother to wonder how Lena had grown so astute. Over the years, the two of them had been drinking buddies but no more. Evidently, she'd absorbed far more about his past than he would have thought he'd revealed. "Nothing."

She shook her head. "Don't you think you should tell her more?"

"Why?"

"Why?" Lena echoed. "Because you're crazy about her."

"I've been crazy about other women before."

"Not like this. Not so much that you started taking chances with your heart."

He made a snorting sound of disgust. "Haven't you heard? I haven't got a heart."

"That's not true. Maybe you've hidden it beneath those mean eyes and that nasty disposition, but you're a man who cares about things. Otherwise you wouldn't risk your life for people you don't even know."

Logan was growing more and more uncomfortable with such talk. Deciding it was time to uncover the thrust of her questions, he demanded, "Is this leading somewhere?"

She toyed with the piece of grass in her hands, shredding it between her dainty fingers. "Yes." Tossing the grass aside, she stood. "This is to warn you that there are things in this world a whole lot more important than anger. Take it from someone who knows. I spent most of my life like you—blaming my past, cursing my future. I didn't have the courage to put it all behind me and move on, to thumb my nose at what society thinks is good and proper and make my own way in the world. You see, I was blind to the fact that not everyone cares about pedigrees and appearances. There's folk out there who are willing to judge us on our merit, but we've got to give them a chance first." She brushed the grass from her skirts. "Think about that, why don't you?"

Then she was striding away, leaving Logan with his thoughts as well as a guilty conscience.

Lena was right. It was time he started trusting, especially in his own emotions. He cared about Felicity. More than he ever had about another woman. If he had the chance, he would bind her to his side and never let her go.

But he'd promised himself that he wouldn't make any more overtures toward changing the course of her future until Everett and Ezekial's boys were safe. He owed them that much loyalty and single-mindedness. As much as he wanted to confide in Felicity, to tell her why he'd become so brooding and preoccupied, he couldn't. He'd gone too long on his own and he didn't know how to allow another person into his life.

WILD ESCAPADE

"Logan! Logan, come quick."

He jerked from his thoughts to see Clarice shouting from the back porch. The moment he saw the pallor of her skin, the wildness of her eyes, he knew she'd received some sort of news from Doc Wanger.

And it wasn't good.

205

Fifteen

As the day progressed, Felicity discovered that she was looking forward to the literary meeting scheduled to occur. She knew it was a trap of sorts, that Logan expected her to use the opportunity to assert her own code of values. But he was wrong. Frankly, she'd been cured of judging anyone of anything. She'd learned the hard way that appearances could be deceiving, and as far as she was concerned, Felicity Pedigrue was the last person who had the authority to say what was right and what was wrong.

At the appointed time, Felicity marched into the parlor, the tattered novel clutched to her chest, ready to show Logan Campbell that she wasn't quite the prissy miss he thought her to be. She'd been sure that Logan would join them if only to torment her, so she'd purposely chosen the most shocking and sensual passages she could find—a fact that had not been appreciated by Miss Grimm when she'd discovered the planned event for the evening.

The room was empty. No lamps had been lit. The windows were tightly closed, and a heated airlessness pervaded the space.

Turning, she saw that even Miss Grimm, who had

shuddered at the content of the literature they had been asked to discuss but had agreed to make a small speech on similes, nonetheless, was confused.

"Where have they all gone?"

It was at that precise moment that Felicity realized they were alone. Not just in the parlor, but in the house itself. The noises she'd grown so accustomed to hearing—muted laughter, conversation, music, and the occasional squeak of the floorboards—were entirely absent.

The thought was enough to cause Felicity to shiver in foreboding. After spending so much time with these people, all but living in their pockets, it was downright eerie to discover that they'd left the premises without her being the wiser.

She and Miss Grimm shared a glance.

"Maybe they've gone to the privy," Miss Grimm provided.

"All at once?"

But a glance out the back door assured them that there was no one outside, no one in the orchard.

"What should we do?"

It was Miss Grimm who spoke, and Felicity was momentarily perplexed. Wasn't it Miss Grimm's position to dictate the proper course of action?

"I'm not sure," Felicity responded slowly.

"We could leave this place and go back to our own house. The quarantine must have been lifted. It is the only possible explanation."

"Surely someone would have told us."

"They might have assumed we'd heard the news."

The explanation seemed incredibly weak even to Felicity. Days earlier, she would have jumped at the opportunity of leaving this house, but now . . .

"No. I think we should stay here until we hear from Doc Wanger ourselves."

"Then I believe we should retire to our own room,"

Elmira Grimm said with unaccustomed forcefulness. "I will not have it said that either of us spent our time snooping into the living quarters and activities of the other inhabitants of this . . . this *place.*"

Unfortunately, that was precisely what Felicity wanted to do. This would be the perfect time for her to investigate the latch she'd found in the larder, but she couldn't confess such a thing to her chaperone. So she complied quite docilely with the idea but not before suggesting she select a book for their own enjoyment. Just because the rest of the household had forgotten the literary hour did not mean that they must follow suit.

Miss Grimm agreed wholeheartedly, especially since she'd thought the original choice of literature lacked "substance." And when Felicity remarked on how flushed the woman appeared, Miss Grimm even took a bit of "tonic" in her tea, although in Felicity's opinion there wasn't much tea but there was a good deal of tonic.

After encouraging Miss Grimm to lie down, Felicity opened the copy of *The Iliad* she'd brought from downstairs. She began to read in that slow, modulated tone her father had always insisted she use. One that, in Felicity's own opinion, offered no drama and could curl the paper from the walls for sheer dullness.

Sure enough, within a quarter hour, Miss Grimm's head had grown limp, her hands lax. Another quarter hour and she was fast asleep, snoring like a grizzly bear in mid-January.

Felicity's words trailed away, and she grinned. All of those years spent caring for her father had not been wasted.

Setting the book facedown to mark the spot, she rose from her chair, wincing when the wood squeaked in protest. But she needn't have worried. Elmira Grimm was dead to the world, her hands and feet twitching as if in her dreams she enjoyed a rollicking polka.

Tiptoeing to the door, Felicity opened it far enough for her to slip through. Then she crept down the hall, breaking into a run at the head of the stairs and dashing to the bottom.

Night had fallen while she'd been upstairs, and thick shadows clung to the corners of the room. Choosing one of the lamps in the parlor, she lit it and adjusted the light to a barely perceptible glow.

The silence of the house was positively eerie, and she wondered for the hundredth time where the other occupants had gone. Perhaps Miss Grimm had been right in assuming the quarantine had been lifted. If so, Felicity thought it was cruel that no one had informed them. That Logan hadn't informed her.

No. Something else had happened today, and she sensed that it had something to do with the way Logan had been so on edge. It had something to do with the house, the quarantine, the businesslike rapport the occupants shared with one another. Felicity would find an explanation, even if she had to dig one up herself.

If there was one thing that Felicity would say about herself, it was that she learned from her mistakes. After being caught snooping in the larder once before, she'd taken better precautions with tonight's excursion. She'd kept her cotton apron over her dress and had concocted a host of excuses should it prove necessary for her to explain why she was searching the larder.

Once there, she took further steps to make her trip downstairs seem perfectly normal. She put a pot on the stove over low coals, splashed a bit of milk into the depths as if to warm, and even grated nutmeg on the top.

There. If anyone were to peer into the room—even

Miss Grimm—Felicity could say she'd been unable to sleep and had come to get some milk. If asked why she'd gone into the pantry, she could explain that she'd needed some honey to sweeten the brew.

Pleased with her own cleverness, she set the lamp opposite the shelves she'd examined earlier. Bending, she found the lock, pulled it . . . *click.*

The sound of the latch giving way was enough to make her heart begin to pound in her breast. It was a silly reaction, she knew. She might not find anything interesting at all. This whole contraption could merely hide another shelf behind it, but Felicity sensed there was more to the situation than that. Something that would account for the secrecy she encountered each time she tried to get more information about Logan's past.

Tugging, she was astonished to find that one side of the case swung free from the wall, affording her a glimpse of a yawning black void with a set of steps that led into a cellar of sorts.

Retrieving her lamp, she held it high over her head, but the light wasn't bright enough to show her anything past the first few steps. Hesitating, wondering if she had the nerve to be so inquisitive, she clutched her skirts in one hand and began to descend. Once at the bottom, she held the lamp up, then huffed softly in disappointment.

It was nothing more than an old wine cellar. One that was now being used to hold foodstuffs and supplies. There was nothing secretive here, nothing dramatic.

As she turned to make her way upstairs again, she was arrested by another doorway that was shielded from view by a blanket tacked at either corner. Pushing the fabric aside, she frowned when she encountered a very different sort of space. One furnished with two dozen cots, a table, chairs, and even a settee.

What in heaven's name? Why in the world would anyone want to *stay* down here, let alone the number of people the cots would hold?

She stepped into the room, absorbing the faint smell of woodsmoke, noting the pegs nailed to the wall, one holding a threadbare sunbonnet. Beside it was an old bookcase, its shelves stacked with neatly folded piles of trousers, shirts, socks, shoes, and dresses.

Why, if she didn't know better, she would think this was some sort of orphanage. Or a refuge center. Or . . .

The skin on her arms prickled in warning before the thought was even completely formed. In an instant, Felicity knew what she'd found.

Dear heaven above. Slaves. Escaped slaves. She had stumbled across some sort of stop for the Underground Railroad.

"So . . . you couldn't leave well enough alone."

She jumped, the lamp nearly dropping from her nerveless fingers. Felicity managed to right it before it could fall but could not disguise the way the flame leaped in a telling manner. Stepping out of the room, she confronted Logan Campbell.

The man was angry. Furious.

"I . . ." But all of her careful explanations sifted into the night. For the life of her, she couldn't remember what story she'd concocted to allow her to be here in this old, converted wine cellar. All she knew was that this man was part of the Underground Railroad. In Boston, she'd heard about his kind, people who risked their lives over and over again to help men, women, and children find their way north to freedom.

"Damn you, Felicity," Logan ground out between

clenched teeth. "Do you have any idea what you've just done?"

But she didn't hear him. She was looking at the two figures at his side. Boys. Mere boys. In an instant she was impressed with dark, curly hair, eyes big and wide and brown, and skin the delicate shade of caramel. But that was not what caught her attention and held it in horror. It was the iron bands still circling their necks, the broken links striking against the metal with the barest hint of a *chink*.

"Mama?" one of the boys—not more than three or four years old—cried out, holding out his hands. "Mama!"

He wriggled free of Logan's clasp before the man knew what the child was doing and ran across the room, throwing his arms around Felicity's legs, skirts and all. He began to sob, heart-wrenching cries that tore at her very soul.

Bending she wrapped her arms around his frail body, rocking him back and fort. "Shh, now. Shh. Don't cry. I'll take care of you. You'll see." But she was looking up at Logan, at the other boy who stood stiffly beside him, his body radiating a pride that was strange to see in one so young. "Where have they come from?"

Logan didn't appear inclined to answer her, but when she refused to cow beneath his stare, he finally relented. "Georgia."

Georgia. So far away. They were dirty and hungry and tired to the bone, she'd bet.

"Take them upstairs, Logan. They need to be cleaned and put in a proper bed." Lifting the small boy to her hip, she clucked her tongue. "He doesn't weigh any more than a feather. I'd say he hasn't had a proper meal in months—or his brother either."

Logan stiffened as if she'd said something wrong. "How did you know they're brothers?"

"It's as plain as the nose on your face. Look at them. How could they be anything but brothers?"

His lips pursed, but he didn't comment.

When she tried to move past him, however, he grasped her arm. "They need to stay here."

"But, Logan—"

"No. They stay down here."

"Why?" she demanded obstinately.

"Because they can't be seen."

"During a quarantine?" She sniffed. "No one will be coming in or out . . ." At long last, she had the answer to her riddle. The truth sank into mind and into her heart. "There's no threat of disease here. None at all," she added pointedly. "You used the idea of some unknown disease to keep people away from this house so they wouldn't discover these children."

Logan's eyes sparkled. Not with amusement, but with some harder, more brittle emotion. "So you think you've figured it all out, huh?"

"I think I know enough. There was no small myslexia scare—I doubt the disease even exists. This is a stop for the Underground Railroad, isn't it?"

He didn't respond, but he didn't need to.

"I must admit the quarantine was a very clever idea."

"It didn't keep *you* away."

"And a good thing too, judging by the fix you're in. I'd say you know nothing about caring for children."

"You'd be surprised," he growled.

"Nevertheless, you'll scare these boys to death with all your grumbling, and since Clarice and Lena have both disappeared—"

"They've gone to gather supplies for my trip."

He would be leaving soon. He would be going north without her.

Felicity pushed her own concerns aside. "That leaves only me to see the boys are taken care of for the next few hours." She offered him a tiny satisfied smile. "It appears as if you need my help, Mr. Campbell."

The cellar grew strangely quiet, fraught with tension. "Oh, yes, Felicity. I need you," he said slowly, deliberately, in a way that made her think he was referring to far more than her ability to aid him with these urchin children.

"Th-then you'd best be heating some water."

"Why?"

"For their baths."

"I see."

"Then I'll gather linens and some of your shirts."

"My shirts?"

"They can wear them to bed until something else can be found." She gestured to the other room with a nod of her head. "I saw the clothes you had stored in there, but I bet they're dusty from being kept in the cellar. We'll let the boys bed down in something clean tonight."

"Very well."

"Then I want you to wake Miss Grimm and put her to work making some soup."

"No." He'd let her go this far in giving her orders, but now his grip tightened on her arm. "I don't want you involving anyone else in this."

"I don't see how you plan to keep this a secret from her. These children will be under the same roof after all."

"There have been many more people than that down here without anyone but Clarice and Lena being the wiser. Slaves were shuttled in and out while upstairs business continued as normal. You may have wriggled your way into this affair, but I'll not have you dragging anyone else into it as well."

"I think—"

"No," he cut her off. "You will not think. These children are my responsibility. Mine. You have no idea what they've already been through to get this far north, and they'll need Providence on their side for me to get them all the way to Canada unscathed since I won't be able to use most of the normal routes. The men who are looking for them wouldn't think twice about harming them or anyone who dares to help them. They are stolen property after all, of little consequence to those who seek them other than the price they might one day receive. Their owner would be glad to make an example of you as a warning to anyone else who might decide to indulge in helping slaves escape to the North."

The reality of the predicament hit her like a slap in the face.

She was about to aid escaped slaves.

An act that could be punished with death.

"If you want to back out now, Felicity, then do it. Go upstairs to your chaperone, say nothing to her, and no one will think you ever knew anything about them. As soon as these children are gone, you can go on with your life as you planned. I'll trust you not to go to the law with what you've seen."

Again, the silence filled the room, broken by the soft smacking sound the youngest boy made as he sucked his thumb and sniffled.

Felicity knew it had cost Logan a great deal to extend such an offer her way. He was willing to let her go. All she had to do was leave.

But Felicity also knew that she'd been given a rare gift. A shred of trust from a man who did not give such a thing lightly. "If you'll bring a tub and your shirts down, Mr. Campbell, I'll let you do the bathing while I see to the soup myself. I won't let such sweet things go to bed hungry."

He knew what she meant, even though she hadn't said the words directly. She intended to help him and care for the little boys, regardless of her own safety.

"Very well, Miss Pedigrue. If that's all you think you need, I'll see to it right away."

The words were innocent. Simple.

But the fire in his eyes held a note of respect that warmed her straight to the heart.

Boston

The curtain fell to a roar of applause and echoes of "Encore!" But as soon as Louise Chevalier saw the slim gentleman standing in the wings, she gestured to the stage manager, conveying quite clearly that she had finished taking curtain calls.

Rushing to Etienne, she stood on tiptoe to kiss his cheek. "Well, Etienne? How is my girl?"

Etienne's gaze swept over the actors and technicians roaming the stage, reminding Louise that she'd always used great caution when referring to her private life. For years, the cast had assumed she was a childless widow. It would not be wise to blurt out the truth here, where some greedy soul might decide to sell the rumor to the press.

"Come with me."

Twining her fingers with Etienne's, she hurried back to her dressing room. Only when they were safely cocooned inside did she ask, "What's happened?"

Etienne sighed, releasing her to rake his fingers through his dark hair. "I'm afraid that the man we hired to keep an eye on Felicity has some bad news."

Louise felt the color drain from her cheeks. "Tell me."

Etienne helped himself to the bottle of liquor on her

dressing table, splashing a healthy dose into a glass. "According to the missive he sent, Felicity has become embroiled in a bit of a sticky situation."

"How? We were so careful about securing a house and a position that would allow her to taste the western life. It was what she wanted, remember? You saw the journal. The one a former governess we interviewed had in her possession. She saved the book after Alexander threw it into the fire, proclaiming it to be trash."

"Yes." He tossed back his drink and poured another. "We were careful. But not careful enough. The house we purchased was located next to a bordello."

"A *what?*"

"Our investigator saw her enter the establishment. Evidently she was making some hospitable calls. Unfortunately the dwelling was under quarantine."

"Quarantine!"

Etienne nodded, taking Louise's hand in an effort to calm her. "Our detective didn't want to make a scene, so he began watching the nearby homes. Evidently, Miss Grimm disappeared inside the house as well. In any event, as soon as Felicity's whereabouts are ascertained, her reputation will be completely compromised. Even with a chaperone, there would be no way to rid herself of the fact that she spent time in a bordello."

Louise waved that comment away. "I don't give a damn about her supposed reputation. We can always relocate her somewhere else. What I want to know is whether she's been hurt."

"Not that he's been able to determine. In fact . . . he says he's seen her sneaking around the property."

"Oh?"

"But she doesn't try to escape. She's been making her way into a certain man's bedroom. A Mr. Logan Campbell."

Louise's brows rose, and a smile toyed at her lips. "Oh, really? And she's doing this of her own free will?"

"So it appears."

This time she chuckled. "I'll be jiggered." She knew her smile was growing positively smug, but she couldn't help it. Evidently Alexander Pedigrue hadn't completely molded his children in his own didactic image.

"What about the sheriff? If our man has seen her, why hasn't the local law?"

"From what I've been able to gather, the sheriff received a false sighting of her leaving the city. He conducted a search, but when some escaped slaves were thought to be heading toward Saint Joseph, Grigsby and his men canceled the hunt for Felicity."

Louise was immediately grateful that they'd paid their own detective man well. At least he'd proven to be discreet in his handling of this whole affair.

"Tell our man to keep an eye on her. But he's not to interfere unless she screams for help."

"Fine."

"Then arrange for my understudy to take over the next few performances."

Etienne's brows rose. "Why?"

"I have this sudden urge to take a rest-cure in Missouri."

Sixteen

It was close to dawn when Felicity made her way back down the cellar steps again, this time carrying a tray with two steaming bowls of soup, thick slices of bread, and an array of sliced cheese and fruit.

She wasn't quite sure what the boys were accustomed to eating or how long they had been without regular meals during their flight. Therefore, she chose things she felt would be easy to digest but would still be warm and filling.

Her skirts lapped against the staircase as she made her way down. She could hear Logan's voice and childish laughter, but it wasn't until she crept closer that she realized he was telling them a story.

Stopping in her tracks, she stared at the sight spread out before her, positively transfixed. Logan sat on one of the newly made bunks, his shoulders propped against the wall, a little curly-topped head tucked under each arm. His voice was deep as he read to them, but the boys must have found the tale vastly entertaining because they giggled and patted his chest to urge him to continue each time he threatened to stop.

Moving as quietly as she could, she set the tray on

the rickety table and strained to hear what was being said.

"'The brigand stood in the fiery embers of the brilliant sunset, his shape huge, powerful, with arms of banded steel. He glared at her, the thrust of his audacious indigo gaze piercing the very bed curtains, tearing her equilibrium asunder.

"'Madam,' he murmured as he prowled toward her with the grace of a jaguar stalking its next meal.

"'*Thump. Thump.*

"'His boots echoed hollowly against the scarred parquet floor.

"'*Thump. Thump.*'"

Felicity stiffened. She knew that particular phrase, that story! They were reading her dime novel, *The Ruffian's Revenge.*

"Mr. Campbell," she shot out so abruptly that the boys jumped.

Logan merely grinned at her. "Yes?"

"Do you really think that's something you should be reading to such youngsters?"

"They're enjoying it."

She huffed in irritation. "Nevertheless, I don't think it's the type of literature you should be using as a bedtime story for such impressionable lads."

"I see." One of his brows arched. "Then what would you suggest?"

"When my sisters and I were small, my father generally read to us from the Bible."

"How awful."

Her lips pursed. "It can be quite illuminating."

"Really? With all that murder and mayhem and thou-shalt-nots?"

She stuffed the book into her pocket. "I think it's time for the boys to eat. Then they'll be needing their sleep."

"Yes, ma'am."

As he rose, the younger child ran to Felicity, wrapping his arms around her skirts and holding her with a vice grip.

"Mama," he whispered.

The cry tore at Felicity's heart. Hadn't there been many times in her own life when she'd longed for a mother to comfort her? Yet, like this boy, her mother had left without explanation. This boy's through death; Felicity's through abandonment.

Lifting the boy, she carried him to the table and held him tightly on her lap. "Here you are." She gestured to the older child. "You take the other stool. Be careful now; it might have slivers."

The boy climbed onto his chair, eyeing the food with obvious longing—so much so that it tore at Felicity's heart.

"Go on," she encouraged. "Eat."

When neither child responded, she moved the bowls of soup closer to them both and extended spoons in their direction. "I want you to clean these plates of as much as you can so the tray won't be so heavy when I have to carry it upstairs. Understand?"

She'd barely finished the admonition before the older child reached for his soup and the younger one began gnawing on a piece of bread.

She waited until the tension had eased from the youngster's body before suggesting, "Can you sit by your brother on the other stool?"

At the mere suggestion, the child flung down his spoon and clung to her neck. "No! Don't leave me! Don't leave me like Mama. Like Everett."

Everett? Wasn't that the name of Logan's brother?

She looked at Logan, who had turned away from her. The stiff line of his shoulders told its own tales. Something had happened to his brother along the way.

Felicity was immediately filled with the need to

know so that she could comfort Logan. His pain was so tangible, his worry so evident, she was surprised his body didn't shake with the effort to contain it.

"Just sit here for a minute. I'm going to talk to Logan, that's all. I won't leave."

It was obvious the child didn't believe her, but when she moved him to the chair, he didn't move. He merely watched her, his eyes wide with fear, huge tears rolling down his cheeks.

Retreating to where Logan stood by the archway, she asked, "When did they eat last?"

Logan started at her question, looking at the boys in a way that made her ache on his behalf. "I'm not sure. It's been too long, judging by the way they look under those shirts.

Felicity shuddered. "It's awful how they've been treated. Just awful."

He looked at her then, his eyes dark and stormy. "Is it?" Not allowing her to respond, he added, "Am I to believe Felicity Pedigrue is an abolitionist at heart?"

She didn't know what he wanted her to say, so she remained silent.

"I have to go out for a few minutes," he finally said.

Felicity winced at the choked quality of his voice. "What has happened, Logan?"

He shook his head, refusing to answer.

"Is it Everett?"

When he looked at her in surprise, she offered, "The younger boy said Everett had left them. Where is he?"

She saw his Adam's apple move convulsively. "He's with Doc Wanger."

Felicity had already surmised the doctor was part of this particular Underground stop since he operated Mother LaRee's, but she sensed there was far more to Everett's disappearance than that.

"My brother was . . . wounded during the escape."

She gripped his arm, wishing that she knew the words to reassure him. "You should go to him."

Logan shook his head. "The boys—"

"The boys will be fine with me. Go to your brother. He needs you." Logan opened his mouth to argue, but she put a finger over his lips. "Go."

"Where's Miss Grimm?" he asked.

"She's passed out on the bed."

"What did you give her?"

Felicity felt a flush creeping up her neck. "Whiskey."

"Good girl."

Good girl? She'd rendered a woman unconscious by serving her liquor.

"Lena will be back soon," Logan said. "I sent her to gather some things I'll need for the journey north, and Clarice is helping Doc Wanger. Lena can keep Miss Grimm diverted if she wakes up. Miss Grimm might even be persuaded to have a drink or two with her."

Knowing that statement to be all too true, Felicity nodded.

But as she watched him take the stairs two at a time, she could not control the shiver of fear that coursed up her spine.

She prayed with all her heart that Everett Campbell would be all right.

Logan moved through the dark streets of Saint Joseph as quickly and as quietly as he could, making his way to the alley leading to Doc Wanger's office.

Before taking the staircase, he stood in the shadows for several long minutes, making sure he had not been followed. Then he was hurrying up to the second floor. Once at the door, he issued a secret combination of knocks and waited.

He was admitted into the office by Doc Wanger himself, and what little moonlight reached this far into the alley glinted ominously off the rifle in his hand.

"Logan?" He squinted at him in disbelief. "What the hell are you doing here? You're supposed to be with the youngsters."

"I've got someone watching them."

Doc Wanger wasn't really surprised, partly because Logan hadn't bothered to tell him who was with the boys. He knew that Doc Wanger had assumed Lena had volunteered her services.

Logan stepped inside, and the door was closed behind him, bolted, and braced with a chair.

"How's Everett?" Logan asked, almost dreading the answer.

Doc Wanger shook his head from side to side. "Not good. Not good at all."

Logan's stomach clenched, and he damned the sensation. On his way here, he'd tamped down his instinctive hope for a miracle, but his optimism had sprung up time and again despite his efforts at self-protection.

"Can I see him?"

Doc Wanger nodded sadly, knowingly, and swept his hand wide. Then he crossed to his desk, sank down in the chair, and leaned his elbows heavily on the blotter.

Stepping into the examining room, Logan was immediately assaulted by the stench of death. There could be no other description for it—that heavy atmosphere of fear and pain that could only be eliminated in one simple way. By completely escaping the world and its cares.

Crossing to the bed where Clarice held vigil, he noted that the sheets bunched at Everett's chest were saturated with blood despite Doc Wanger's efforts to pack the bullet wounds and bind them with strips of cloth. He'd been shot not once, but twice, and Logan was sure that it was nerve alone that had allowed him to get this far north. Judging by the blood he'd lost and the black hint of gangrene surrounding his wounds, he should have died days ago.

Clarice stood. "I'll go home and check on Lena's progress."

Logan nodded, but he couldn't speak.

Everett must have sensed that Logan was near because his eyes flickered and his lips twitched in a grimace that Logan supposed was meant to be a smile.

"Boys . . ." he croaked.

"They're fine. Just fine," Logan whispered, sinking onto the side of the bed and taking his brother's hand.

Everett clutched at Logan with a strength that belied his condition. "Logan, I want—"

"Shh," Logan said gently. "Don't talk. Save your energies for getting well."

Everett grimaced. "Don't lie . . . to me . . . now," he panted. "I'm not . . . getting . . . better."

Logan wanted to deny such a claim, but he couldn't. Not when they both knew the truth.

Everett's face contorted in a spasm of pain. Once it had passed, he began again. "I want . . . you to . . . go . . . away . . . north . . . tonight."

Logan shook his head. "Samuel and Joseph need their rest—"

"No!" Everett hissed, then flinched when he paid for his vehemence. "Tonight . . . go . . . promise . . . me."

Logan knew he should do just as Everett proposed. He should leave Saint Joseph. Now. Before the slave catchers and bounty hunters found Everett's trail.

But he couldn't do it.

He couldn't let Everett die alone.

"Please, Logan. Please . . ."

Everett appeared so desperate, so worried, so scared, that Logan could not deny him.

"I'll leave before dawn," he promised. "Until then, I'm staying right here."

Even as he uttered the words, he knew his brother would not live to see the morning's light. And meeting Everett's eyes, he realized that the wounded man had come to the same conclusion.

Everett's mouth twitched again, and he eased closer to unconsciousness. "All . . . right"—his eyes closed—"little . . . brother."

Soon after midnight, Everett died.

There were no dying words, no grand gestures. Merely a hitch in his breathing and a total relaxation of his body.

Then the guilt. The overwhelming, unmitigated guilt.

Damn it, Logan should have stopped him. Everett hadn't been prepared to go to Georgia. He didn't have the experience or the training to infiltrate plantation society. It should have been Logan who'd gone. Logan who'd been shot. Logan who'd died.

"You can't blame yourself."

He didn't even look up when Doc Wanger entered the room.

"It was my place to go."

"Why?"

"I was the one who promised Ezekial I'd get his kids out."

"You promised you'd help arrange it. You didn't promise to do it yourself."

The fact offered Logan little comfort.

"What makes you think that you could have done any better than your brother?" Doc Wanger demanded. "It was *you* who had the biggest possibility of being recognized. If Everett hadn't gone south, we might not have those kids here today. It could have been all your deaths."

When Logan didn't answer, Doc Wanger sighed. "I'll take care of the burial."

"No. I'll do it."

Doc laid a hand on his shoulder and shook his head. "You can't. You've got to be heading north. Within the hour."

Logan knew the older man was right, but that didn't make him feel any better. It seemed the ultimate betrayal to leave Everett this way, alone and cold and still.

"I'll do him proud, Logan. You know I will. I'll find a nice spot in the churchyard—"

"No." Logan's voice was firm, if tight with emotion. "No. He always hated church. He couldn't sit still. Said it made him feel all antsy inside. I won't bury him next to one. Pick a spot by the river, a cool grassy place—maybe on a hill with some trees . . ." His words trailed away, and he couldn't go on.

Why, Everett? Why? Why you and not me?

"Logan!" Lena burst into the room. Her hair was wild as if she'd run the entire way from the boarding house.

Logan immediately stood, a chill seeping into his bones.

"Logan, you've got to get out of here. Clarice and I went to gather your horses when a ruckus broke out in town. Bloodhounds were spotted ten miles south. Grigsby and Moon are riding out to rendezvous with the plantation owners. They abandoned their search for the Pedigrue woman when they received word the bounty hunters arrived."

"Damn it!"

The curse came from Doc Wanger. Logan didn't speak. Grasping his rifle from where it had been propped against the wall—the same rifle he'd given Everett to take into Georgia—he strode from the doctor's office into the black night.

There was no more time for thinking. They had to act. He and the boys had to be out of Saint Joseph in less than a half-hour.

And heaven help them all if the plan they'd already orchestrated didn't work.

Felicity's first warning that something was amiss was the slam of the door upstairs and shouting. Lots of shouting.

Not sure what had happened, she woke the children, damning the fact that she'd been so wrapped up in her own musings she hadn't taken the time to see if there was some other way of escaping this place rather than the trap door to the larder. But even as the thought sprang into her head, she knew it was too late to wonder about such things. Whatever had happened, she must hide the children. She would not let them be captured.

Scooping the smaller child into her arms, she cautioned the boys to remain quiet. She took one of the carving knives from the tray and hustled the children behind a pile of steamer trunks stored in the corner. Crouching in the darkness, she plastered an encouraging smile on her face despite the way her heart threatened to pound from her chest.

There was a scraping from above, and her eyes closed in silent prayer, her arms tightening around both of the boys. "Shh, shh," she warned again so quietly that she wasn't sure if they heard her at all.

Nevertheless, they must have understood the gravity of the situation, because they leaned into her, making themselves as small as possible.

The clatter of boot heels rushing down the steps filled her with a terror unlike any Felicity had ever experienced before.

The thump of boots on solid earth made her freeze, her blood stilling in her veins. She realized now that she should have blown out the lamp that she'd left low when the children had been frightened of the dark, musty cellar.

"Felicity?"

It took her senses several seconds to comprehend that the intruder had called her name, then another second to comprehend it was Logan. Logan!

Standing, she revealed herself.

Logan caught her eye, then smiled broadly murmuring, "Good girl."

She could not account for the way her heart warmed at the simple praise. Neither could she speak. Not when she saw the stark worry, the almost primordial sense of caution that radiated from his body.

Then the doctor appeared behind him, and Felicity automatically pulled the children more tightly against her skirts.

"Damn," the doctor growled under his breath. "What's she doing here?"

Logan didn't even bother to answer.

"What's happened?" she asked.

"The children were followed."

"Followed? By whom?" But she knew even as she asked. She'd heard the stories of southern plantation owners who searched for escaped slaves.

"Bloodhounds, bounty hunters, and the law."

Having him say it aloud was even more ominous than relying on her own imagination.

"What do you want me to do?" Felicity asked, her heart pounding.

"Take your chaperone back to the house next door. She's been in an alcoholic stupor since early this afternoon. Keep her that way. Put her back in her bed with a bottle and see that she doesn't leave for at least a day or two."

"What are you going to do?"

"I've got to leave with the boys. Now." Logan

reached for the younger child, who began to scream, gripping Felicity's neck in a stranglehold.

All of the adults jumped, automatically looking overhead as if the noise had betrayed them.

"Mama!" he cried, sobbing. "I won't leave Mama."

Logan turned to Doc Wanger. "I'll need some sleeping powders to drug him."

Felicity knew by the statement that Logan had used such methods before.

Doc Wanger shook his head. "It would take nearly an hour to put him under, and I'd be afraid of giving the medication to one so young. The bounty hunters will be here any time."

"Damn it."

"Even if you drugged him, you'd have to strap the boy to your body. You've got to go the first leg of the journey on horseback. He'd be nothing but dead weight."

Logan tried again to take the child, but the boy screamed. Even a hand over his mouth couldn't drown out the noise.

Felicity took him back in her arms, stroking his hair. "I won't leave you, honey. I won't leave."

As soon as the words left her mouth, she knew they were true. Glancing up, she realized Logan had come to the same decision.

"You'll have to take me with you, Logan."

He shook his head. "No. We can give him the powder—"

"The bloodhounds will be on your trail by then."

Logan took a deep breath, held it, then released it with infinite care. Then he turned to Doc Wanger.

"We need another horse. Take the supplies Lena gathered and divide them into two bags."

Doc Wanger nodded and hurried up the staircase.

Felicity was already mentally reviewing the supplies available to them and which of those items would be the easiest to carry.

"I've already set their clothing to soak. We can't dress them in wet things."

Logan's eyes gleamed with a touch of wonder as well as something far more precious. It was clear he hadn't thought that far. "Wrap them in my shirts and some blankets. We'll be stopping several times on our way to Canada. Several of the safe houses are operated by families with young children. Someone will have something we can use."

"Very well."

Shepherding the children from behind the trunks, she instructed them to don their shoes. Using the carving knife, she cut one of the blankets in half, sliced a hole for each boy's head, then wrapped the woolen fabric around them like an ill-fitting cape.

Through it all, the children were quiet and obedient, sensing—even at this tender age—the seriousness of their predicament. Nevertheless, the younger boy clung to her as if fearing her promise to stay with him would not be fulfilled.

As she passed Logan on the steps, she couldn't prevent herself from reaching out, stroking his cheek. She could see that he regretted putting her in danger. What warmed her was that his regret was more personal than professional.

"You've done this before, haven't you?" she asked. "Taken children north."

"Yes."

"Under hazardous conditions like this?"

"I've had the law on my trail at least a dozen times."

"Then you obviously know what you're doing." She rubbed her thumb over his lips. "Don't worry about me. I'll do whatever you ask."

As she stepped away, he snagged her hand.

"Go, Felicity. Leave this place. Head out into the night and forget you ever met me. I can take care of everything."

"Oh, Logan," she sighed. "You know that would be impossible. If he were to find me gone . . ." She shuddered. "One scream, one shout, and you could be found."

"But you don't have to risk your life to help me."

She wrapped her fingers around his wrist, feeling the pulse there, that strong, beating force. "You're a part of me now. And I intend to stay with you as long as you need me."

He looked up at the ceiling, squinting at some unseen spot. "Do you know what you're doing, Felicity?" His voice was gruff and filled with emotions she couldn't begin to define.

"Yes. I do."

She knew he didn't believe her, that he didn't think she was prepared for all that might occur, but she was. The journey they were about to take would be dangerous and fraught with pitfalls. By the time it ended, she could be branded a criminal—or worse, she could be dead.

But she didn't care. Just as she'd told him, her place was by his side. For as long as he needed her. For as long as he would have her.

Briefly she considered asking him about Everett, then brushed the thought aside as she noted the redness of his eyes and the gauntness of his features. She knew Everett had died without being told, and she sensed that Logan's hold on his emotions was tenuous despite the seriousness of the situation. Now was not the time to allow Logan to dwell on his grief.

"Come along, boys," she said, reaching behind her to take their small, trusting hands. "We need to raid the larder of all the kinds of things you like to eat."

As they climbed into the main portion of the house, she felt Logan's gaze upon her. It was a comforting sensation as well as a daunting one.

Did he know the power he had over her? That he could affect her moods with a single glance? If he did, what would he do with such knowledge once they were free from danger with their whole lives stretching in front of them.

How ironic, she thought. When she'd journeyed to Saint Joseph, she'd longed for some sort of adventure.

Well, she was about to have one—whether she wanted it or not.

Seventeen

The night was thick and heavy when Felicity led the children out the back door. Kneeling so that she could meet them at eye level, she said, "Are you ready for our thrilling adventure?"

The boys blinked up at her as if it could be inconceivable to them that their escape could be regarded in any way as fun.

"We're going to have a grand time, you know." As she spoke, she tucked the collars of the shirts they wore more securely beneath their blankets and tightened the string used as a belt for their makeshift outfits.

When they were dressed as well as she could manage, she smoothed their tousled locks, commenting, "As soon as we get you safely away, I'll have to trim your hair, hmm?"

Again the boys stared at her as if she'd used a foreign tongue.

She tugged at the older boy's collar. "Will you tell me your names? I heard them once, but I want to make sure I remembered them properly."

They exchanged suspicious glances.

"I'm Felicity."

They shifted shyly, but the older boy finally offered her a fleeting smile and said, "M' name's Joseph."

"Joseph! My, what a wonderful name."

"I'm Samuel," the younger one responded.

"Samuel! That's a strong-sounding name too. Do they ever call you Sam?"

Both boys nodded.

"Then that's what I shall call you. Little Sam." She tucked the blanket more firmly around his frail body.

Samuel yawned.

"I bet you're tired."

"Whenever we stop, he spends most of his time sleepin'," Joseph supplied.

"That's because he's so little. Soon, you won't be able to catch him. He'll be racing you down the street." She touched each boy's cheek. "Do you know where you're going?"

The boys looked at one another again as if they shared a guilty secret.

"We're going to join our papa."

"And where is he?"

The hesitation returned.

"He's in heaven," Joseph whispered reluctantly. "That's where we're going, isn't it? Heaven."

Felicity's heart melted. "No. Oh, no. You're going to a wonderful place called Canada." She was thankful that Doc Wanger had briefly taken her aside to explain that the boys' mother had been killed in a previous escape attempt and that they were going to be reunited with their father in Canada.

"Canada?" Joseph echoed. "But before she died, our mama said Papa had died."

Again she touched their cheeks.

"I know, sweetie. Your mama didn't know your daddy had arrived safely in Canada. But he's not dead. He's as alive as you and me. Logan's going to take you to him. But in order to get there safely, you must do whatever he says, understand?"

They nodded, although it was clear they didn't comprehend what she was saying.

"And you must be quiet as mice."

"Yes, ma'am," they whispered.

She patted their tiny shoulders, at a loss as to how to convey the import of following instructions. But then she pushed such misgivings aside. They knew they had to be careful. They might not fully understand why, but they sensed the care being taken on their behalf.

"Ready?"

She looked up to find Logan watching them and wondered how long he had been there, how much he'd heard.

"Yes. We're ready."

"Then let's go."

Logan led Felicity and the boys into the orchard, where he paused long enough to help Felicity wrap a shawl around her body and pin it in place so that a portion of their food and water could be kept in a cloth bag hung from her neck. Then, strapping a knapsack to his own body with the rest of their supplies, he turned to shake the doctor's hand.

"I'll be sending you a letter from Canada," he said.

Doc Wanger's grip was firm and lingering. "You see that you do."

Logan led them to a pair of waiting horses.

"Can you ride astride?" he asked peremptorily after hefting Joseph onto the front of his own horse. When Felicity didn't immediately respond, he threw her a quick glance. It was apparent from her wide-eyed expression that she wasn't accustomed to riding at all.

"Can you at least stay on?"

She nodded. "Yes, I'll stay on."

He wasn't sure if she was trying to convince herself or him, but he was proud of her spunk. Spanning her waist with his hands, he lifted her onto the gentle mare, then set Sam on her lap.

"It's a good horse. It won't throw you."

She was clutching the pommel with one hand and Sam with the other, so he took the reins and tied them to his own saddle. He didn't bother to tell her that the ride ahead would be rough. They would have to take the back roads out of town, then head north six miles to where one of the midnight freight trains took on water. Twice before, Logan had used such a means of escape when taking young children who weren't accustomed to the rigors of the trail. But if they were going to make the rendezvous point at the railway spur, they would have to hurry.

"Samuel, you hold tightly to her skirts, you hear? Don't let her fall."

The boy nodded.

Logan angled his horse close to hers and paused to touch Felicity's knee. "If you get into trouble, just call out."

"I'll be fine," she said firmly.

He stroked her through the layers of her dress. "Good girl."

Settling Joseph more firmly on his lap, he clucked to the horses. "Let's go."

He could tell by the expression Felicity wore that she was terrified of her mount, the unfamiliar gait, and the distance to the ground. To her credit, she didn't complain. She clung in equal measures to the saddle and to the boy until Logan feared that he wouldn't be able to pry her free when the time came.

Cautiously, he made his way through the trees, cursing the fact that the sun would be up in a few hours. Normally, he would have liked to leave much sooner than this, but it had taken too long to prepare to leave and he didn't dare stay in town another second.

After only a few blocks, he paused, drawing their horses to a stop, his head cocking.

"What is it?" Felicity whispered.

"Listen."

From some distant place came the barking and howling of hounds.

"Dear sweet heaven above," Felicity murmured. "What are we going to do?"

The decision was instantaneous. All of Logan's former routes and contacts would have to be avoided until he could escape the search party. He couldn't risk disclosing any of the safe houses in the area. From this instant, Logan would have to rely on instinct and experience. If they could only make it as far as the train, they could use the means of escape as a diversion.

"We make a run for it. Hang on!" Digging his heels into his horse's sides, he urged it to a full gallop, praying that they would make it to the creek and from there to the train.

Praying they wouldn't be caught.

What followed was a nightmare for Felicity. Until now, she never would have thought it possible to be so afraid—so down-to-the-bone afraid—and still manage to function in some normal capacity.

First, there was the race to one of the narrow runoff streams just outside of town. The summer heat had shriveled it to little more than a few inches of depth, but Logan explained that he hoped it would be deep enough to cover their trail.

Hoped.

She didn't like the fact that their escape could be thwarted by a lack of water, but she didn't complain.

Nor did she protest when they wasted precious time crossing and recrossing their own tracks, wandering in seemingly aimless circles that she supposed were meant to confuse the dogs. Only when the baying of the bloodhounds became too close for comfort did Logan leave the water for good, this time heading southwest in an effort to confuse the men who chased them, then east, then finally north.

Through it all, Felicity clutched Sam and the saddle horn and prayed for a miracle. But with a sliver of gray appearing on the horizon and miles of open countryside ahead of them, she didn't know how such a thing could take place.

And then she saw it. A train strung with boxcars and flatbeds had paused for water on one of the distant spurs.

Logan must have noted it at the same time as she did, because he bent low, urging the horses into a gallop. Within a few yards, she saw the way a ramp miraculously appeared from one of the cars, and she knew they were about to ride into the yawning opening full steam.

Huddling as close as she possibly could, she tried to remember that Logan knew what he was doing. He wouldn't kill them. He wouldn't lead them into a trap. Somehow he must have known the train would be there, just as someone had known to expect them.

The pace of their flight eased as they approached. Logan directed them up the ramp before bringing the animals to a shuddering stop. Without pausing, he swung down and helped Joseph to his feet.

The huge wooden door was already being rolled shut, and Felicity saw a quick glimpse of a stranger's face. Then they were closed in the shadowy confines, and she dared to take a deep breath.

"Come on." Logan held out his arms. "We're only going to be here a minute or two."

Felicity's brow furrowed. "What?"

"We can't stay on the train. As soon as the bounty hunters think we've used it for our escape, they'll have it stopped at the next station."

She was still bent over animal's neck, her pulse racing.

"But—"

"Come on, Felicity," he urged with a tinge of impatience. "We've got to jump. There's a place about a dozen miles away where we'll get off."

He took Sam from her arms, setting him on the ground, then all but dragged her from the saddle. When he tried to release her, she sagged, her legs numb from their precipitous ride. Seeing no other alternative, she clung to him, and bit by bit, his arms circled her waist, taking her weight.

"I can't do it, Logan," she whispered next to his ears so that the children couldn't hear her. "I can't jump from a moving train."

Tugging at her hair, which had come loose and was streaming down her back, he forced her to look at him, to meet those clear, vibrant eyes. "Yes, you can. I know you can."

Then his mouth closed over hers, passionately, hungrily, instilling in her a portion of his strength. When he released her, she was determined to do it. Not because she had lost her fear, but because she couldn't disappoint him. Not now. Not ever.

"Can you swim?"

She gazed at him in confusion. "I—I suppose. I could stay afloat."

"Good. That will make things easier."

"Why?"

His mouth spread wide in an audacious grin. "Because we're going to jump into a river."

"What? With these children?"

"We don't have a choice. It's our best hope to lose the search party." He released her to begin gathering their things together. "Give me your shawl."

She didn't even bother to ask why. Unfastening the knot, she gave him the sack of supplies as well as the huge woolen square. She watched in utter amazement as he took everything they would need for the journey, wrapped it in the shawl, then drew the edges together and knotted them.

Stepping to the door, he opened it a crack, allowing the already-hot air to swirl around them and lap at her skirts.

"How long before we jump?"

He held out his arm, and she went to him, allowing him to tuck her against his side. "Another ten or fifteen minutes."

She shuddered but didn't speak.

"What am I supposed to do?"

His embraced tightened in tacit approval as he said, "We'll throw the supplies out first, before we get to the trestle." He turned to the boys, who had huddled together in a mound of straw. "Joseph, can you swim?"

"Yes, sir."

"What about you, Sam?"

Sam didn't answer.

"Well," Logan said after a time, "this is what we'll do. I'll take Sam with me. That way I can help keep his head above water. Joseph, you'll take Felicity's hand. When she jumps, you jump. As soon as you hit the water, start swimming to shore."

"What about the horses?"

"We'll have to make this jump on our own."

Logan caught Felicity's eye. "Ready?"

As far as Felicity was concerned, there was no way to be ready for such a thing as jumping into a river

241

from a moving train, but she didn't complain. It took all her energies to keep from grabbing the side of the car and holding on for dear life.

Logan bent to murmur in her ear, "I won't let anything happen to you. If you need me, just call out."

She nodded. It was all she could manage in the way of a response. Especially when the lazy glint of water curled into view up ahead.

A tiny hand wriggled into her own, and Joseph gave her a squeeze. "Don't you worry, Miz Felicity. I'll help you too."

The assurance, coming from one so small and so brave, was enough to fill her limbs with steel.

"We'll do this together, won't we, Joseph?"

He nodded and grinned.

The train's whistle squealed.

"That's our signal," Logan said. He pointed to the narrow trestle that could be seen in the bend of the track. "That's were you'll be jumping. Make sure you take a running leap to clear the bridge."

Felicity's heart flip-flopped in her chest, but she managed a gruff "Fine."

"I'm going to throw the bundle as close to those double pines as I can. If we get split up, we'll meet there, OK?"

"Yes."

He tipped her chin and kissed her again. "Good luck."

She and Joseph backed to the far side of the boxcar. As soon as Samuel realized that he was about to be separated from her, he began kicking and screaming, trying to free himself from Logan's arms.

Felicity tried to drown out the sounds, knowing that she couldn't help the boy, couldn't soothe him. Not until they met each other after their jump.

A minute passed. Two. Then Logan threw the

bundle into the air and lifted his arm as a signal. Felicity knew instinctively that when it dropped, she should make her running leap.

"Now!"

His hand fell to his side.

Clasping Joseph's hand, Felicity offered a quick prayer for all their lives, then sprinted to the opening so that she wouldn't have to think about what they were doing or the possible outcome.

In a blur, she saw the bridge, the water, her own swirling skirts. She was falling, falling, her mind ordering her to take a breath now while she still could. Then the water rushed up, slapping her hard, swallowing her, dragging her down. Somehow she lost hold of Joseph. The fact scared her more than anything else. She began to kick toward the surface, her lungs bursting, her body aching, dots of blackness swimming in front of her eyes.

Her head popped out of the current into the air above, and she took a quick inhaling gulp and swiped the hair from her eyes. The current tried to suck her underneath again, and she flailed with her arms, whirling in the water, searching, searching.

"Joseph? Sam?" She fought the swirling eddies with her hands. "Logan?" A sick dread plunged into her stomach. She couldn't have been the only one to survive. She couldn't!

"Over here!"

She twisted in the direction of the shout, seeing Joseph a few yards away. Beyond that, near the bank, was Logan and Sam.

Seeing them safe and sound was all she needed to fill her with the strength she needed to swim against the current.

Laughing, dripping, shouting, she joined them on the bank. Her knees trembled so badly she found herself unable to stand. Throwing herself at Logan, she sent them all tumbling to the ground, where they lay stunned, gripping one another.

Then, as it sunk into her mind that she had survived her headlong leap, she threw her arms around Logan, hugging and kissing him and exclaiming, "We made it. We made it!"

He held her close, his body trembling in a way that filled her with strength when she realized how worried he'd been through the whole scene. A familiar, intimate warmth spread through her body, and she found herself staring at him. She was hardly aware of the way the boys had flopped on the ground and were chattering to one another.

"Yes," Logan murmured, wiping the hair from her face and staring deep into her eyes, his own alight with pride and pleasure. "We made it."

He took her lips, warmly, tenderly, one hand rubbing her shoulder.

"Logan?" she whispered. "Are we safe now?"

He didn't move for some time. "We won't be safe until we cross the border. Never drop your guard, Felicity. Don't allow your emotions to cloud your judgment."

She sensed the warning had been directed more to himself than to her, and she cupped his cheeks.

"Everett died."

It wasn't a question, but he nodded all the same, his eyes squeezing closed.

"Oh, Logan," she sighed, pulling him close, allowing him to bury his face against her shoulder. His body shook as sobs pushed from his chest.

Her own eyes squeezed closed, tears seeping from her lashes. The fact that this strong, proud man wept for his brother made her feel his grief that much more keenly. She knew his heart was breaking, just as her own cracked on his behalf.

Gently, tenderly, she cradled him next to her,

thankful that Samuel's fears had forced her to come on this adventure. If she had stayed in Saint Joseph . . .

She didn't even want to think of such a thing. She couldn't bear to imagine Logan being forced to deal with this situation on his own. He might have experience in taking slaves north, but he had never had to do so when his own emotions were taxed to the limit. She might not know the procedures he used to get to Canada, but she could be here to comfort him, to calm him, to ease some of the burden from his shoulders.

Above their heads, the sky turned to pink, then a sunny yellow as dawn pushed away the nighttime stars.

When Logan rose to his feet, she feared he would regret dropping his emotional guard. Instead, he reached out a hand, helping her to stand. Stroking her still-wet cheeks, he murmured, "Thank you." His kiss was light and sweet, and although the pain still radiated in his eyes, she knew he was ready to move on again.

"What now?" Felicity asked, her limbs still trembling as she attempted to brush the sand from her wet skirts.

"We find our bag first," Logan said, already searching for the twin pines. "Then, if we can locate a bend in the river with some trees as cover, we'll choose a patch of sunshine, dry out our clothes, and get ready to move on."

Rest. He was offering her a respite from their wild dash even if it was only for the hour or so it would take to repair the state of their clothing. For now, it was enough.

"Come along, boys," she called. "Let's go find our things."

Eighteen

~

It was quiet when Felicity returned from tucking the boys into their haphazard bedrolls. Despite the hot summer sun that hung like a molten button overhead, they'd fallen asleep the moment they'd lain down, and she couldn't blame them. For the past two days, they'd kept up a grueling pace north. One that had allowed little rest or food.

Once, Logan had disappeared for a few hours and returned with a pair of fresh horses, clothes for the boys, and food. She didn't ask where he'd been; she didn't want to know. Just as she didn't want to know if the items had been donated by some friendly face along the way or if he'd found a way to steal them.

Even after so many precautions, so many miles, Felicity knew they weren't safe. Another time, Logan had hidden them in an abandoned barn and doubled back on their own trail. It was then that he'd discovered that the original search party had been lost somewhere along the way, but Hap Grigsby and his deputy had taken two dogs and were still in pursuit. The distant bark of bloodhounds now and again was enough to remind them that they still hadn't lost the two men.

Her skirts rustled through the grass and leaves as she made her way back to the tiny, smokeless fire Logan had allowed them to light so that the boys could dry their shoes after several hours spent wading up a narrow creek.

"How are they?"

Logan didn't look up from the flickering flames, and Felicity was glad. Glad that he wouldn't see her face, see the emotions that must be written there as plain as the noonday sun. How she loved him body and soul. How she'd come to the realization that she would never be happy without him, never be complete.

Why? Why had she been so blind to what was happening? Oh, she'd freely admitted the passion between them, the attraction, the allure. But love? That wasn't something that she would have openly allowed if it were even possible to dictate such feelings. Passion held enough risk, but love . . .

Love could be dangerous with this man.

Leaning against the trunk of a gnarled oak tree, she stared at him, trying to imprint every feature, every nuance, into her mind so that later she might dissect it all and determine what it was about him that held her so securely. He was a difficult mixture of personalities. Sometimes witty and teasing, other times angry and reckless. Wild.

Yes, that analogy might suit him most. He was like a wild animal that had been tamed—not completely, but just enough to allow him to fit into society. Nevertheless, he didn't really belong there. He needed open spaces. Land, sky, and wind.

"How did you ever grow to be so independent, Logan?"

He sighed. "My father was probably like yours in many respects. He felt the need to punish those around him. My activities with the Underground

Railroad have always been a show of rebellion against him even though he's dead now. I suppose I have him to thank for my vagabond ways."

Felicity sank onto the ground beside him, absorbed by the way Logan was willingly telling her these things.

Taking a stick from the ground, he began to break it into small pieces.

"What did your mother think of your lifestyle?"

"She didn't disapprove, but she would have liked me to be more settled, I suppose. I'm sure she would have relished grandchildren."

Felicity's heart skipped a beat. "Why haven't you married?"

The smile he sent Felicity's way was wry. "Personally, I never found anyone who could compare with my mother."

"She was beautiful?"

"Yes, as well as kind and loving and serene."

Felicity sighed. "It must have been wonderful to grow up with a mother like that."

His gaze was understanding. "I always thought so." He took her hand. "I wish that your own mother could have been the same."

She shrugged as if the thought was not important. "I was only a baby when she left me, but sometimes, I think I can remember her. Or someone like her. But then I think my imagination must have fabricated this woman who teased me and made me laugh."

"Why would you say that?"

"Because if she'd loved me, she wouldn't have left."

Logan squeezed her hand.

After several minutes of silence, Felicity asked, "What will you do once the boys are safely north?"

Her voice should have startled him, coming so suddenly from the stillness of the afternoon, but he didn't start. Not at all. "Why do you want to know?"

He looked at her then, his gaze so direct and intense that she shivered, knowing that she had to tell him at least a portion of her feelings.

"Because I care."

Her words hung in the hot air, and Logan grew so quiet that she feared she might have offended him with her blunt reply.

He sighed and tossed the twig into the blaze, watching as it was consumed.

"I don't know what I'll do when I make it to Canada."

It was an honest answer, but it offered her no comfort.

"Why do you do this?"

He didn't pretend to misunderstand. Even so, he didn't immediately speak. The air crowded around them, broken by little more than the snap and pop of the fire. At long last, he looked at her, his gaze so direct, it was nearly painful.

"My mother was born in Dublin, Ireland, but all her life, she wanted to come to America. She was so sure that she would find happiness here. Her fortune.

"When her family died during a cholera epidemic, she felt there was no better time to build a new life for herself. Making her way to London, she signed on with an immigrant ship, agreeing to serve as an indentured servant to pay for her passage.

"According to her stories, the journey was horrific. Upon her first sight of the American coastline, she cried, praying that her travels would soon be at an end. The man who bought her seven-year contract was a plantation owner in Georgia. A Mr. Isaac Campbell."

Felicity's lips lifted in a smile, recognizing that as Logan's last name. His mother must have come here to find romance as well.

But the hard cast to Logan's features didn't ease, and the lighter mood faded. "He put her to work in the house, and because he never married, my mother became a . . . surrogate wife of sorts since he needed someone to tend to the servants and organize the house for his guests."

His jaw became tight. "He seduced my mother. Not so much with passion, but with words. At first he promised to marry her, to make her the mistress of his home. For that, she bore him . . . two sons." He stumbled over the number as if it pained him to admit it.

"What happened?" Felicity breathed.

"Over the next few years, he humiliated her, he debased her, he crushed her spirit. Yet even when her contract was finished, she stayed. As long as she remained his mistress, he was willing to support my brother and I as if we were distant relatives. We were allowed to live in the guest house. We went to school, were introduced to a limited circle of his friends and neighbors. Through it all, my mother kept hoping he would soften completely and name one of her sons his heir."

Logan took a deep shuddering breath. "In the meantime, Everett and I moved on to other pursuits. My older brother was given money enough to attend a college up north, and I joined the army." His hands balled into fists. "We never should have left her alone."

Felicity didn't dare speak, didn't dare breathe. She sensed she was about to be handed the final piece to the puzzle that would help her to understand this man as well as his motives.

"While we were gone, she befriended another house slave." His head dipped in the direction of the sleeping children. "Ezekial worked as a butler and his wife,

Nancy, was one of the cooks. Soon after Joseph was born and Samuel had been conceived, my father had an argument with Ezekial and threatened to sell him. Ezekial, who had been thinking of escaping for some time, decided he couldn't wait any longer and went to my mother, begging her to help them."

Felicity's eyes closed, sensing what he was going to say even though she wasn't sure she wanted to hear it.

"The plan was discovered. Nancy and Joseph were caught. Only Ezekial managed to get away."

"And your mother?" Felicity whispered, opening her eyes.

When he looked at her, his expression was bleak. "She was shot for her involvement. My father tied her to a post in the yard and shot her in front of the other servants and slaves."

Felicity's stomach clenched, and she feared she was going to be sick. Her mind was flooded with images and emotions her imagination conjured on behalf of his mother as well as the pain Logan must have suffered in hearing about her fate.

"Nancy and Joseph were spared because they were valuable property. But my mother, who now received a modest wage, was only a liability to him. Once she was gone, he could forget about the promises he'd made and the bastard sons he'd supported for so many years but had never claimed as his legitimate heirs." He shook his head as if to rid it of his own dark images. "I vowed then and there that I would finish what my mother started to do. I would see to it that Ezekial's family escaped as well as any other slave who wished to do so."

"What about Nancy?" Felicity had to know. "I thought she was dead."

"Yes. She died giving birth to Samuel." Logan's features clouded. "Now Everett is gone too." His hands closed into fists. "He was shot twice bringing the boys to me. He managed to bring them hundreds of miles on his own, but then he didn't have the strength to help himself."

She gripped his hand, knowing that Logan's pain had not eased since that afternoon they'd jumped from the train. The guilt in his tone was overpowering.

"I was supposed to be the one to go into Georgia, but Everett convinced me to let him take charge this time."

Felicity's throat was tight with emotion, tears for all those who had been so cruelly treated. She understood now why Logan had always appeared so single-minded, so hardened, so alone. After all that he had borne, all the anger, all the grief, was it any wonder that he couldn't find a place in his heart for a woman?

She opened her mouth to say something, then closed it again, at a loss. Vainly, she wished she could go to him, hold him, ease his pain. But he had grown stiff and unapproachable, and she knew that after exposing a portion of his soul, he needed time alone to think.

"You'd better get some rest, Felicity," he said.

She nodded. Standing, she walked beneath the shade of a thick stand of poplars and sank onto the blankets next to the children. Her arm draped over their bodies to reassure herself that they would be safe. But she didn't dream.

She could only lie in the shadows and weep—for the boys, for herself. And most of all for Logan.

Logan sat quietly. Even with the overwhelming heat of the day and the dancing flames, he felt chilled to the bone.

She knew the truth. That his life had been one long

fight against authority. That he had no family, no job, no real future. That he was a bastard.

So what would happen now? Would he ever be allowed to touch her, to kiss her, to hold her?

Lena was right. He should have confessed the sins of his past long ago before Felicity had committed herself to a flight north. It wasn't fair to drag her into his problems and disrupt her own plans in the process.

Damn. Damn, damn, damn.

His hands ground into fists, and he rested his head on his up-drawn knees. He was tired, so tired. Tired of fighting and worrying and running. Maybe he was getting old or soft or . . . who knew what. But he was ready for a change. He wanted a little plot of land and a house he could call his own. He wanted a warm bed in the winter and a cool, shady porch in the summer. He wanted the time to enjoy a sunset now and again and some sort of work that involved his hands and good honest labor.

But did he deserve such a thing? Especially after Everett had died.

Everett . . .

His throat grew tight, and his hands balled into fists. Damn it. Not here, not now. Not again. But try as he might, he could not control the sobs that rose within him or the tears that scalded his cheeks.

Impatient at his own weakness, he bounded to his feet, grasped his rifle, and strode into the trees, not really paying attention to where he was going. But when he heard a faint bark in the distance, the murmur of voices, he froze.

Who else shared this particular knoll?

The breeze dried his skin of all but the nervous sweat that broke out on his back as he crept upwind, an inch at a time. Twenty yards away, he knelt behind a rock, peering over the top.

What he saw made him blanch.

Grigsby. Hap Grigsby stood staring out at the creek, sipping coffee from a battered tin mug. As Logan watched, another man came from the trees, fastening his trousers.

"When do you want to break camp, Sheriff?"

The man thought for a minute, then said, "Wake me just before dusk. I doubt Campbell even knows we're still on his trail. He won't dare to travel by day, so he won't get more of a lead on us. I'd go after him now, but the horses have got to rest before we push them any farther. If Campbell leads us on a wild goose chase, we could have an animal come up lame."

"Yes, sir."

"Hell!" the sheriff exclaimed, slapping his hand on his thigh. "I can't believe that man has been working out of my town all this time. If it weren't for those bounty hunters spreading the news that the Campbell brothers were their number one suspects, I wouldn't have believed it. The only time I ever saw the man, he was sleeping or drinking as if he didn't have a care in the world. I thought he was nothing more than a saddle bum, damn it."

Logan didn't wait to hear any more. Inch by careful inch, he made his way back in the direction he'd come, knowing that it was useless to run. The fact that Grigsby had managed to track him this far was evidence of that.

His only other alternative was to confront the man. But first, he would have to hike the last five miles to the spot where Doc Wanger had arranged to have Brant Rassmussen bring the wagons. He wanted to be on horseback once he and Grigsby met.

Breaking into a trot, Logan began to run in the direction of the rendezvous point. He didn't have a minute to spare.

* * *

Felicity jerked awake, uneasy dreams and half-formed nightmares skittering into the shadows.

Instinctively, she didn't cry out, but her arm tightened around the children, causing them to stir. Seeing that it was Logan kneeling above her was a relief but one that was transitory, because she instinctively sensed that something had happened. He was filthy and covered in sweat, and judging by the late-afternoon sun, he'd allowed them to sleep much longer than originally planned.

"Follow me."

He led her to where a battered wagon had been hitched behind one of their horses. In the center of the bed lay a small wooden coffin.

When she jumped, he chuckled.

"Relax. It's empty, and you'll never know what a bother it was for Doc Wanger to get it to one of our safe houses so quickly."

A gangly man—a boy really—stepped from where he'd been checking the team.

"This is Brant Rassmussen, one of my assistants."

Brant touched the brim of his hat.

"He's going to escort you to a Quaker family that helps us from time to time. They'll shelter you while he takes the boys north to Canada."

"But why? I thought you were going to take them?"

"I will. But I have some business to tend to first. I'll meet up with him a few miles up the road."

"But what about Samuel? He'll be beside himself if I'm not there."

He took a deep breath, saying, "I don't have a choice any longer. Doc Wanger gave me a bottle of chloroform before we left. He had reservations about using it on children so young, but we've got to take the risk."

When she would have protested, he lay a finger over her lips. "Trust me to take care of them as well as I

255

can." He took her by the shoulders, forcing her to look at him. "Promise me you'll stay at the safe house, then head back to Saint Joseph."

"No."

"I don't have time to argue, Felicity. The law is only a few miles away."

"No! No, no, *no!*" She stamped her foot in the dust. "I know what you're going to do. You'll send me to stay at the safe house, and Brant will go north. Then you'll go back to handle these men on your own."

He opened his mouth to speak, but before he could say anything, the baying of a hound split the silence.

"Damn it!"

He pulled her back to where the boys were huddled in their blanket.

"What are we going to do?" she whispered.

He thought quickly but knew his original plan was the only solution.

"Take the boys and go with Brant." He framed her face between his hands, forcing her to look at him and acknowledge the intensity of his emotions. "There's no other way, Felicity. The bounty hunters won't be looking for you or Brant. Put the children inside the coffin, then ride hell-bent-for-leather north. If something should happen to Brant, keep going. Don't stop for anything. Just over that rise, there where you see the copse of trees, is a narrow canyon. Follow the road about three miles until you see a red brick farmhouse. That's the safe house. From there, they'll help Brant get under way for Canada. Then they'll protect you until it's safe for you to contact Miss Grimm and go home."

Her fingers dug into his skin, and he realized at that moment that no one had ever cared for him this way, so deeply, so completely, that she shook with her concern.

"I'll be fine, Felicity."

"No. No, you won't. You'll try to be a hero, you'll try to lead them away, and you'll take stupid chances that will get you killed."

"Felicity . . ."

When he tried to calm her, she shook her head, her hair spilling about her face. That lovely, earnest face.

"Nothing will happen to me."

But she didn't believe him. He knew that by the gleam of tears in her eyes.

No one had ever cried for him before. No one.

"I'll come for you, Felicity. As soon as I can. If you don't want to contact Miss Grimm, stay at the safe house. The Rosses will take care of you. Just remember it could be some time before I can get back."

She finally nodded, conceding to his plan no matter how foolhardy she thought it might be.

He helped her to gather the children, then took a bottle from his pocket that Doc Wanger had provided him before they'd left. Spilling a small amount onto his handkerchief, he instructed the boys to breath deeply. Soon their eyes sagged, and they grew limp. Working quickly, he carried them to the coffin and covered them with a woolen cloth. He pounded a pair of nails loosely in the lid to keep it closed, then turned to Felicity.

She was standing in a puddle of sunshine, her hands clasped together, her eyes wide with fear.

"There's a pistol under the wagon seat if you need it."

She nodded, wide-eyed.

"Get the boys out of here as soon as you can, Brant."

The boy nodded, swinging onto the wagon seat.

"Remember. If anything happens, go to the Rosses for help, Felicity." Such instructions didn't need to be given again, but he had to keep talking to her, had to keep reassuring himself that he was doing the right thing.

Then, needing much more than words, he hauled her into his arms, kissing her with all the passion and emotion that he could not express, must not express. Only when his desires threatened to completely over-whelm him was he able to let her go.

She climbed onto the wagon seat, and Brant took the reins. Still her eyes were trained in Logan's direction, filled with such beseeching entreaty, he could scarcely credit that it was directed toward him.

Knowing that he couldn't bear this a moment longer without surrendering to her silent supplica-tion, he slapped the mare on the rump. The wagon jolted forward.

As the wheels rumbled past him, he didn't turn to follow Felicity's progress. Instead, he made his way to their camp, quickly obliterating all signs that anyone had ever been there. Then, taking his rifle and swing-ing onto the back of his own horse, he began to make his way south.

Directly into the path of his nemesis.

Nineteen

Brant Rasmussen drove toward the canyon road just as Logan had said he would. But as each moment passed, every nerve in Felicity's body screamed for him to turn around and go back. Back to Logan. He needed their help.

But she didn't say a word. Not because she was afraid of what sort of confrontation Logan might be engineering, but because she couldn't bear it if he were ever disappointed in her. He'd given her a set of instructions, and by thunder, she would see them through.

"Only a few minutes more, miss," Brant Rassmussen said.

She nodded, thankful that the boys were oblivious to what was happening outside their macabre hiding place.

As the wagon crested a hill, she thought she saw a house ahead. The lazy drift of smoke from a chimney. She was almost there, almost—

"Whoa!"

The horse reared as a pair of men darted from the underbrush. Felicity screamed as one of the men grabbed at the reins, bringing the horse and the wagon to such a halt that Brant was jolted from his seat and pitched onto the ground.

Scrambling for the pistol hidden beneath the wagon seat, Felicity didn't see that the other brigand had run toward her until she was lifted high in the air, then pinned close to his body.

Filled with a rage like she'd never experienced before, she began to kick and scream and claw, ignoring the man's curses. Every muscle of her body, every thought racing through her head centered on one thing. Escape.

Escape.

She barely heard the carriages that approached, but when she caught the movement from the corner of her eye, she screamed even louder for help, hoping that whoever was inside them would come to her aid. To her infinite relief, both conveyances came to a stop and a woman's head appeared in the window.

"Très bien, Etienne. *Très bien."*

The door opened, and the unknown female stepped to the ground. She was beautifully attired in the latest fashion—her dress made of a dull, heavy, plum-colored satin trimmed in black fringe. A black bonnet covered most of her dark, sleek hair, a veil of black Nottingham lace concealing her face.

Growling low in her throat, Felicity tried to lunge free, knowing that if this woman had come to get the boys, Logan had probably been led into a trap.

"The little boys?" the woman asked, her voice laced with a lilting French accent.

"In the coffin," the man holding the horse said.

"Will you get them out, please, Pierre. Put them in the second carriage with Marie, where they will be more comfortable."

"Yes, ma'am."

"No!"

Again Felicity tried to free herself, but she was held fast.

The woman swept the veiling over her head, revealing one of the loveliest faces Felicity had ever seen—dark eyes, pale skin, a petite mouth. From deep within her soul, Felicity experienced a faint glimmer of recognition. She had seen this woman before, not so handsomely attired, but . . .

"There is no need to fret, *chérie.*"

The voice struck a chord of familiarity, and Felicity could have screamed in frustration that she could not place where she'd heard it before.

"I've come to help you on behalf of your family."

"Liar," Felicity spat. "No one in my family knows where I am now."

"Don't they?" The woman motioned for her servant to let Felicity loose.

Reluctantly, the man released her. Felicity considered storming toward the woman and knocking her down, but judging by the pair of henchmen waiting for just such an overture, she decided against it.

"The children, Pierre," the woman reminded one of them, and he rushed to the wagon. Then she turned her attention back to Felicity. "I'm so sorry that we have been reunited under these circumstances, *ma petite.* I arrived in Saint Joseph expecting to orchestrate a charming get-together. As soon as I discovered that you were gone, I did my best to find you again. But it took some time to convince Dr. Wanger that we were genuine in wishing to help. The man I hired to follow you insisted that you'd left the house one night with Logan Campbell and two children. But the doctor was not willing to admit such a thing to a stranger until I explained our relationship. I finally convinced him that you were not accustomed to such . . . precipitous adventures as helping slaves to escape and should be given the opportunity to return home."

"Who are you?" Felicity demanded, catching only half of the information the woman had volunteered.

"My name," the woman said slowly, "is Louise Chevalier. I am your mother."

"My mother?" Felicity's brow creased, and her eyes narrowed in disbelief. "You've obviously made some mistake. My mother abandoned me years ago."

The news caused the woman to blanch and steady herself against the carriage wheel.

"What?"

"My mother abandoned me—probably to meet up with some lover she met behind my father's back."

"No," the stranger whispered. "It isn't true. He took you from me. He stole you."

Felicity waved the remark aside. She didn't have time for this nonsense. She had to get the boys to safety. She'd promised Logan. Obviously a local asylum had lost one of its inmates, but she couldn't deal with the woman's misconceptions now.

"I swear, it's true, Felicity." She scrambled for some means to prove herself. "Tell me, did your father ever speak of his life before moving to Boston?"

Felicity grew still, the hair on her arms standing on end. Unbidden, she thought of the images that had plagued her since leaving her home, the recurring bouts of déjà vu.

Sensing her unease, Louise continued. "Perhaps you can recall those years yourself. Tell me, Felicity. As you traveled west, did any of the scenery look vaguely familiar to you?"

The prickling sensation was growing more intense now.

"We lived in a place very similar to this, your father and I."

Hazy images swam to the fore. A log house. Grass. Lots and lots of grass.

"But then, you were so small when Alexander took you away, you probably don't remember a thing."

Felicity didn't bother to inform the woman differently.

Louise sighed. "This is a shock, I know, and I didn't mean for us to meet this way." She nervously patted her bonnet. "But you should know it was I who sent you to Missouri in search of adventure, Felicity. Your father had plans to send you on a mission to India."

India. Felicity had been so sure that she would be forced to go there.

"No," she whispered. But deep in her heart, she knew she was hearing the truth. This woman was either her mother or she knew a good deal about Felicity's early years.

"How did you know about Logan? About the slave boys?"

Louise frowned. "I have not yet had the pleasure of meeting Mr. Campbell. I have only heard about him through Pierre's reports. He's the detective who has been watching you since you arrived in Saint Joseph. If not for him, we wouldn't have known the trouble you were in."

"But I've been staying—"

"In a bordello. I know. Frankly, even Pierre didn't catch on to the establishment being involved in the Underground Railroad until he saw you and the two children being taken away. That sight combined with the arriving search party helped him to reach the proper conclusions."

The man in question was returning, a groggy Samuel held tightly in his arms. He put the child in the carriage, where another young woman waited to hold him.

"Who is the other . . . ?" Felicity couldn't manage to finish her query.

"That is my maid, Marie. A judge I know was so

kind as to give her the proper papers she will need to prove the boys are the sons of her footman. They have already been booked on a train that will journey from Addington to the Canadian border. We sent a telegram to Dr. Wanger so that he can notify those who need to meet them. All that remains is to get them to their train connections in time."

"H-how did you get here so . . . ?" Felicity began.

"I have found that money can resolve a good many details, *ma petite.* As soon as I convinced the doctor to help us, we were on our way here to intercept you."

Felicity knew she should remain suspicious of the woman, especially considering her preposterous assertion of motherhood. But there was something about her, something innately good, that caused Felicity to lower her guard.

"But . . ."

Louise approached and stroked her cheek. At that moment, there was a glint in her eyes that reminded Felicity of Constance. "Later, my dear. All of your questions will be answered when there is time. For now, we need to see about getting everyone to safety."

Safety.

Logan.

In an instant, the woman's fantastic claims were banished by another, more overwhelming need.

"I've got to go." Felicity looked wildly around her. "I've got to go!"

Brant Rasmussen groaned, pushing himself upright.

"You!" Felicity said, pointing a finger at him. "Make sure you accompany the boys every step of the way." Her gaze flicked to Louise. "She might be lying."

When Louise would have stopped her, Felicity dodged past her, running to where two horses waited in the trees, presumably belonging to Pierre and Etienne.

Tugging the mount to a rock, she clambered onto its back, grabbed the saddle horn, and kicked it into a gallop.

"Etienne, Pierre! Follow her."

Felicity vaguely heard Louise's command. If the two men accompanied her, she would be grateful for the help, but right now, she couldn't take the time to see if they would come.

Twenty

The wind whistled past Logan's ears as he galloped full speed toward the men who had been sent to hunt him down. Two men. Sheriff Grigsby and his deputy, Nathaniel Moon.

Not for the first time, he thanked heaven that Brant Rassmussen had used enough foresight to supply him with a horse. Automatically, he reached for the rifle at his side. It was loaded and primed, as was the pistol he'd shoved into the back waist of his pants.

Once he reached Grigsby, he knew there wouldn't be time to reload. His shots would have to be true and his knife ready should he need more protection.

His heart was pounding, his body filling with an energy he had never known possible. He kept thinking about Everett, his mother, and all the men and women he'd helped north. Men like Grigsby were responsible for perpetuating the institution of slavery with their displays of hate and intolerance. That in itself would be enough to spur Logan into action. That and a promise to avenge his mother's and brother's deaths.

But now, there was so much more to his anger. If Logan hadn't taken measures to thwart Grigsby, he and his deputy would have descended upon Felicity and the children. And Logan could never have lived with himself if they'd been hurt.

The baying of the dogs Grigsby had brought with him was louder now, more excited. Logan reached low to unsnap the strap to the scabbard. Sliding the rifle free, he damned the fact that he was on a strange horse, one that wasn't accustomed to knee commands as his own mount would have been. But there was no helping that now. His horse had been left on the train out of necessity.

Topping a rise, he saw two liver-colored bloodhounds streaking toward him, tongues lolling from their mouths. Behind them was a pair of men on horseback.

In that instant, when he saw them look up, Logan was consumed with a body-numbing anger. Logan wanted to see these men afraid. He wanted them to cower as countless slaves had done when they'd surrounded them, tormented them, and tortured them. Logan had heard the stories from the slaves who had managed to escape them. He knew what Grigsby and Moon were capable of doing.

Leaning low over his horse, he twisted his rifle so that it was aimed butt first. Grigsby was racing toward him but had looked down to grasp his revolver; Moon was watching Grigsby for some sort of sign.

They were fatal mistakes.

Moon was the first to collide with Logan's rifle. It took him by surprise, crashing into the bridge of his nose and propelling him onto the ground where he lay unconscious, blood spurting over his face.

Logan whirled his horse into Grigsby's path next, grazing his ribs and the arm he'd held straight out, revolver aimed.

Grigsby swore as he was thrown to the ground.

Barely slowing his animal, Logan swung down and

was running toward the man. Visions of his mother's face as seen in her coffin and Everett offering that last sigh of death filled Logan's brain. Throwing his rifle to the ground, he dove onto Grigsby's supine form, pummeling him with blows. Emotions he'd submerged for years bubbled to the surface and were expended on his unwitting target. In this man, he found an outlet for the betrayal he'd felt from his father, the horror of his mother's death, the helplessness of watching slaves being subjugated by their masters.

Over and over again, he lashed out. The smack of flesh against flesh and the crunch of breaking bones came to him from far away, and Logan felt as if he had stepped outside of his body and was viewing it all from some distant vantage point.

Grigsby was part of the whole slavery system that had destroyed Logan's family. And for what? Money? The ability to own another man's life? How could you place a monetary figure on a person's soul? How could you deny any man his freedom or his future?

"Logan!"

Far away, he heard his name being called.

"Logan?" it came again, this time nearer. Much nearer.

His hand came back for another blow, but something caught his wrist.

Someone.

Looking up, he saw Felicity standing there, her hands tightly wrapped around his wrist.

"Stop," she pleaded.

It was then that the reality of the situation came rushing back to him. He looked down at Grigsby's bloody face, then at his own battered hands.

He trembled, wondering what had come over him. How long had he been here? Lashing out at a man who had long since lapsed into unconsciousness.

Taking a deep breath, he tried to still the pounding of his heart, but his pulse continued to race, fueled by a purging of an anger as old as time itself.

Felicity's grip tightened, and he looked up at her, wondering how she'd come to be in this place. She'd promised him that she wouldn't come back. She'd promised.

She looked up at him. Her eyes were filled with such concern that his body shuddered and the tension seeped from his muscles.

"Let's go, Logan," she whispered. "It's over."

Logan shook his head, sure that there was more he needed to do, but he was too exhausted to remember what steps he should be taking to flee again. To get them all north.

Felicity's thumb rubbed over his wrist in a silken caress. "Please, Logan."

The whisper pierced the haze of indecision, and he exhaled, ridding himself of the blacker emotions that had possessed him. Needing an anchor, he focused instead on the sight, the scent, the sounds, of the woman beside him. Then, knowing he couldn't face her reaction if he didn't do as she'd bade, he released Grigsby and the man crashed to the ground, unconscious.

"I'll have someone put Grigsby and Moon on a boxcar back to Saint Joseph," Logan rasped, unsure why he willingly left the man there, still breathing. "I'm sure Doc Wanger can arrange something to keep him in Saint Joseph until his temper cools and he realizes I've left the country." He straightened, his muscles still quivering in reaction, and allowed Felicity to lead him away.

He vaguely saw two men racing toward them, both riding a single horse, and a little farther back, a carriage.

"The boys?" he managed to gasp.

"Later. I'll explain everything later." Her eyes narrowed. "I'm not really sure what has happened myself. I refused to take the time to demand an explanation, but I'm sure I'll have one soon. Right now, we'll go to the Quaker house you spoke of and see to your hands. Once you've gathered everything you need, you can head for Canada yourself. You know you can't stay in the United States. An officer of the law knows that you've helped escaped slaves. If you were ever caught, you'd be hanged for breaking the Fugitive Slave Act. Go north. The boys are already on their way."

He stumbled and looked back at Grigsby, but Felicity forcefully turned his head away. "It's over, Logan. Let him crawl back home in defeat. By that time, you'll be long gone and he won't be able to find you."

A spark of anger kindled, and he tugged against her grip.

"No." She said again, gesturing to the two figures who had ridden up on horseback and held the lawmen at gun point. "Those men will see to him. It's time to look to your own future."

Logan stared down at her, at her earnest eyes and sweet face. He wanted to tell her he had no future. Not without her.

But how could he ask a woman such as Felicity Pedigrue to share her life with a man who wouldn't be welcome in this country? A man who was a bastard, literally and figuratively.

He stopped and stroked her cheek with his knuckle, wincing when it left a faint streak of dirt and blood. He wished he could find the words to tell her how she'd touched his life, his heart, his soul.

But even as he opened his mouth to try, he shut it again. He couldn't do such a thing. She had her whole life ahead of her. She wouldn't want to abandon all her plans to follow an American outlaw to Canada. He had to leave her without any protestations that might return to haunt them both some day.

He had to let her decide her own future. He had to let her go.

Then he had to pray that one day she decided her future belonged with him.

Louise folded her arms under her breasts and stared out at the carriage that had been summoned to the Rosses' home in order to take her to the railway station. Once there, she would take her private car back to Washington, D.C. and the performance that waited for her.

Two days had passed since she'd encountered her daughter. Two days of watching Felicity with a hunger beyond any she'd ever known before. How Louise wished she could have experienced her daughter's childhood with her. Felicity had been less than three years old when Alexander had taken the children. Louise found it hard to believe that the rambunctious toddler had become such a beautiful woman.

"Louise?"

Etienne took her shoulders, drawing her against his body. She welcomed the strength he offered, the heat.

"They thought I'd abandoned them, Etienne," she said forlornly. How could she possibly make any of her children believe that their father had deceived them?

His thumbs caressed her, making circles against the tense muscles of her spine.

"I know, *chérie.*"

A tightness gripped her throat. She'd shed so many tears since discovering the lie that Alexander had told his daughters she hadn't thought it possible to cry any more.

"In all these years of searching and waiting and

hoping, I never even considered that he would explain my absence in such a manner." Her breath emerged as a ragged sob. "How could I have been such a fool?"

Etienne turned her in his arms and held her close. "Shh. Don't think about it now. The past doesn't matter."

"But it does, Etienne. Felicity hates me for what I've supposedly done."

"Is that why you haven't made an effort to speak to her privately?"

She nodded against his shirt.

"Perhaps you are as foolish as you claim to be."

She started, glaring at him. But when he smiled at her, that warm, loving, toe-curling smile, she knew the statement had not been meant as a rebuke.

"You've waited all this time to meet your girls, yet now that the moment has come, you hesitate because you are afraid of what they will think about you."

She nodded guiltily.

"Don't *you* think such actions are absurd?"

She plucked at his shirt. "I suppose so."

"Good. Then I want you to go to Felicity's room and tell her everything you've wanted to say during the years you were separated."

Louise's stomach flip-flopped as if she were about to perform for a multitude of patrons and hadn't learned her lines.

Etienne bent, kissing the tip of her ear. "She will love you, Louise. I do."

Knowing that if she didn't confront her daughter now, she would rue her own faintheartedness, Louise pulled away from Etienne, straightened her shoulders, and strode to the staircase.

"That's my girl!" she heard Etienne call, and she nearly laughed.

Nearly.

Once at the top of the stairs, she made her way to the room Felicity had been given.

Louise's steps slowed. How many times had she come down this hall? How many times had she lifted her hand to knock, then reconsidered and turned away?

Well, it wouldn't happen again. Felicity might order her from the room, but at least Louise would have made an attempt at a reconciliation.

Her knuckles rapped against the door.

"Come in."

The call was eager, and Louise took courage from the fact, opening the door.

Felicity looked up expectantly, sure that it was Logan, that he'd finally come to talk to her.

But when she discovered that Louise Chevalier stood at the threshold, her body wilted, and she sank onto the edge of the bed.

"It's you," she said disappointedly, knowing she was being rude but unable to hold back her distress.

"You were obviously expecting someone else."

"Yes. I thought Logan would . . ." Felicity's words trailed away. She'd thought he would what? Come to beg her to join him? Come to say good-bye? Come to kiss her one last time before he left for Canada?

"I believe he is gathering provisions for his journey north."

Felicity had suspected as much, but hearing the words spoken aloud caused her heart to drop in her chest. He was going to leave her. He truly meant to leave her.

"I've spent a good deal of time with Miss Grimm since she arrived this morning," Louise announced.

Felicity fought the urge to roll her eyes. Miss Grimm had taken over her role as chaperone with a vengeance, probably because she feared her position would be terminated after all that had occurred to Felicity in the past few weeks. Since the old woman had stepped through the Rosses' front door, Felicity had barely been able to draw breath without Miss Grimm's permission. She'd finally closed herself in her room to escape.

"Miss Grimm is very impressed with your manners, Felicity. She thinks you are a lovely girl."

The news was completely surprising to Felicity, but not knowing how to respond, she remained silent.

"I think so too," Louise remarked.

"Do you?"

Felicity couldn't help the snappishness of her tone. Couldn't this woman see that Felicity didn't want to talk to her? That she didn't want to be reminded of the way Louise had left the Pedigrue girls to Alexander's strict care.

Louise sighed, stepping into the room and closing the door. "Felicity, I know that you think you have every reason to be angry with me. But I would like to tell you my side of the story."

Felicity sniffed. "I know your side of the story. I found the packet of letters in one of your trunks."

Louise frowned. "Letters?"

"There was a packet of love letters tied with a ribbon. They were all signed, 'Your Beloved.'"

Louise clapped her hands, her eyes shining. "Alexander didn't throw them away? Those letters were written by my father to my mother."

"Your father?" Felicity breathed.

Louise sat by her on the bed, taking her hand. Immediately, Felicity was enveloped in a faint cloud of perfume. One that reminded her of being small. Of laughter, warmth, and security.

But such emotions were a figment of her imagination. Weren't they?

"Felicity, I want to tell you what happened. Then it is your decision whether you see me again or not."

Felicity didn't want to hear any of her stories, but if the woman promised to leave her alone, she was willing to listen.

"Very well."

"My parents were performers for a traveling burlesque show. They had a dog act—you know, where tiny trained poodles jump through hoops and do tricks?"

Felicity nodded.

"When I was sixteen, Mama and Papa were killed in a horrible train accident outside of Pittsburgh." She shuddered. "Most of the troop was lost or injured. I found myself on my own with no means of support. Not knowing what I should do, I went to a local church for refuge. That is where I met your father."

Even though Felicity wanted to remain removed from Louise's story, she found herself intrigued.

"He was so handsome. So tall and dark and intense." Louise laughed. "I was immediately smitten, of course. And being young, I made mistakes."

"What sorts of mistakes?"

"Your father assumed that I lived in the parish, had always lived in the parish. When I tried to explain my parents' deaths, he assumed I had no one to care for me and he proposed. I wanted to marry him so much that I didn't tell him that my parents had earned a living in the theater. I knew he would not approve."

On that point, Felicity would have to agree. Her father had continually railed against the ungodly actors and the sinful stages that polluted society with their lies. She could only imagine what he would have said about burlesque performers.

"We were really quite happy those first few years,

Felicity. We moved out west to homestead, and your father built us a house."

"A log house," Felicity murmured, thinking aloud.

"Yes! It was small but comfortable. Soon it was filled with three growing girls." Her voice became thick with emotion. "I loved you all so much. So very much. Never think that I didn't."

"Then why did you leave us?" Felicity cried, all the old hurt and anguish bubbling to the surface. "How could you do that?"

Louise's features became fierce. "I didn't. I swear to you, I didn't. Not willingly." She took a breath to calm herself. "Your father had a horrible temper."

That was a point Felicity didn't need to have explained.

"One day, when we were returning home from church, an old friend of my parents saw me, recognized me, and . . ." The sentence trailed off in a sob.

"He told Papa," Felicity answered faintly.

Louise nodded. "I thought Alexander would beat me for my sins. After all, I'd lied to him for years about my background. But he didn't say a thing; he didn't even seem to notice the information he'd been given."

She gripped Felicity's hands even harder, and Felicity noted that her skin was like ice.

"He persuaded me to go to a quilting bee in town the next afternoon. It was an all-day affair, and I agreed to go because I wanted to please him. He even offered to take you, Patience, and Constance on a picnic. I was overjoyed that he meant to spend some time with you. But when I returned late that night"— her chin wobbled—"you were gone."

Felicity stared at the woman, horrified. She didn't want to believe the story she'd been told. She didn't want to believe that her father had been so cruel. But deep in her heart, she recognized the truth.

Her father was a hard man; he'd always been that way. Living with him for so many years, Felicity had grown wary of his blacker moods and the way that he'd been so intent on ridding his children of their supposed sins. She could only imagine how furious he would have been to discover that his wife had lied to him—moreover, that she'd lied to him about her roots.

Suddenly, so many things became clear to Felicity. She knew now why her father had been so adamant against his daughters' going to plays or recitations, why he had been so blatantly prejudiced against actors of any sort. Those things had reminded him of his wife. A woman whom he was sure had betrayed him by failing to confess her iniquitous past.

Louise was watching her expectantly, and Felicity stared at her in return, noting that her eyes were so much like Constance's eyes, her chin like Patience's. *But her stubborn determination is just like mine.*

"I tried to find you, Felicity," Louise continued, stroking her cheek. "But when your father left, I had no idea where he'd gone. I returned to the stage in order to provide for myself. Does that shock you?"

Felicity shook her head. After all that had occurred the last few weeks, she didn't think she could ever be shocked again.

"I became quite successful and quite wealthy. But all my money, all the detectives, all the prayers and dreams, couldn't unearth your hiding place . . . until just before your father died."

"*You* changed the will," Felicity said faintly, remembering that in previous drafts Alexander had decreed she should serve a mission in India.

"Yes. I bribed a clerk into helping me. I changed the original documents for new ones and sealed them with the signet ring Alexander had given me as a wedding present."

"Then you offered each of us the chance to chase a dream."

"I wanted you to be happy. I wanted to make up for the years I'd been unable to spoil you. By unearthing old governesses and nannies, it wasn't hard to determine what sorts of adventures you'd craved."

Felicity gently disengaged herself, moving to the window, her mind whirling with the new information she'd gathered. Peering down, she saw Logan leading his horse to the house.

"You must not have bargained on the trouble I'd bring you in the process," she said quietly.

She heard the rustle of Louise's skirts as her mother approached and looked over her shoulder.

"You've given me no trouble at all, Felicity." She hesitated, then smoothed the hair from Felicity's cheek. "Do you love him?"

Felicity nodded. "More than I would have thought possible."

"Does he love you?"

"I believe he does, but he's never said the words aloud."

"Some men are not prone to flowery speeches. That doesn't mean their emotions aren't real."

Tears gathered in Felicity's eyes. "But he's going to leave me. What can I do?"

Louise wrapped her arms around Felicity's body, drawing her close.

Felicity stiffened for an instant, then willingly succumbed to the embrace, finding in it the peace, comfort, and motherly love she had craved all her life.

"I don't know what you should do, Felicity. Only *you* can make that decision. But I will tell you one thing. The only things in life that I've regretted were the times I didn't follow my instincts. Trust yourself. Trust your heart. It will never lead you astray."

She held Felicity near, rocking her back and forth as

if she were a child. When she drew away again, it was with obvious regret on both their parts.

Smiling, Louise wiped the tears from Felicity's cheeks, then from her own. "I wish I could stay here with you, Felicity. I wish we could spend a week or more talking and laughing and getting to know one another." She tipped her head to the man out the window. "But right now, I sense that the time for your own confrontation with destiny has arrived and I am in the way."

"No, I—"

Louise placed a finger on her lips. "I want you to settle things with Logan one way or another." She removed a small card from her pocket. "Then when you are ready—any day, any time—contact me here. I look forward to getting to know you, my dear."

Felicity took the card, and on impulse, she threw her arms around Louise's neck. "Thank you, Mother."

Louise's eyes were bright with unshed tears. "You don't know how long I've waited to hear you call me that." Then she was gone in a rustle of skirts and a waft of perfume.

Felicity stood for several long moments, absorbing the stillness. The contentment. The hunger for happiness.

During her years with her father, she'd been kept isolated from the world and its problems. She'd been allowed no real range of emotions. Yet in the past few weeks, she'd experienced the gamut of anger, frustration, pity, ecstasy, fear, and love. She'd had a part in a great adventure and had found a way to help someone in a way that was truly meaningful. Yet now . . .

What? What now?

That, she supposed with a sigh, was the root of her problem. For so long, she had been living from day to day, problem to problem. She'd been challenged to the end of her patience and her abilities, and now that she was finished, she discovered that she was no longer needed.

No longer needed. What a sad phrase. What a horrible thought. Only weeks before, she'd been reaching out for room to dream, a place of her own, privacy, personal adventure. Inexplicably, she'd developed a need for belonging. She wanted . . .

Logan.

A tightness gripped her throat, tears crowding close behind her eyelids. Drat it all, she'd always detested those sniveling sorts of women who resorted to weeping when all else failed. But at this particular instant, she couldn't seem to help herself. What else could she do? Logan might find her alluring, even interesting, but he wasn't a man accustomed to being tied down. Especially to a woman. She'd known that from the first time she'd seen him, and to think otherwise now would be foolhardy.

A soft tap on the door had her swiping at her cheeks and stiffening her spine. She might be quivering inside like a bowl of custard, but that didn't mean that anyone else had to know such a thing.

"Yes?"

"Miss Pedigrue? 'Tis Edith Ross."

Felicity jumped from the bed and rushed to admit the woman.

As soon as the door had opened, Edith beamed, clasping her hands at her waist. "Thy chaperone is wondering when you would like to leave, Miss Pedigrue. She said something about needing to relocate thy tea house in another city."

"Oh." Felicity couldn't prevent the disappointment that rang from her tone. "Thank you, Mrs. Ross."

Edith's head tipped inquisitively. "Was thou expecting someone else?"

"No," Felicity said quickly. "No, I just didn't think

Miss Grimm would be ready to go so soon. I have enjoyed resting here at your home. I'm not looking forward to journeying again so soon."

Her explanation apparently pleased Edith. But there was a twinkle to her eyes that Felicity couldn't completely explain.

"I'm so glad thy needs were met. I will send one of my sons for thy things." Then she was rushing down the hall with the sense of urgency that Felicity was beginning to associate with everything Edith did.

Turning back to her room, that clean spartan room, Felicity gathered her things—the dress, the petticoats, her stockings. Miss Grimm might not have been a welcome addition to the safe house, but the clothing she brought had been appreciated.

Felicity's gaze scanned the chamber one last time. She didn't know why she lingered. Perhaps because she had expected something more. Some sort of private leave-taking from the man who had dragged her from pillar to post.

But, she thought steeling her spine, such a thing was not going to happen, would never happen, could never happen. So she'd best be on her way. Whirling, she took two determined steps and stopped. Her mouth dropping ever so slightly.

"Logan?" It was said with a note of doubt as if the man might be a mirage.

"You're ready then?"

"To leave?"

"Yes."

Her lips thinned ever so slightly. The man sounded positively anxious to have her gone.

"I suppose so."

"Good."

A sticky silence descended over them both. One filled with the haunting echoes of their banter and lovemaking.

It was Logan who cleared his throat first. "You've been a good sport, Felicity."

One of her brows arched. Of all the things she'd expected him to say, this was not it. "Good sport?"

"Other women might have screamed or hollered at me for all you've been through."

"I see." Her tone was quite flat, quite emotionless, but she was far from unaffected inside. A slow anger had begun to smolder. He was speaking of what they'd endured as if it had been a game and she'd managed to catch on to the rules.

"Other women would have cried and carried on, fallen into hysterics."

"As I recall, I did some of that."

"Yes . . . well, that's all over now. You can return to your life as it was before."

But she couldn't. That was the crux of the matter. She would not be welcome as a teacher in Saint Joseph. Not after spending her time quarantined in a bordello. The prospect of opening a reading club and tearoom was out of the question. Louise had invited her to stay with her in Washington, D.C., but she really didn't think she'd accept. In essence, she was back at the same place she'd been once before, searching for a niche for herself.

"I don't believe I'll stay in Saint Joseph."

"Oh?"

She wasn't sure, but she thought that he grew inestimably still. His eyes grew darker, more intent.

"Why not?"

"I don't think that's possible now." She didn't bother to sugarcoat her answer. Let him know the truth. Let him know that he was partially responsible for her current dilemma. "I will never be given a teaching position there and opening a tearoom is out of the question."

"Where will you go?"

"Does it matter?" she shot back, suddenly weary of the civilities that had never been a part of their relationship before.

"Yes. It does."

"Why? You intend to go your own way as soon as I've left, so what does it matter?"

She saw the way his hands balled into fists. "I merely wanted to ensure that—"

"That I was safe? Happy? Well, don't bother yourself about such matters, Logan. I have things to do. Lots and lots of things. I have a life ahead of me—one without you. I intend to be an important woman some day, and no one will ever know what you've done to me, how you've diverted the course of my life." She took a deep breath when her voice began to quaver. "Now, Logan, if you will let me pass, I'll be on my way."

She saw the muscle of his jaw working as he ground his teeth together, but he moved aside. Lifting her head high, she began to sail past him, but at the last moment, he grasped her arm and pulled her tightly against him, his head swooping low, his lips taking hers in a swift, powerful kiss.

Just when her knees threatened to buckle and she was tempted to throw her arms around his neck and beg him to let her stay at his side, he released her.

"Good-bye, Felicity," he murmured, his voice low, dark, and deep. Then he was gone.

Felicity stood for several long moments, absorbing the silence, the pain, the regret.

And then the anger.

Damn him.

Damn him for being a fool. A stubborn, hard-nosed, can't-see-a-good-thing-right-in-front-of-his-face fool.

Tossing her bundle of belongings on the bed, she marched to the door, whipping it open so hard that it slammed against the wall. "Logan!" she shouted to the house in general. "I haven't finished with you yet!"

Striding through the hall to the front of the house, she ignored the open-mouthed Ross children and the ramrod-stiff Miss Grimm. As far as Felicity was concerned, her purpose was clear, her need well defined. Moving through the doorway to the wide front porch, she spied Logan checking the cinch to his saddle.

"Logan!"

His head rose, and he stared at her.

"I'm not finished with you yet," she repeated, stalking down the two shallow stairs to the dirt path that led to the barn.

He turned away from her and adjusted the strap to his side scabbard, infuriating her even more.

Taking a handful of his sleeve, she tugged, forcing him to look at her. "How dare you?" She stabbed him in the chest with a finger. "How dare you treat me this way?"

His expression darkened, but she didn't allow the fact to daunt her.

"I gave my heart to you." She poked him. "I gave my *body* to you."

He glanced over her shoulder to where the Ross family was gathering on the porch. This time, it was his cheeks that held a hint of pink.

"I don't know where you learned your manners, but where I come from, such liberties with a woman demand some consideration on your part."

"You're right."

"You should . . ." She lost some of her steam when she realized that he'd agreed with her. "Well . . . hmm . . . at least we see eye to eye on this point."

She huffed, trying to gather her scattered thoughts.

"You can't just walk away," she finally said.

He absently rubbed the leather of his saddle with

his thumb. "What do you want me to do?" When she opened her mouth to reply, he added, "Think carefully, Felicity. Take every possible repercussion into consideration."

"What are you saying, Logan?"

For the first time since encountering him on the train, since storming into the bordello, since becoming his lover, she saw the mask he usually wore drop. Not even when he'd told her of his brother's death had his emotions been so naked. For the first time—and maybe the last—she saw to the heart of this man. The facade he usually wore was one of pure, tempered steel. But hidden underneath was a lonely, needy man. One who craved love and acceptance but would never bring himself to ask for it. One who felt his illegitimacy was a badge of honor to wear but who secretly, inwardly, wanted to belong.

"I just want you to love me, Logan."

He looked away, blinking quickly. Felicity thought she saw a glint of moisture there.

"I do, Felicity. Sweet heaven above, how I do."

Her stomach tensed. Gooseflesh raced up her spine. Expressing his feelings did not come easy to this man. She knew that. Especially those emotions that might form an invisible bond.

She touched his cheek. "Was that so hard to say?"

He grasped her wrist. "You aren't thinking this through, Felicity." His voice had a harsh edge to it. "I'm not the sort person you should get tangled up with. I'm not the sort *any* woman should get tangled up with."

"Why not?"

"I'm a bastard, damn it."

"Your personality isn't the point."

He scowled. "You know what I mean."

"Yes, I do," she said more seriously. "But I don't really care."

"You should."

"Why?"

He seemed at a loss as to what to say, and she stepped closer.

"You see, Logan, neither of us is what we would seem. All this time, I've been told my mother abandoned me. Now I discover she was a victim too." She sighed, realizing she wasn't expressing herself very well. "What I'm trying to say is that I don't care where you've come from or what you've done. I fell in love with the man you are now. All of him. Everything that's ever happened to make him what he is." She gripped his shirt with both hands. "I love you just the way you are."

The ensuing silence was almost more than she could bear, but when he laid his hands lightly at her waist, she felt a glimmer of hope.

"So what do you want me to do, Felicity?" he asked slowly.

He was going to make her say it. He was going to make her spell out every detail.

Taking handfuls of his shirt, she pulled him closer, murmuring, "I want to marry you, you big oaf. I want to build a home with you. I want dozens of babies, some chickens, and a garden. I want a guest bedroom where my family can visit and maybe even a safe place for escaped slaves to rest for a bit before moving on. As for you, you'll never be happy as a farmer. We'll have to find something more exiting for you to do—ranching or even law work. You would make a wonderful sheriff. You already know the dirty tricks someone would use to escape. Then there's a matter of schooling for the children, so I suppose we would have to be somewhat close to a town but not too close. I wouldn't—"

Logan hauled her tightly against him, crushing his mouth over hers, kissing her intensely, deeply, passionately. His tongue thrust into her mouth, raiding the sweetness he found there, involving her in an intimate duel for suppression. When at long last he drew away, Felicity was breathless.

"You've got it all worked out, haven't you, Felicity?"

She could only nod.

"Well, at least I've found a way to silence you when it's my turn to talk."

"Your turn?" she echoed.

"I'll marry you, Felicity."

She caught her breath. She hadn't thought he would capitulate so easily.

"But as for your other plans, I've got a few of my own details to add."

"Oh?"

His hands dropped to spread wide over her hips, pulling her flush to his hard, tempered thighs. "We'll settle in Canada, because I'm an outlaw here."

"Fine."

"I'm not quite sure I could handle a dozen children, so we'll start with one and work our way up."

Her knees were turning to jelly.

"I like the idea of working with the law but nothing that would take me too far away from you." His head bent, and he murmured next to her lips. "After all, we have a future to build together, don't we?"

"Yes," she sighed, throwing her arms around his neck. "Oh, yes."

From the direction of the porch came a smattering of applause, then Miss Grimm's weak mewl of distress.

"Does this mean I'm out of a job?"

Epilogue

Canada
July 21, 1859

My Dearest Patience,

I know that I promised to write again soon—and you are probably frightfully worried about all that has occurred since my last letter when I explained about my adventure in Saint Joseph and my encounter with our mother.

As you can tell by the postmark, I have since relocated in Canada, but do not worry. I am happy and healthy and very much married.

I know the news of my nuptials will surprise you no end. After all, when I left you and Constance in Boston, I never dreamed of falling in love. But my current state of adoration for Logan Campbell is so complete, I know I could not survive without him.

Logan and I left for Canada a mere hour after exchanging our vows. Logan wished with all his heart that we could return to Saint Joseph where we'd met, but it would be too dangerous for Logan to live there. According to the Fugitive Slave Law, he could be put to death if someone successfully charged him with helping escaped slaves. I will never allow that to happen.

Even as I write this letter, I find myself watching him. He is leaning against the stone railing of our home, surveying the fields where he hopes to raise horses. He sips from a mug of coffee I brought him minutes earlier, and a contented smile lingers on his face even though he claims that my coffee could peel the paint off a wagon. We both know he drinks it because it gives me a sense of purpose here in this huge, rattling, old house until we can fill it with children.

I regret that you and Constance could not be at my wedding. Thankfully, Mother was able to stay long enough to be there with me. Please, dear Patience. She means to visit you next. Listen to what she has to say, and decide for yourself whether or not she is telling the truth. As for me, I have no doubts.

Mother has since sold my house and its furnishings, then forwarded the money to me. She was very upset that she could do nothing about my inheritance from Father. Because I did not stay in Saint Joseph for a year, fulfilling my "supposed" task from Father, the money was given to charity. Frankly, I don't care one whit. After all our father did to our family over the years, I would rather provide for my own future.

I am pleased to report that such a future looks bright. Last week, Doc Wanger appeared on our doorstep to announce that he'd decided he would be safer living in Canada as well. He stayed with us for only five days, but during that time, he'd reported that Grigsby and his cohort, Moon, had been shot and killed during an altercation with a gambler at one of the local saloons. Clarice and Lena have relocated in California, where they have opened a boarding house—a real boarding house—to serve the influx of unmarried women moving west. And Miss Grimm has returned to Saint Joseph, where she has opened a "wine and spirits" emporium. Imagine that woman in charge of liquor!

It wasn't until Doc Wanger was about to leave that he took Logan aside and told him about Everett. Doc Wanger never had a chance to see to the burial arrangements because Clarice and Lena took matters into their own hands. They brought Everett's coffin with them on their journey west. When they reached the first slopes of the Rocky Mountains, they left the train and hired a wagon. After searching long and hard through the verdant hills, they chose a beautiful place in a bend of the Colorado River.

Logan has been touched beyond belief by the generous actions of his friends—Doc Wanger, Clarice, and Lena. Without them, he is certain his life would not be nearly so happy. He holds them responsible for helping us to fall in love and survive the obstacles pitted against us.

But I digress.

I see that Ezekial has brought the wagons from the barn. He and Logan have begun to escort escaped slaves from the Canadian border to our own home, where they stay until they are ready to move on. It pleases me no end to see Joseph and Samuel scampering around the older men like frisky pups since I had a hand in bringing them here safely.

Logan will be coming to get this letter so that it can be posted to you, so I will quickly close. I have not received a single letter from you as of yet, dear Patience. Please write as soon as you can. I have heard about your employer from a neighbor who once lived on his island, and I must say I am intrigued. She speaks of him in a whisper, giving the impression that he is part ogre and part god. If that is the case, I wish I could have been a fly on the wall when the two of you met.

Tell me, Patience, in all honesty—

How long did you spend in his company before you lost your infamous temper?

Your loving sister,
Felicity